The Passageway

The
Passageway

Laurel Mouritsen

Covenant Communications, Inc.

Published by Covenant Communications, Inc.
American Fork, Utah

Printed in the United States of America
First Printing: February 1994

01 00 99 98 97 96 95   10 9 8 7 6 5 4 3 2

Library of Congress Cataloging-in-Publications Data

Mouritsen, Laurel, 1948

Passageway, The

p.   cm.

ISBN 1-55503-688-0 : $10.95
1. Fiction. 2. Historical Fiction. I. Title

CHAPTER ONE

THE MORNING WAS already going badly when Professor Bowen came stomping into my office with a scowl on his florid face. He had misplaced his notes on Colonel Thomas L. Kane's participation in the Utah War, and I knew immediately that I was about to get the blame for the lost notes.

"Ms. Garrett, do you have the notes on Kane?" he growled.

I hated it when he called me "Ms." It reminded me of a cantankerous old cat I'd once owned named Mitzy. "No, sir. I gave those papers to you last week when you asked for them."

"That's impossible. I don't have them." He shuffled through several pages of my handwritten notes which he carried in his fist. "You must have put them somewhere else. I'd appreciate it if you'd locate them for me, Ms. Garrett. Immediately."

"Yes, Professor Bowen."

He made a swipe across his balding head, and muttering under his breath, crossed the hall and disappeared into his office.

I watched him go, indignation flaring up inside me. If Professor Edgar A. Bowen couldn't keep track of his notes, how in heaven's name was he going to be organized enough to write an entire book? I shook my head. As his research assistant, I was a natural target for venting his frustrations, which he'd frequently done over the past three months that I'd been working for him. A girl named Sally Perkins, who did the typing of the manuscript, and I occupied one corner of an office across from Professor Bowen's own cluttered cubicle. Sally was near my own age, twenty or so, but from the first day on the job she ran our tiny corner of the world like a general on the field of battle.

In exasperation I began searching through my research papers for the wayward notes. I knew the task was useless, for I had put them in Professor Bowen's care the previous week; but I had to make the gesture.

"You'll never find them, Kallie. Bowen's lost the notes and you know it. You'll have to do the research over again," Sally said briskly from behind her desk.

A computer monitor hid Sally's face so that all I could see was her short brown hair. "I'll find those notes if I have to turn over every scrap of paper in this office. It took me two solid weeks to search out that information and I don't intend to repeat it, thank you."

"It's a lost cause," Sally replied in a clipped voice.

I glared at the dozens of sheets of paper stacked in piles across the top of my desk, then commenced going through the first stack. Across the top of each page I had written the general category to which that page belonged. "Causes of the Utah War." "Background of the Utah War." "Participants of the Utah War." The Utah War—a rather pompous name for such a trifling dispute. I wished the Utah War had never happened. It would have saved me a good deal of time and trouble.

Professor Bowen came charging out of his office with his textbook and lecture notes tucked under his arm. He was a bull of a man with a thick neck and a head too small for his blocky shoulders. A few strings of iron-gray hair lay plastered across his head, and the rest was shorn short. His eyes were round and protruding, his nose bulbous, and his lips quivered with each drawn breath. He tossed Sally and me an impatient glance, then clomped down the hallway to his class.

This was Bowen's second term of teaching at the college. He wasn't a regular member of the staff, but a visiting professor from some obscure university in the East. Why he was so interested in the history of Utah, I didn't know. The man wasn't a Mormon, so apparently it wasn't the Church's involvement in the Utah War that interested him. I suspected his sympathies leaned with Johnston's Army. Perhaps he was trying to unearth some historical bit of evidence which would turn Johnston into the hero of the whole muddled affair.

By the time five o'clock came around, I was thoroughly frustrated. I hadn't found the missing notes, and I had wasted most of the day looking for them. Aggravated beyond words, I threw on my jacket and prepared to leave.

"I'll see you tomorrow," I grumbled to Sally.

"Maybe your notes will turn up by then," she replied.

I glanced at her with a sardonic expression. "Yeah, sure."

She smiled, a quick exercise affecting only the corners of her mouth. Sally's face was round and plain, her nose large, and her eyes set like hard little raisins. Her short brown hair curled around her face, making it appear even more rotund. She was a healthy-sized girl, to put it politely, but she was a fine typist. As I left the room I heard her gallantly attacking the keyboard.

I hurried down the stairs of the weathered old building and climbed into my car. When I turned the key in the ignition, the engine leaped to life. I smiled appreciatively. I had taken great pains in choosing a car to buy. After looking at dozens of automobiles, I had decided on the handsome silver Mustang with maroon interior. I hadn't been wrong in my choice. The sporty little car hadn't given me a minute of trouble. As I pulled away from the curb, the Mustang slipped easily into the flow of traffic, humming at my touch.

I skirted the downtown area with its modern glass and steel office buildings mixed among the older brick edifices. The stately spires of the temple and the domed Tabernacle quickly fell away from view as I traveled the curving highway. The mountains to the east loomed outside my car window. Usually I feasted on the beauty and grandeur of the mountains as I drove the highway hugging the foothills, but today I barely gave them a glance. I was too engrossed in my own problems. The difficulties at work had left me feeling anxious and edgy, emotions which I disliked dealing with. By nature I was a cheerful person, but no one would be able to guess that today. The misplaced notes and the attendant pressures of the job were beginning to rattle me.

I pulled into the driveway of my parents' home just before six, climbed out of the car carrying my notes and books, and started toward the house. Our red brick rambler sat well back from the road, its porch shaded by two huge blue spruce trees whose breadth filled nearly the entire front yard. Along the front porch of the house ran a rock planter box. Inside the box, Mom's spring flowers strutted their colors. Snowy white crocus grew alongside brilliant red tulips and sunny daffodils. As I mounted the porch steps I watched the tulips sway in the cool canyon breeze, and heard the wind sing through the pines.

I could smell dinner cooking as soon as I walked in the door. It made me suddenly ravenous. Mom greeted me from the kitchen as I dropped my armful of things into our newly-purchased Queen Anne chair, which occupied a prominent spot in the room.

"Don't put your things on my new wing chair, Kallie." Mom's voice from the kitchen told me she'd anticipated this indiscretion on my part. I moved my books and papers from the chair to a nearby table.

The television was blaring from the corner of the living room. As I walked past I caught a glimpse of a spindly black child on the screen, her arms and legs thin as chicken bones and her belly distended. I knew without listening to the newscaster that he was reporting on the famine raging in Africa. The picture of the starving little girl was a familiar one; I had seen it and others like it a dozen times. I made a mental note to eat every scrap on my plate at supper, lest Mother remind me again of the malnourished people of Africa.

"Hi, Mom," I said, coming into the kitchen.

"Hello, sweetheart. How was your day?"

"Don't even ask," I groaned.

"That bad?"

"That bad," I affirmed, nodding my head.

"Well, some hot supper will do you a world of good."

I frowned slightly. Mother relied on a hot supper to cure any ailment, physical or emotional. Her old-fashioned sentiments often rankled me. I tried not to let my irritation show.

"You shouldn't leave the television on when no one is watching it," I said brusquely.

"It keeps me company, Kallie. With your brothers grown and gone, I get lonely when no one's about. Now go wash your hands for supper."

By the time I came out of the bathroom, Dad had arrived home from work and was seated at the kitchen table. When I sat down, he leaned over and kissed me.

"How's my girl?" he asked.

"Don't ask her," Mom replied, waving a long-handled wooden spoon in the air. She bent over the stove and briskly stirred the gravy bubbling and roiling inside the roasting pan. Dad gave me an understanding wink, then set about carving the roast beef Mom had set on the table.

It was a delicious meal. Mom must have spent half the day in the kitchen preparing it, and she hovered over each bowl of mashed potatoes and dish of carrots like an artist inspecting her latest canvas.

The three of us chatted about the usual dinner-table topics while we ate, and in the background the gravel-voiced anchorman of the six o'clock news droned on. From my place at the table, I could easily see the television screen. Now it was filled with the picture of a large city, drowning in a smoky haze. "Scientists predict that by the year 2000, pollution from our cities will cause worldwide climatological changes," the newscaster drawled. The next picture showed a drawing of withered and dying trees, with animal corpses littering the barren ground. All of this had been caused, presumably, by the buildup of pollution.

I shoved a spoonful of mashed potatoes into my mouth, idly watching the screen. I wondered about the pollution level on the island of Fiji, where my older brother, Mark, was serving a mission. I grinned at the thought of Mark feeling his way among the coconut and palm trees, his sight blinded by a thick sea of pollution.

"Do you think you can arrange time off from work to go with us?" I suddenly heard my father saying.

My eyes shifted to Dad, who was obviously waiting for some kind of answer from me.

"What? I'm sorry, what did you ask?"

"The trip to California. We've been planning it for months, remember?" he replied, his eyes crinkling in amusement.

"Oh, the trip. I don't know yet, Dad. I have a lot of work to do for Professor Bowen. He's misplaced some important research I did, and I may have to do it over." I frowned, thinking of my harrowing day at the office.

"You promised us you'd try your very best to get the time off, Kallie. Your father and I will be very disappointed if you don't go." Mom's mouth was set in a tight line.

I dropped my eyes so I wouldn't have to see the accusation spelled out on her face. Mom was constantly on my back about not spending enough time with the family. Time with the family meant Mom, Dad, and me—which was not a whole lot of fun from my perspective. Since Mark had left on his mission and Darrin was away at college, most of the pleasure had gone out of family togetherness. When the three of us planned to be together, it usually meant that I was expected to take part in my parents' activities. These generally revolved around church-related functions. This planned trip to California was no exception. Dad had a series of church meetings coming up in Sacramento that he had to attend, and he wanted to combine the trip with a family vacation.

Truthfully, I had no desire to go. My parents' idea of a good time did not coincide with mine. I had no inclinations to follow the path they had marked out for themselves. My parents expected me to adhere to their standards, and for years I did so without complaint. No family attended their church meetings more regularly than ours. Diligently, we studied the scriptures together. Dad usually managed to wring a spiritual lesson out of every activity. But when I started high school, I realized I'd been viewing all of life's decisions through the spectacles of Mormonism. Discarding them brought freedom from the set bounds and restrictive patterns of behavior my parents had established. I began to shed some of my old, stale friends and cultivate new ones. My social life picked up. I started staying out late and enjoying myself. Soon my attendance at Sunday meetings slackened, and I found excuses to absent myself from the nightly ritual of scripture reading and prayer. To their credit, Mom and Dad did not try to force me into the old mold. But they took every opportunity to let me know they disapproved of my actions.

I looked at my watch, anxious to end the conversation before it evolved into a sermon. "Boy, I didn't realize it was getting so late. I promised Terri I'd come over to her house after dinner to hear her new tape. Would you mind if I ran over for a few minutes, Mom?"

"I guess not. Maybe your father will help me with the dishes tonight."

Dad nodded as he reached for another slice of homemade wheat bread.

I hurriedly grabbed my car keys and purse, then started for the door. The newsman was still talking—something about weapons reduction between the United States and Russia. I flipped off the TV set and let myself out the door.

Terri's bedroom vibrated to the rock music blaring from her cassette player. She closed her eyes and gyrated to the beat, seemingly oblivious to my presence. Even if I'd wanted to, I couldn't have collared her attention. The music was turned up so loud that she would have had trouble hearing a locomotive roar past her window. I sat patiently listening to her newest tape until it had run its course. As the last guitar screamed and the final drum roll exploded, Terri dropped down on the bed beside me.

"What do you think?" she beamed. "Wasn't it great?"

I nodded enthusiastically. "Great," I echoed.

She sighed contentedly. "I think they're about the best band I've ever heard."

I didn't share her feelings, but I didn't tell her so. Although the music was well crafted, the lyrics to several of the songs had been vulgar and explicit, and I had been offended by their message. As sophisticated as I liked to think I was, I didn't approve of the obscenity and violence that permeated today's rock music.

Terri took the tape out of the tape deck and slipped it into her dresser drawer. "I think I'll play this for Kevin when he comes home from school next weekend. It'll drive him wild."

I knew what she meant. Her older brother, Kevin, was a returned missionary attending Brigham Young University. He was as straight as an arrow when it came to things of the spirit. I was sure his indignant reaction to the new tape would give Terri a good laugh.

I gazed out her bedroom window, absently thinking about the tape. The sun was just setting in the west and its fading light cast purple shadows across the craggy slopes of Mt. Olympus. Terri's view of the eastern mountains was magnificent. If this were my bedroom, I'd be at the window regularly to witness the ever-changing hues on the mountainside.

"Oh, I almost forgot to tell you," Terri blurted out excitedly. "Kevin is bringing his roommate home with him next weekend. I haven't met him, but Kevin says he's a cool guy. I thought we could invite a few friends over and have a party while Kevin and his roommate are here. Good idea, huh?"

"Sure. I guess."

"You guess? I thought you'd love the idea. I've never known you to miss a party, Kallie." Terri grinned knowingly at me.

"It's just that I might have to work extra hours for the next couple of weekends. Research problems."

"Do it the following weekend," Terri urged.

"I can't. My parents want me to go to California with them that week."

Terri rolled her eyes in sympathy.

"I'll see what I can arrange, okay?"

"Sure. But you'll miss a good time if you don't come."

I chuckled aloud. "If you're referring to your brother's room-mate, once he sees you, he won't give me a second glance."

Terri snorted, but I caught the quick smile of pleasure my comment had brought to her lips. If Terri Gilbert suffered from an occasional show of self-pride, in my mind it was justified. She was blessed with perfect features. Her large blue eyes were framed by long, honey-colored lashes. A slender nose, a dazzling smile, and an eye-catching figure shouted instant appeal. Terri's thick blonde hair fell in smooth waves down her back. My own unruly brown locks resisted every effort at curling. I wore my shoulder-length hair straight, with a side part. The style probably did not do a lot to enhance my looks. My eyes were small and a very ordinary brown. My nose was puggish, and my mouth a bit too wide. I did have a good eye for clothes, choosing patterns and lines which accentuated my narrow waist and hips, but I was short in stature. Terri, tall and leggy, towered over my small frame.

I glanced again toward the window. The sun had disappeared from the sky now, leaving the mountains wrapped in darkness. I stood up and retrieved my keys from the bottom of my purse.

"I'd better be going. I have a long day ahead of me tomorrow," I said.

My brows puckered, thinking of the unhappy prospect of repeating the research on Colonel Thomas L. Kane. It would entail hours of work, probably taking up my evenings and

9

weekends, and I much preferred to spend those cruising with Terri in my Mustang. Aside from my job, I didn't give much consideration to how I spent my free hours. My main ambition was to have a good time with my friends. Dad proved to be the proverbial thorn in my side, however. He kept reminding me how I ought to have some goals—some long-range plans for myself instead of "drifting," as he termed my leisure activities. I didn't see any need for change. I was perfectly happy—especially when I learned to ignore the prickings of my conscience. I'd once overheard Dad telling Mom that it would take a miracle to bring me around. Well, I knew I wasn't in need of any miracles.

Terri walked with me to the front door of her large, beautifully furnished home. Both of her parents worked, and the fruits of their labors were prominently displayed.

"Get your party shoes ready, Kallie, and we'll have ourselves some fun next weekend," Terri said as she opened the door for me.

"Right." I gave Terri a thumbs-up sign. "I'll do my best to get the time off."

"That's the girl."

"See you later," I said lightly.

Terri stood on the porch until I drove off.

When I got home, my parents were asleep in their room. The house was still except for a low murmuring of voices coming from the corner of the living room. I walked over to the TV set and firmly clicked it off.

CHAPTER TWO

THE FOLLOWING MORNING held the promise of another difficult day. Professor Bowen still had not located his notes. In addition, he wanted me to begin an immediate search of certain pioneer diaries for entries concerning polygamy. Normally, I would not have minded such a search. I had digested dozens of books on history, and I had the nose of a bloodhound when it came to tracking down tidbits of historical information. In fact, I kept a row of history books on the shelf above my bed at home for quick reference. I was fascinated by the historical beginnings of nearly every topic. If I had a personality quirk, it was this—I could be charmed by anything from the invention of the automatic milking machine to the founding of nations.

This search of pioneer diaries, however, did not interest me. The early Latter-day Saints' practice of plural marriage had been hashed over by historians for decades. I was already acquainted with the events which introduced polygamy into the Church, as well as being versed in the history of the Church itself. I knew the story of the Saints' persecution. Driven out of Ohio, Missouri, and Illinois, the Saints had migrated to the valleys of the Great Basin in an effort to escape their enemies. Eventually, however, the Saints' problems followed them even there. Plural marriage, which the Saints viewed as a commandment from God, became the focal point around which hostilities flared.

From my research, I knew that the practice of polygamy

came to be the scapegoat for the Mormons' troubles in Utah. Professor Bowen knew it, too. Nevertheless, he seemed intent on dredging up all the sullied stories of plural marriage that he could find. Or rather that I could find. Any disparaging remark I might unearth in some impoverished, overworked polygamous woman's diary was fair game for Professor Bowen. He pounced on it like a lion making ready for the kill.

Professor Bowen's tactics and slanted writing didn't matter to me. I felt no kinship with the Mormon pioneers. It seemed to me that they had brought their problems upon themselves through their fanatical devotion to their religion. Rather than research the complexities of a religious tug-of-war, I would have preferred working on some topic of real historical significance. I had hoped to secure a position at the Custer Battlefield National Monument in Montana, where field work was taking place on the famous battleground. The area had suffered a fire which burned a good portion of the famous battlefield, and it had unexpectedly proved to be a boon. With the tall prairie grass burned away, the barren ground lay exposed to the scrutiny of archaeologists and historians. Their labors had turned up some fascinating evidence. I had applied to work at the site, but the job openings were restricted to those experienced in archaeological procedures.

Needless to say, I was disappointed. I was beginning to sense that a bachelor's degree in history was virtually useless. I wanted to research new frontiers, and instead I was sitting in a stuffy little office reading Mormon trivia.

"Ms. Garrett!"

My head jerked up from the copy I was reading.

"Have you found the Kane notes yet?"

"No, sir. I haven't. They're nowhere on my desk." I gulped, waiting for the blood to rise in Professor Bowen's face. It always did when he became agitated, and this time was no exception. Bowen's face grew beet-colored, starting at the neck and climbing to the roots of his sparse, stringy hair. His eyes bulged in their sockets, and his lips puffed out in a deep shade of purple.

"Need I remind you, Ms. Garrett, that time is money?"

"No, sir," I answered meekly.

"And on this project we do not have enough of either to repeat ourselves." The veins in Bowen's thick neck swelled until I thought they would burst.

I understood his meaning clearly enough. He stood glaring at me, red-faced, a moment longer, then proceeded to make a cursory search through the notes stacked on my desk.

I darted a glance at Sally. She was leaning back in her chair, her arms folded across her ample bosom, watching us with a bland expression. I wished she would offer an encouraging word or show me some gesture of support, but she remained seated stoically behind her computer.

Having finished his search through my notes, and leaving them in a jumbled heap, Professor Bowen wordlessly returned to his office. I had scarcely taken a breath when he abruptly returned carrying a bundle of papers.

"I want you to read through these files, making notes on anything you may find pertinent to our research," he barked, depositing the papers on my desk.

"I'll do that right away, Professor Bowen."

"Finish it as quickly as possible so you can get back to the Mormon diaries."

"All right." I immediately picked up the top paper on the stack and began examining it, not daring to lift my eyes from the page until I heard Bowen's office door slam shut behind him.

After a few moments of cursory reading, I realized that Professor Bowen's "files" were nothing more than a collection of anti-Mormon literature. It contained copies of the standard disreputable histories and articles, along with some other material I had never seen before. As I flipped through the pages, I noticed several comments in the margins made in Bowen's own hand. One in particular caught my attention.

The text to which it made reference concerned Brigham Young and his plans to transport the Saints across the plains.

Beside it, Bowen had written in ink, "Mormon followers witless as sheep!"

The comment stung me, even though I didn't know why it should. I had no reason to care what Bowen thought about the Mormons. I replaced the pages in their proper order and straightened the pile. Sally had gone back to her typing, for I could hear the steady clicking of the keyboard. I wished I knew her views concerning the anti-Mormon literature, but I lacked the nerve to ask her about it.

My head had begun to ache and my back cried out for a change of posture. I stretched in my chair, but it did little to relieve the stiffness settling throughout my body. What I needed was a good, brisk walk. I looked at my watch. Eleven-thirty. Too early yet for lunch. I tried concentrating on the papers lying before me, but the words began to blur in front of my eyes.

"Sally, I'm going out. I'll be back after lunch," I said, rising from my seat. I smoothed the wrinkles out of my green and navy blue plaid skirt, then slipped on the navy hip-length jacket. This two-piece outfit was my favorite. I usually wore it with a plain white cotton blouse, but today I had added a kelly green vest over the blouse. To complement the outfit, I had put on big, dangling earrings.

The blouse felt cool and soft against my skin. I straightened my jacket, grabbed my lunch sack and prepared to leave.

"Wait, Kallie. The Church Historical Department called. They have those diaries you asked them to pull from the shelf for you."

"Thanks. I'll stop there first and take a look at them. You can call me at the Historical Department if Bowen needs me."

Sally nodded in reply.

I hurried out the door and down the steps of the building to my car. It was the last day of April and unusually warm for the time of year. My wool jacket was ideally suited for the weather. The day was calm and clear, the sky a flawless blue. There wasn't a cloud to mar the azure ocean overhead. I drove the few blocks to the towering Church Office Building on North Temple which housed the Historical Department, and parked my car in a thirty-minute parking zone. A light breeze caressed my hair as I stepped from the car. The weather was so delightful and my body so tired from sitting that I decided to take that walk I had promised myself before going into the office building.

I crossed the street and headed up the slight incline of First Avenue. My feet were left to decide their own course, for my mind was crowded with thoughts of Professor Bowen's "files." Now I understood Bowen's intentions concerning his book on the Utah War. Undoubtedly, he planned to write it in such a way as to fuel anti-Mormon sentiment. To my surprise, I felt unsettled by that realization. It bothered me to know that Bowen planned to write such a slanted version. I thought I had purged myself of every loyalty to the Church, but this dilemma shook all my defenses. I wondered if I should express my feelings to Bowen and perhaps offer a word of caution, but I immediately decided against taking any action. My job was already hanging in the balance. If I didn't find those notes on Colonel Kane soon, I could be seeking new employment by the end of the week.

My pace quickened as thoughts of Colonel Kane, Mormon polygamists, and Bowen's projected book whirled in my head. A few moments later I found myself in front of the black wrought-iron gate leading into the Brigham Young family cemetery. I paused, my hand on the gate, conscious of the fact that I hadn't been to the cemetery in years. I traced with my finger the ornamental ironwork on the gate—the letters "B" and "Y" woven together, the initials of Brigham Young. The cemetery looked quiet and peaceful; its large shade trees and abundant shrubbery beckoned me inside. I put away my troubled thoughts and let myself through the gate.

A carpet of green grass and half a dozen trees, whose leaves ranged in hue from emerald to a deep purplish-brown, dominated the grave site. Encircling the cemetery were thick lilac bushes, whose delicate blossoms of cream and lavender filled the air with sweet perfume. The fragrance reminded me of my grandmother; she had always smelled of lilac.

The place was nearly deserted. Besides myself, only two others were present. An older woman with gray frizzing hair and thick glasses was seated on a bench eating her sack lunch. The other, lying on the grass reading a paperback book, was a plump young woman wearing rust-colored slacks and an orange top. Her short, curly hair was reddish-orange as well, and her face was as round as a pumpkin. She looked like the last vestige of autumn.

I nodded at the young woman as I walked down the five or six stone steps leading to the area where the graves were located. I paused at each marker, cement slabs set into the ground, reading the names and dates of the deceased. Most were wives or children of Brigham Young. Located in the southeast corner of the cemetery was the prophet's grave, surrounded by the same type of iron fence which enclosed the whole cemetery. The iron bars of the fence were topped with decorative spiked tips. As I stood beside Brigham Young's grave, peering between the bars, I wondered what he would have thought of the city as it was today. He had colonized Salt Lake City over a hundred years ago—would he be pleased with the changes? What would be his thoughts on pollution or nuclear disarmament? I mused silently.

I moved to the south end of the cemetery, a foot or two away from the prophet's grave. At this point the site was above the street, and the cars rushed past below me in a noisy stream of motion. Beyond the street, the city stretched away with only a few tall buildings to block the view. I could see for miles in every direction. The mountains, purple and serene, presided over the city. On the valley floor, the buildings of the business district gradually gave way to the gentler structures of homes and schools. Nature's finery claimed every space not occupied by man's handiwork.

I nibbled at my sandwich as I surveyed the scene. The big green Mountain Fuel building, with its rotating sign perched on the roof, stood prominently in the foreground. I was mesmerized by the turning sign and the blinking time-and-temperature display below it.

The noisy bawling of a trucker's horn interrupted my pleasant reverie. I turned away and yawned, suddenly sleepy from my leisurely lunch. To the west of the cemetery stood an old brick building with climbing vines clinging to its walls. On the east side spread a vacant grassy lot which looked inviting.

I squinted up into the sun. It was almost directly overhead. I walked to the shade of one of the emerald-leafed trees and sat down. The trunk was gnarled and knotted, and the branches twisted like old bony fingers into the air. Thick ivy, the color of jade, wound up the tree, reaching to its highest branches. The tree looked a hundred years old. I wondered if it had been here when Brigham Young was laid to rest.

In the cool shade of the tree I felt content—the most contentment I had known since beginning work on Professor Bowen's project. This place was such a peaceful spot, nestled in the heart of the noisy city. It gave me an opportunity to forget my worries. I leaned back on my elbows and relaxed. The sun filtered through the leaves, making a pattern of light and shadow on my arms. I watched as it weaved its gilded design.

By this time, a few more people had come into the cemetery—two young men in T-shirts and a middle-aged woman clasping a child's hand. None of them paid any heed to me as I lay stretched out beneath the tree. They read the gravemarkers and then drifted away. The sun's golden warmth bathed my face as I lay on the cool grass. I closed my eyes to let the heat soak into them.

The sound of footsteps on the stone staircase jarred me to attention. I jerked open my eyes to find an elderly man dressed in old-fashioned clothing slowly making his way across the grounds. He had on a pair of black and gray striped trousers, a knee-length loose fitting coat, and a black cravat tied around his neck. His head was bare, revealing thin gray hair parted low on his head, just above the ear. I noticed an ornately-worked black metal key hanging from a chain, one end of which was hooked to the top button of his vest and the other concealed in his vest pocket.

I turned away, amused by the man's appearance. Nothing people wore these days surprised me. A few days ago I'd seen a young man dressed in ragged levis, a sportcoat, and leather tie. His hair was shaved in a checkerboard pattern on one side of his head, and left long over his ear on the other. The outlandish fashions of the day were all too commonplace to cause much of a stir.

I wouldn't have given the old man another glance except for the fact that now he was standing at one end of the fence surrounding Brigham Young's grave, trying to fit his key into a lock on the gate. I hadn't noticed a gate or a lock before on the little fence; but now as I watched, the man's key clicked and turned, and the gate swung open.

I scrambled to my feet, surprised by the man's actions. Surely he had no business inside the fence of Young's grave. My eyes swept the grounds. No one else was about. I wondered where the pumpkin-faced woman had gone; I hadn't seen her leave the cemetery. My gaze went back to the old man. He was standing motionless beside the open gate, as though waiting for someone or something. I couldn't figure out what he was doing there. I decided to question him as to his purpose.

I hurried over to the grave. As I approached, the old man turned as if expecting me. He didn't seem surprised in the least by my presence. Before I could say a word, he slowly and delib-erately reached into his vest pocket and pulled out an old-fash-ioned timepiece. I was close enough to see the flowery etching on its shiny gold case. He flipped the timepiece open. The numerals on the face were of bold size. He studied the clock face for an instant, then lifted his eyes to meet mine. They were the strangest eyes I had ever seen—deep, clear, piercing.

His eyes bored into mine. As I stared into the depths of those strange, bottomless eyes, I felt curiously light-headed. I blinked, trying to fight off the dizziness. At that instant I experienced a falling sensation, as if hurtling backward through space and time. When I recovered myself, I was astonished to see that the old man and I were no longer alone in the cemetery. A great throng of people pressed about us. So many men, women and children were crowded into the graveyard that I couldn't take a step. I caught a glimpse of the old man through the crowd, closing his timepiece and replacing it in his pocket. Then he was blocked from my view.

For some seconds I gaped, speechless, at the people pressing on all sides of me. To my amazement, I realized everyone was dressed in attire similar to that worn by the old man at the grave. The men wore dark trousers, vests and topcoats. Many had on tall beaver hats. The women were clothed in long full dresses of a dark color, with shawls around their shoulders. Each face was somber. Some of the ladies pressed handkerchiefs to reddened eyes.

Panic welled up inside me. I had to get out of the cemetery, away from all these people. I glanced toward the street where my car was parked, trying to gauge the distance from it to me. I couldn't see the road because of the crowd, but I knew it wasn't more than a few yards away. In the safety and security of my Mustang, perhaps I could make some sense out of all this.

As I managed a step in the direction of the street, I felt something soft brush against my legs. I looked down. My heart nearly took flight as I discovered I was dressed in the same ankle-length, billowing skirts as the women around me. I gasped. Gone was the plaid skirt and wool jacket I had donned that morning, and in their place I wore a calico print, plum-colored dress, with a row of black buttons running down the front from neck to waist.

My gasp and look of consternation must have attracted the attention of the woman standing next to me. She patted my hand and whispered, "There now, child. Brother Brigham didn't want any tears shed on this day. Try to be courageous."

The woman gave me a brief smile, then turned away.

It wasn't until then that I realized the crowd was breaking up, moving out of the area of the cemetery. Perhaps now I could get to my car. If I didn't hurry, I would be late getting back to work. I had no idea what the woman meant when she spoke to me, but I followed her woodenly out of the cemetery.

As we walked toward the street, I noticed with a start that the building to the west had disappeared, and in its place was a large empty field. Confused and frightened, I jerked my head around to the south. The tall green Mountain Fuel building with its rotating sign was gone, too. All I could see were a few brick and adobe buildings, and vast fields of cultivated land. Beyond that, nothing but raw ground. I couldn't understand what had happened to the buildings or why I was dressed in this strange outfit.

I was nearly to the street now. I strained to see over the heads of the crowd, but the men's tall beaver hats obstructed my view, making it difficult to see much of anything. In a few more steps I should have the car in sight, and this whole business would be over and I could . . . I stopped cold in my tracks. Instead of my sporty Ford Mustang parked down the street, the whole area outside the cemetery was filled with carriages, wagons, and buggies. Horses snorted and stamped their feet impatiently as they waited for their owners. I stood rooted to the spot with my mouth open while the people around me began climbing into their carriages and driving away. What was going on here? The twentieth century was twisted all out of shape.

"Katharine!"

The voice to my left was loud and insistent. I turned to see a man with a full beard and dark eyes scowling in my direction.

"Katharine," the man repeated, looking sternly at me. "Come get into the wagon."

"Me?" I asked, pointing a shaky finger to my chest.

The man gestured for me to hurry.

I looked around me, thinking the man must be addressing

someone else, but everyone seemed occupied. Not knowing what else to do, I started slowly toward the man's wagon. When I was within a few steps of him, he reached for my arm and said in a deep voice, "Get in the wagon, daughter. It's time for us to leave."

His firm grip fairly lifted me off my feet and into the wagon parked at his side. Two of the biggest horses I had ever seen were tossing their heads, straining against the traces that ran along their broad backs hitching them to the wagon. The bearded man climbed into the wagon seat beside a slight, dark-haired woman, the same woman who had spoken to me in the cemetery, and with a slap of the reins the wagon lurched forward. Unprepared for the sudden movement, I pitched head-long into the straw lining the wagon bed. Four pair of blue eyes turned to stare at me. I self-consciously righted myself, pulling pieces of straw from my disheveled hair.

The eyes belonged to persons ranging in age from about seven years to slightly younger than myself. They were seated, cross-legged, in the wagon beside me. The two children, a young boy and a girl of about twelve, finally ceased their staring and began weaving pieces of the straw into a chain, talking between themselves. The oldest of the group, a fellow with brown hair and broad shoulders, continued to stare at me, a smirk tugging at the corners of his ample mouth. I ignored him, fastening my eyes instead on the young woman sitting next to him. She had lighter hair than the young man and light blue eyes, but still the two looked very much alike.

"What's the matter? You look like you've just swallowed a hot coal," the young woman said testily to me. "Surely you're not that upset by Brother Brigham's passing."

"What?" I replied, confused by her words and the whole circumstance which had befallen me.

"Oh, never mind," she answered crossly.

The young man chuckled, then turned away.

Not knowing what to make of any of them, I concentrated

on my surroundings. We had pulled away from the cemetery and were headed down First Avenue toward town. Since that was the direction I needed to go in order to get back to my car, I sat expectantly in the wagon. Within a moment, however, I realized that everything was changed. The towering Church Office Building was nowhere in sight. It had completely vanished! The street we traveled on, too, was altered. It was unpaved and rutted, and dust churned in the air from the constant motion of hoof and wheel on the dirt road.

I scrambled to my knees, searching desperately for a glimpse of something familiar. The long dress I wore tangled around my legs and I became acutely aware of the heat. It was much hotter now than when I had first come to the cemetery. Beads of sweat were collecting along my forehead. I wondered what had become of the cool April breeze. On the crowded road ahead, I caught a quick glimpse of someone I recognized. I strained to see through the dust and the dozens of carriages jostling up and down the road. My breath caught in my throat as the man's face came clearly into view.

"It's him!" I shouted. "Stop! Please stop, I have to speak to that man."

Just up ahead, the old man with the iron key whom I had seen in the cemetery was patiently walking beside the road. In a matter of seconds our wagon had pulled up even with him, then began to pass him.

"Wait a minute!" I cried, gripping the edge of the wagon. "Please!"

"Katharine, what is the meaning of this outburst?" The bearded man in the wagon seat turned to glare at me. His gruff tone ground into my ears. "I will not allow you to behave disrespectfully on a day such as this."

I cowered under his harsh stare.

He looked at me with a steely gaze for a second longer, then he faced forward again, giving the reins a shake.

During that brief exchange, our wagon had left the old man

in the street far behind. With a sinking heart, I stared after him. I still had no idea how I had come to be in such peculiar circumstances, but somehow I knew the old man with the pocket watch and key had the answers. I'd have to find him, and the quicker, the better.

The four people in the wagon bed were watching me curiously, surprised, I supposed, by my outburst. The young woman, who I guessed to be about sixteen or seventeen, gave me a particularly scornful look. I couldn't comprehend why all of them behaved as if they were acquainted with me. I was certainly a stranger, yet they treated me with familiarity. And even more puzzling was how they knew my name. Although I had been given the name of Katharine at my birth, I was never called that. I disliked the name and all its usual dimunitives. For as long as I could remember, everyone had called me Kallie. I resolved to ask them about it.

"Pardon me," I said boldly, addressing myself to the young woman, "but have we met before?"

Her eyebrows raised a fraction of an inch, then she lifted her chin and haughtily looked away.

I tried again, this time with the younger boy, who by now had strung a necklace of straw which he proudly wore around his neck.

"Do you know me, by any chance?" I inquired, with somewhat less resolve.

"What d'ya mean, Katharine?" he answered innocently.

"Well, I don't know any of you. Yet you seem to be acquainted with me."

The boy cast a quick glance at the little girl sitting at his side, and they both started to giggle.

I was somewhat taken aback, to say the least. I watched the children laughing together, not knowing what else to say.

"If it's temporary memory loss you have, Katharine, I'll be happy to oblige you," the strapping young man sitting across from me volunteered. His expression communicated the fact that he was obviously jesting with me. "Allow me to introduce myself.

23

My name is Thomas Kane Walker, and this lovely creature to my right"—he gestured toward the older girl, who sniffed in derision and turned her back on him—"is Lacy Walker. Those giggling hooligans at your feet are Marinda and Jesse Walker. And you, Miss Walker, are our dear sister, Katharine."

I was stunned speechless. I guess my face must have shown it, for Thomas Kane Walker's grin slowly faded and was replaced with a genuine look of concern.

I finally found my voice enough to croak, "And those people?" I pointed at the two figures in the wagon seat in front of us.

"Henry and Rachel Walker. Our parents." Thomas frowned. "I think you've carried this little charade far enough."

"It's not a charade," I replied desperately. "Something terribly wrong has happened here. I'm not who you think I am, at least not entirely. My name is Katharine, but not the Katharine you take me for." My words were tumbling over one another in my rush to explain to him. "You see, I had come to the cemetery to eat my lunch and think over what to do about Professor Bowen's . . ."

"Stop. Just stop it, Katharine," Thomas commanded in a low voice. "All of us are upset by Brother Brigham's passing, but I'm beginning to worry about you. You act as if you've slipped a cog. Everything's going to be fine. I know how much you loved the Prophet—all of us did—but I can assure you things will work out as the Lord intends they should."

I clamped my mouth shut, totally at a loss for a reply. Evidently, they really believed me to be their sister. It was incredible. Slowly, the fact dawned on me that all of us had just attended Brigham Young's graveside service. This was the reason for the crowd at the cemetery and the reason why everyone was talking about his death. And, of course, it was the reason for the ladies' teary eyes. But that was impossible! Brigham Young died over a hundred years ago. Had I gone crazy? Slipped a cog, as Thomas said? I fought the terror rising inside me. I had to find that old man and get him to tell me what had happened. I felt sure he was the key to freeing me from this nightmare.

CHAPTER THREE

I WAS SILENT for the rest of the ride. We turned left off of First Avenue onto Main Street, and down past South Temple. I watched speechlessly as we drove near Brigham Young's Beehive and Lion Houses. The houses looked much the same as I knew them, but I couldn't remember seeing the tall cobblestone wall which surrounded them now. There was a large gate directly beneath the Eagle Gate Monument, which was swung open on its hinges; and a schoolhouse across the way, with a white steeple.

As we traveled down Main Street, I was astonished at the homes and buildings lining the road. I had never seen any of them before. Many of the buildings were made of adobe brick and sported signs advertising wares and services. Shades or awnings were drawn against the afternoon sun, and these too exhibited painted advertisements. A tailoring shop called Buckle & Son boasted "Punctuality! Fashion! Economy!" on its overhead sign. We passed by the company of Calder & Careless, who were advertising Hamlin organs for sale. The Deseret Carriage and Wagon Company offered vehicles from the farm wagon to the family carriage. All kinds of shops and businesses were represented along the streets—Day & Co. dry goods store; Jake Heusser & Bro., dealer of guns, pistols, ammunition, and fishing tackle; Sierra Nevada Lumber Association; Deseret National Bank; Morton & Tullis, who sold wines and liquors; C. W. Stayer, attorney; Dr. A. W.

Calder, practitioner in dentistry; the barbershop of E. Cox & W. J. Wright; and Mr. George Reynolds who sold walnut, mulberry, and locust trees. There were dozens more.

For every unfamiliar building we passed, my mind pictured the edifice which should have been there instead. There was no Brigham Young Monument at the intersection of Main and South Temple. The magnificent old Hotel Utah was gone. The Deseret News building had been replaced with a square, two-story structure built of adobe and red sandstone. Not only had the Church Office Building disappeared, but the temple—the most distinctive landmark in the entire city—was built to a height of only about fifty feet or so. Private homes were sandwiched between public buildings on both sides of the street. The city wore a whole different face.

We drove to an area I could only estimate to be near 1700 South and 500 East. The buildings had thinned out considerably since we had departed the downtown area, leaving only a few scattered homes set on generous tracts of ground. Mr. Walker turned the horses into the yard of a home set well back off the street. He pulled up beside the two-story house, stopping to let us climb down from the wagon. Thomas remained seated with his father. Walker gave the reins a shake, and the huge horses plodded down the worn path to the barn and pasture beyond.

The younger children, Jesse and Marinda, hurried into the house. Mrs. Walker followed silently behind them with Lacy at her side. I paused on the dusty path next to the house, gazing about at my surroundings. Behind the house stretched an orchard of fruit trees and a large vegetable garden. The whole was encircled by a split rail fence. The barn, located to the side and behind the house, showed a graying coat of paint, and there were pens for pigs and goats. I started in surprise as a scrawny chicken suddenly ran, squawking, in front of my feet.

Slowly I walked toward the house. It was built of adobe brick painted a straw yellow color, with narrow windows on both the upper and ground floors. The roof was gabled and I spotted three chimneys from where I stood. Bright flowers bloomed beside the door in a profusion of pinks, reds, and yellows. I heard the chirp of a robin nesting in the branches of an old elm tree growing in the yard.

I hesitated at the door. "What am I doing here?" I said aloud. Questions raced through my mind: Why have these people mistaken me for their daughter? Surely they can tell from my appearance that I am not Katharine Walker. My eyes are brown, not blue like the Walker children. And I'm much shorter than either Lacy or Thomas. What resemblance can they possibly see between us? I stood uncertainly on the doorstep, wondering whether I should turn and run or go inside. Although my initial panic had subsided, I was incapable of making a decision, for I was completely baffled by my situation.

Suddenly the porch door swung open and Mrs. Walker stood in the doorway, the sun on her face. "Come inside, Katharine," she said in a gentle voice.

She held the door open for me, a slight smile parting her lips. I noticed for the first time what a pretty woman she was. Her eyes were kind and gentle and her face, though careworn, had an expression of contentment. Her dark hair was beginning to gray at the temples, her waist to thicken, and lines had begun to burrow their way into the corners of her blue eyes, but her whole person radiated a kind of dignity and quiet strength.

Hesitantly, I moved through the door and found myself in a large, comfortable kitchen. A square oak table dominated the room, the wooden chairs placed around it with the seats facing outward. My initial glance took in a big black iron stove standing in one corner and a hand-crafted cupboard set against the wall. An open door at the far end of the kitchen led to what appeared to be a pantry stocked with goods.

"Change out of your best dress, Katharine, and help me with the meal," Mrs. Walker said to me.

I could only stare at her.

"Go on, child," she encouraged. She glanced toward the hall leading from the kitchen, where a set of stairs rose to the upper floor. All I could see of the staircase were the first two or three steps. Obediently, I started toward the steps. Evidently I was headed in the right direction, for Mrs. Walker gave me a final glance and then set about preparing the afternoon meal.

I paused at the foot of the staircase and looked up. It seemed like an unusually steep set of stairs, and at the top a hallway led in either direction. Cautiously I began to climb. I had mounted only four or five steps when Marinda came bounding down, rushing past me on the stair. She smiled brightly at me as she passed. I noticed that she'd put on a white muslin pinafore over her cotton dress, and her blonde hair hung in long ringlets down her back. I watched her skip down the remaining stairs and turn to go into the kitchen.

With a sense of determination, I continued up the stairwell. When I reached the top, I saw a room to my left just off the hallway. I tiptoed over to it and peeked in. It contained a bed with a beautiful tall oak headboard and matching footboard, covered with a lovely quilted spread. A chest, closed and latched, was at the foot of the bed; beside the bed stood a small table with a pitcher and bowl resting on it. A glass lamp, painted with pink and lavender flowers, hung from the ceiling. In one corner of the room sat a large wooden chair with a man's coat draped over the back of it. The room was charmingly quaint and old-fashioned. I sensed that it belonged to Mr. and Mrs. Walker, for it was in perfect order with nothing out of place except for the coat, and that was carefully straightened and hung.

I started back down the hall, past the top of the stairs, and turned right, following the hall where it led into a second bedroom. This room was larger than the first and furnished with a single narrow bed, a large chest of drawers made of dark wood, and a table where three or four books rested beside a pitcher and basin painted with delicate blue flowers. An assortment of girls' clothing lay strewn across the top of an unopened trunk. A shaft of sunlight streamed through the window, revealing flecks of dust dancing in the air.

"I'm glad that's over. I thought this day would never end."

I jerked around to see Lacy pulling a white petticoat over her head. She mumbled something else, but the underclothing muffled her words so that I couldn't make them out. With a puff, she tugged the petticoat off her outstretched arms and tossed it onto the trunk with the other clothing.

"Oh, I'm sorry," I stammered. "I didn't know anyone was in here."

Lacy stood with both hands on her hips, dressed in only her chemise, staring disgustedly at me. I couldn't help noticing her slightly plump figure in the revealing underclothing.

"What are you talking about, Katharine? As much as you'd like it to be otherwise, this room does belong to Marinda and me, as well as yourself." She gave me a final haughty glance and began to rummage through the clothing heaped on the trunk.

I shook my head in disbelief. No one in this entire family seemed to grasp the fact that I was not their Katharine. I considered instigating a serious discussion with Lacy as to my real identity, but decided against it. Lacy was too distant and unapproachable. I thought about talking to Marinda or Jesse, but they were just children and probably could not answer the urgent questions I had any better than I could. Thomas seemed to be my best bet. At least he was willing to talk to me.

"Where is Thomas?" I asked, trying my best to sound casual.

"He's probably still outside with Father, taking care of the wagon and horses."

I bit my lip. I didn't want to run into Mr. Walker right now. His stern countenance loomed forbiddingly in my memory.

"You'd better change quick and get downstairs. Mama will be wanting us to help with supper." With those words, Lacy finished buttoning her green calico dress and started to leave the room.

"Lacy, wait a minute," I said on impulse.

She stopped and turned to look at me.

"What day is this?" I asked in a trembling voice.

A frown creased Lacy's brow. "Sunday, of course."

"No, I mean what month and year?"

"Don't be ridiculous . . ."

"Please! This is important."

Lacy's blue eyes widened at the urgent tone in my voice. "Why, it's September second."

"And the year?" I asked breathlessly.

"What kind of game are you playing, Katharine? I've had just about enough of it, whatever it is."

"The year? Please, Lacy."

Lacy glared at me. "It's 1877, Katharine. As you well know." With that reply, Lacy lifted her nose in the air and swept out of the room.

September 2, 1877. The date whirled round and round in my head. I knew from the research I had just completed for Professor Bowen that Brigham Young had died on August 29, 1877. His funeral and burial would have taken place a few days later. How was it possible that I had become a participant in that burial service? I stared after Lacy's retreating figure, not knowing what to do next.

The room where I stood was hot and stuffy. I glanced down at the floor where a multi-colored rag rug covered the polished boards beneath my feet. My gaze fixed on my feet, which had begun to ache. It was no wonder they hurt; I had on the queerest pair of pointed, tight-fitting, ankle-high leather shoes. Casting a quick look behind me to make certain no one was about, I gingerly lifted up the hem of my skirt. Beneath it was a petticoat of white, very much like the one Lacy wore. I picked up a corner of the petticoat and was surprised to see another of the same style and fabric. Lifting that, I saw yet another! Here was the reason I had felt so warm on the ride home from the cemetery. Beneath the last petticoat, I discovered long cotton stockings.

I let the skirts fall with a quick motion of my hand. How I came to be dressed in these outlandish clothes was a mystery to me. I tried to recall the sequence of events that had led to this moment, but none of it made sense in my mind. How could I have been suddenly thrust backward in time, complete with contemporary attire, without a logical explanation for it? I still felt that the old man I had seen at the cemetery could supply the explanation. I was determined to talk with Thomas about it— get him to help me find the strange old man. I must be careful not to be too impatient, I reminded myself. I must act rational and natural or Thomas would never consent to help me.

With renewed determination, I quickly removed the old-fashioned ankle-length dress I wore. I sorted through the discarded clothing left on top of the trunk, and finding nothing suitable, put them aside and opened the trunk. Some underclothing and three or four dresses lay folded neatly inside. I searched through them, looking for a dress that might fit me. I selected a plain blue muslin and slipped it over my head. The dress had a row of small buttons which took me some time to fasten. When I'd finished the last button and smoothed the skirt with my hand, I was surprised to see how well the dress fit. The sleeves came precisely to my wrists, and the bodice was neither too tight nor too loose. I took a look at myself in the square mirror fastened to the chest of drawers and decided that except for my hair, which was collected into an unfashionable bun at the nape of my neck, I did not look too awful. I wondered briefly what had become of the attractive skirt, jacket, and soft cotton blouse that I'd been wearing earlier. I hoped they'd turn up eventually.

I returned all of the clothing to the trunk, drew a deep breath, and resolutely marched out of the bedroom toward the stairs.

My knees were beginning to ache from kneeling, and my back hurt from hunching over the kitchen chair. I wondered how much longer Mr. Walker's prayer was going to go on. My own parents had always made it a practice to say a blessing on the food at every meal, but we never knelt at the table, nor did our prayers last more than a couple of minutes. Walker's prayer was the most lengthy and the most fervent I had ever heard.

I opened my eyes a slit to look furtively at the family kneeling around the kitchen table. Mrs. Walker's head was bowed, but I could see enough of her face to read the expression of humility gracing her brow. Thomas's eyes were closed, his face expressionless. Jesse and Marinda were squirming on their knees, but other than that, bore the lengthy prayer stoically. It was Lacy's attitude that arrested my attention. She knelt with eyes wide open, making no attempt to disguise the impatience her eyes reflected. I wondered what she was thinking, and why she didn't conform to the example set by her parents and siblings.

Almost without warning the prayer came to an end, and everyone rose from their knees. The sudden "amen" took me by surprise. I scrambled to my feet and in the process knocked over the chair I had been kneeling against. It fell with a loud clatter on the wooden boards of the floor. Mr. Walker's eye fell on me.

"I'm sorry. I didn't mean to—it's just that—" I stammered.

Walker's brows lowered and he scowled fiercely at me. He was a gruff-looking man. Heavy dark brows made almost a solid line across his forehead. His eyes were dark also, and deeply set in his head. His nose was broad, his mouth wide, and his chin completely hidden by a heavy beard. I shrank under his harsh gaze.

While I clumsily righted my chair, everyone else took their seat. Mrs. Walker set a bowl of steaming mashed potatoes in front of her husband, and followed that with bowls of green beans, meat and corn. The dishes of food were passed from hand to hand until all were served. The family ate with relish, wasting little breath on conversation.

I hadn't realized how hungry I was until I'd taken my first bite. The potatoes tasted smooth and creamy in my mouth. I eagerly tried the beans—they were tender and lightly seasoned with some kind of herb. The corn was sweet, the meat succulent. At first I did not recognize the kind of meat on my plate, but after a few bites I determined that it was a mutton roast. I hadn't cared much for mutton in the past, but this meat was delicate of flavor, tender, and juicy. Like the others, I polished my plate in no time at all. Then, feeling full and contented, I leaned back in my chair. My mother would certainly like to have Mrs. Walker's recipe for mutton roast, I mused.

With a start, my present dilemma came crashing back into my consciousness. I had to get home! Mother would have prepared dinner by now and would be waiting impatiently for me to arrive home from work. If I didn't get there soon, she and Dad would be worried.

I wrung my hands nervously. I had to talk with Thomas, and soon. I glanced across the table at him, meaning to give him a silent signal of my need to speak with him. He sat slouched down in his chair, picking at his teeth with a bit of bone from the roast. His eyes were on the empty plate in front of him, and all my mute efforts to attract his attention failed miserably.

"Today has been a momentous day," Mr. Walker said suddenly in a low, solemn voice.

I jumped in my chair, unnerved by Walker's unexpected words.

"A day that will be recorded in the annals of time," he went on soberly.

I wondered if he were referring to me and my present predicament. It had certainly been a momentous day for me.

"I want each of you children to remember Brother Brigham in your hearts," he went on. "Treasure up his words, obey his precepts, follow his example."

Each member of the Walker family nodded his head solemnly.

"A great man has passed beyond the veil. There, friends and loved ones greet him with joy and gladness. For those of us who remain behind, it is a day of sadness. Yet Brother Brigham did not want us to grieve. He expected us to remember that he lived a righteous life and has gone on to his reward."

Walker looked around the table at each individual. I sat rigid as stone for fear he might discern the fact that I was not mourning Brother Brigham. I could think of nothing else but how to escape this time warp I had fallen into. Walker sighed heavily and folded his arms against his chest. I detected a reverence in the room that I did not feel a part of. Each person was quiet, respectful.

"I shall never forget the many kindnesses of Brother Brigham and his great wisdom. A more God-fearing man I have never met, yet at the same time practical and farsighted."

Walker paused, passing a hand over his bearded chin. "I remember when I first came into the valley. I was only fourteen years of age. My father had died at Winter Quarters, leaving my saintly mother alone with six young children. Mother summoned the faith and courage to go ahead without him. The trek was difficult and exhausting. Being the oldest, I did all I could to help shoulder Mother's burdens. But it wasn't enough. Pregnant and ill, she gave birth to a baby girl just two days before reaching the valley. Both my mother and the baby died the following day. When Brother Brigham heard the news, he rode out to meet our wagon, and when he saw my mother along with her baby dead inside the wagon, with all her little children sorrowing around her, he sat down and wept."

Not a word was spoken in the room as Mr. Walker finished relating his tale. In my role as a historian, I had read dozens of accounts of pioneer suffering and death, but none had ever moved me as much as this intensely personal and poignant experience that Walker had just related. I was stunned by the story. My own concerns dissolved away like sugar in boiling water, and my eyes were riveted on Walker's face as he started to speak again.

"That first winter we spent inside the old fort. It was a hard winter and by the time spring arrived, food was scarce. We were put on rations to help preserve what little food we had. My brothers and sisters and I gathered thistles, pig weeds and sego lily roots to eat. The tops of the thistles were cooked to make greens and the roots were boiled and eaten also."

Walker grimaced slightly. "I remember the roots tasted like a combination of watery turnips and beeswax. Boiled sego lily roots weren't too bad, though. Later, many of the Saints cultivated sego lilies in their gardens for their roots."

"The shortage of food was one of the biggest problems in those early days. Many of the Saints fell ill from not having enough to eat, or from eating the wrong varieties of plants, weeds, or berries. When we didn't have the real product, we made do with what we had. Molasses was made from squash, beets, or corn stalks. Potatoes were mixed with flour to make bread. We quickly learned that four barrels of lake water produced one barrel of good table salt, and alkali was used for soda. As a young boy it seemed I never had enough fresh food to eat. There was little fresh fruit, and nearly all of our meat was either dried or salted. I can remember, too, hankering after something sweet many a time."

Walker leaned back in his chair and closed his eyes. I wondered if he was revisiting that hungry, orphaned young boy of many years ago. I had scarcely completed the thought when he resumed his story.

"Brother Brigham suffered with us in all our trials, constantly providing encouragement, help, and spiritual guidance. He never asked the Saints to accomplish anything that he wasn't willing to do first."

I noticed that Mrs. Walker was silently nodding her head in agreement. Tears had come to her eyes; they were red-rimmed and she dabbed at them with a handkerchief. Walker glanced over at her, then covered her hand with his.

"That was a fine meal, Rachel," he said to her. "Come sit with me in the parlor for a spell while the children clean up here."

Rachel Walker rose to her feet, and together she and her husband retired from the kitchen. Their departure signaled a return to activity. Lacy and Marinda immediately began clearing the leftover food from the table, while Jesse and Thomas scraped scraps from the plates into a metal pail. The four of them conversed in low tones, maintaining the reverent atmosphere left by Walker's narrative. No one seemed to mind the fact that I remained seated, wordlessly, at the table. They worked around me, gathering plates and bowls without disturbing my silent reverie.

When the kitchen was tidy, the plates placed face-down on the table in preparation for the next meal, and Jesse had taken the pail of slops out to the pigs, the family reassembled in the parlor—a large, cozy room off the kitchen. At one end of the room was a handsome fireplace with a mirror above it, and at the other sat a glass-fronted bookcase crafted in the Queen Anne style. Several chairs, a couch, and a large desk made up the remainder of the furnishings.

Each of the Walker children was soon busy with some task. Thomas took up a book, Lacy her sewing, and the two younger children commenced playing some sort of game using string and wooden pegs. I sat down awkwardly on one of the chairs, my long dress and layers of petticoats bunching up uncomfortably underneath me. There was the usual conversation that might be expected in this kind of relaxed family setting, but the words passed over me. I felt as though I were an unseen visitor, listening but undetected. I studied the Walkers' faces; for the most part they reflected a common forthrightness and open honesty. My eyes traveled over their clothing—simple and without adornment, but clean and neat. Its old-fashioned style was similar to pictures I had seen in history books or models I had viewed in museums.

My attention moved to the room itself. The walls were painted a rich green; ivory-colored lace embroidered curtains hung at the windows, and the floor was covered with a green and pink floral patterned carpet. The trim around the fireplace was crafted of a dark red wood, fine-grained and polished to a high luster. On the mantelpiece were two matching ruby vases with crystal teardrops, and between them sat a china figurine. The room was lighted with coal-oil lamps, placed on marble-topped side tables. I squinted in the dim light of the room to better see the figurine. It was about the size of a dinner plate and cast in the shape of a shepherd with his lamb.

Although not pretentious, the house was obviously very nice for the period. I wondered what sort of work Mr. Walker did. I exerted all my powers of recall to summon up the facts I had learned about nineteenth century life and made a quick mental comparison to what I saw around me. This information would serve me well in my capacity as historian and researcher.

I felt a mounting excitement as I took in the artifacts around me, committing their shape, size, and texture to memory. I rubbed my hand over the coarse horsehair fabric covering the chair on which I sat, and fingered the intricate patterns of the crocheted doilies that covered and protected the armrests. I was already on my feet to more closely examine the figurine on the mantel when I caught myself. This was not real! I could not possibly be experiencing any of this! Like stepping into a swift, cold stream, the confusion and panic came rushing back upon me, nearly sweeping me off my feet with its force. I gasped and looked wildly around the room. Mrs. Walker raised her eyes from the sewing in her lap and glanced at me.

"You look tired, Katharine. I think it's time we all went to bed. We've had a long day," she said firmly.

Mr. Walker folded his newspaper and laid it on the couch. With a nod of his head he beckoned all of us to his side. Without any further conversation, he and Mrs. Walker knelt in the center of the room, with the children quickly following suit until all were kneeling together in a circle. I quickly fell to my knees, for which I was grateful as my knees were shaking and threatening to fold underneath me.

Mr. Walker called on Thomas to offer the evening prayer, which he did in a considerably condensed version of his father's earlier prayer at the table. When we'd said "amen" and risen to our feet, each of the children kissed their parents goodnight. Not wishing to draw any further attention to myself, I dutifully kissed Mrs. Walker on the cheek. She returned my kiss affectionately and hugged me to her. For a brief moment I felt as if I were in my own mother's arms, and the feeling brought a measure of solace to my harrowed mind. But the reassuring feeling abruptly left as I turned and was met by Mr. Walker's stern countenance looking squarely into my face. I had no choice but to offer him the same dutiful gesture.

He leaned his craggy, bearded face toward me. Trembling and with my heart in my throat, I stood on tiptoe to reach his cheek. He smelled, not unpleasantly, of an odor I could only identify as a mingling of new-mown hay and the aroma of barnyard animals. I brushed his cheek with my lips and would have quickly pulled away except that he put his arms around me and gave me a brusque, but surprisingly gentle, squeeze. When he released me a moment later, I was surprised to see the kindliness in his eyes as be bid me rest well.

I followed the Walker children upstairs to their bedrooms. I assumed from my earlier encounter with Lacy that I was to share the room with her and Marinda. As we reached the top of the staircase, I paused to watch Jesse and Thomas continue down the hallway. At the far end of the hall they turned and disappeared into a room on the left. I heard Thomas call, "Goodnight, girls," as he shut the door behind him.

I felt a certain sense of security in knowing just where Thomas's room was located in the big house. I still had not seen every corner of the home, and I didn't wish to go poking about if I needed to find Thomas in a hurry. I leaned against the polished wooden handrail. I was exhausted. I wanted to speak to Thomas about my situation, but I was just too tired. It would have to wait until tomorrow. Perhaps in the morning's light all of this could be sorted out. I heaved a great, soulful sigh and walked into Lacy's bedroom.

Lacy and Marinda were already out of their dresses and attired in heavy cotton floor-length nightgowns.

"Open the window before you come to bed, will you, Katharine? It's hot as an oven in here," Lacy complained. She

38

turned down the quilt on the single narrow bed and climbed in. "I'm so tired I think I could sleep for a solid week."

She yawned loudly and pulled the quilt up to her chin. All that showed was her round face flanked by a few wispy curls which had escaped confinement under her sleeping cap. Lacy's plump figure took up the whole of the bed. I wondered just where she expected me to sleep. In spite of everything else I'd had to endure during the day, I was not about to squeeze into that tiny bed with Lacy Walker. And I most definitely was not going to put on one of those ridiculous sleeping caps!

From across the room came a sudden whine and then a floor-rattling thump. I jumped at the sound, fearful that Marinda or someone else in the house had met with sudden calamity. I whirled around to find Marinda bent over a bed that had appeared out of nowhere, calmly adjusting the blankets. It took a moment for me to realize that the bed had been stored in what I thought was the chest of drawers, a sort of old-fashioned hide-away bed. I wondered what other surprises were in store.

Marinda crawled into the bed and looked up at me expectantly. I smiled weakly in return.

"Don't forget the window," Lacy mumbled.

I hurried to the window and fumbled with the latch. It took some moments to figure out how the contraption worked. At last I had it open, and cool air streamed against my face. From the window I could see the fields and various buildings on the Walkers' property. The moon was nearly full, sending a golden glow upon the land. The scene looked like a picture out of a calendar. In the distance I heard a cow bellow. Other than that, the night was perfectly still. No sound of cars rushing down a busy highway. No raucous music blaring from someone's stereo. The quietness of the night seemed strange, but at the same time relaxing and peaceful.

"Come to bed, Katharine," said Marinda sleepily.

I silently shed my clothes, put on the nightgown Marinda had thoughtfully set out for me, ignoring the night cap, and slipped under the covers next to Marinda. She stirred and mumbled contentedly. I twisted and turned, trying not to disturb Marinda, but the bed was the worst I had ever laid on. The mattress was lumpy and thin and the bed so narrow I could hardly turn over without bumping into my sleeping partner. I lay on my back, wiggling to find a comfortable spot. It was impossible; I didn't know how I was ever going to sleep. I could hear Lacy snoring in the other bed.

I turned my head so I could gaze out the open window. The curtain rustled in the gentle breeze. From my position in bed, I could see the moon high up in the night sky. It cast a soft beam of light into the room. I lay in the splash of moonlight, thinking about the day's experiences and trying to unravel the mystery of how I came to be a part of the nineteenth century. I thought about it until my head hurt, and still had not come up with a plausible explanation. The moon was rising higher and higher in the sky, brightening the room with its light. Marinda mumbled in her sleep and sighed softly. Probably dreaming, I thought as I tucked the blanket around her shoulders. Dreaming? That was it! That was the answer. I was dreaming all of this! The explanation was so simple that I laughed aloud.

The sound of my voice must have startled Marinda, for she jerked. In doing so, she struck the upper part of my leg hard with her foot. I winced, but gave the blow scant attention because I was so excited by the fact that I had finally figured out what had happened to me. I'd go to sleep now, and when I awoke everything would be back to normal. I snuggled under the covers, confidently shut my eyes, and soon drifted into sleep.

CHAPTER FOUR

Voices from the next room awakened me. It felt early—too early to get up. I pulled my pillow over my head and tried to go back to sleep, but the muffled rise and fall of voices kept me awake. Mom probably had the TV set turned on already; there seemed to be too much conversation going on for just Mom and Dad. Maybe Darrin had dropped in unexpectedly from college, I thought brightly. It had been weeks since Darrin had been home, and it would be good to see him.

I tossed the pillow aside, anxious now to be up but still groggy with sleep. As I turned over, a sudden stab of pain in my upper leg startled me. Feeling along my leg, my eyes still closed, I found the painful spot and rubbed it. I could smell breakfast cooking, eggs and hash-browned potatoes. Mom was outdoing herself. After breakfast and a quick visit with Darrin, I would have to jump in the car and get to work. Professor Bowen would be anxious for me to get started on those diaries, and . . . I reached over to my bedside table to switch on a tape, but my fingers fumbled instead against something smooth and round. I opened my eyes a slit to find the button to turn on my music. I couldn't believe what I thought I saw. I sat up abruptly, opening my eyes as wide as they'd go.

Instead of my stereo tape deck, a blue flowered pitcher and basin perched precariously on the edge of the table where I had brushed against it with my hand. My mouth went dry, as if I'd swallowed a wad of cotton. I squeezed my eyes shut, recounting in my mind every detail of my bedroom at home, from the mauve ruffled curtains to the row of history books sitting on the shelf above my bed.

This was impossible! I must still be trapped in this incredible dream. I scrunched my eyes tighter, then opened them again quickly. The pitcher and basin were still there, and the old-fashioned lace curtains on the window, and the narrow bed where Lacy lay sleeping. I began to feel sick to my stomach. If this wasn't a dream, then what was it?

Next to me in the bed, Marinda stretched and yawned. I shrank to the very edge of the bed, as if her touch would confirm the reality of my presence here. As I pulled my legs up against my body, I became aware again of the painful place on my leg. I pulled my leg out of the blankets, pushed up my nightgown, and looked at the big, purple bruise. It was actually there where I could see and touch it. *I* was actually here, stuck in the nineteenth century with a family who sincerely believed I was one of them.

Facing that realization somehow gave me courage to deal with it. I drew a deep breath and tossed the blankets aside.

"Morning, Katharine," Marinda said to me sleepily.

"Good morning, Marinda," I returned, in as steady a voice as possible.

I walked to the window and looked out. It was early and the sun was just peeking above the mountains, but already there was activity in the yard below. Chickens were strutting about, pecking at the ground. A rooster crowed lustily. I saw Thomas, milking pail in hand, headed toward the barn. He shuffled across the yard, a piece of straw lolling in his mouth.

I quickly dressed in the clothing I had worn the day before and slipped down the stairs. Jesse was in the kitchen with his mother. The voices I had heard earlier must have belonged to Mrs. Walker and the boys. I skirted the kitchen and let myself out the front door. The morning air was brisk and cool. It felt good on my face as I strode around to the back of the house and toward the barn. When I reached the barn door, I paused and listened for any sound. Then I slowly opened the door a crack. There was no one inside the barn but Thomas. He was seated on a little one-legged stool milking a brown and white cow. The straw worked in his mouth as he rhythmically kept at his task. I let myself inside the barn and tentively came to his side.

"Thomas, could I speak with you?" I asked hesitantly.

Thomas looked up at me briefly. "Sure. What is it?" The straw rolled to the opposite side of his mouth.

"Thomas, there's been some kind of mistake made here," I began. "My name is Katharine Garrett—most people call me Kallie—and somehow I've been whisked back in time to this place. I don't know how it happened, or why, but the fact is I'm not your sister. I hadn't even met any of you before yesterday." I paused, holding my breath. "This is all very confusing, but you have to believe what I'm telling you."

Thomas stopped his milking and looked up at me for a long moment. "You're not going to start that crazy talk again, are you?" he asked with a hard edge to his voice.

"But Thomas, I'm trying to tell you . . ."

"Look," he interrupted, "I've got a lot of chores to do here. I don't have time for your foolishness." He glared at me, then went back to milking the cow.

I walked around the cow so that I could look Thomas directly in the face. He was frowning and vigorously working the cow's udders. I put a hand on the cow and bent down.

"Thomas. I'm serious. I have never been more serious in my life. I am not Katharine Walker. I'm Kallie Garrett, from the twentieth century," I said in exasperation.

Thomas said nothing, nor did he break stride in his milking.

"I don't belong here. I have a life back home. I have parents. Brothers. I need your help in getting back to my own time," I pleaded.

"You'd better back away from Elsie. You know she's liable to kick while she's being milked," was all he said.

I stared at Thomas. He had no intention of even discussing the matter with me. I knew that well enough, though I was acquainted with Thomas only slightly. I sighed and moved away from the cow. She tossed her head and mooed mournfully.

"That's how I feel, Elsie," I said under my breath.

I turned and walked out of the barn.

Thomas was right about the chores. There was enough to do around the farm to keep a person occupied all day long. I quickly learned that Mr. Walker was engaged in farming, and that every member of the household was expected to share in the work. Mr. Walker and the boys labored outside feeding the animals, cutting and storing hay, mending farm implements and tools, while the women and girls kept busy inside. There was cooking to do, and mending, cleaning, sweeping, and clearing away ashes from the three fireplace hearths. Each day of the week had its specific chores: washing on Mondays, ironing on Tuesdays, bread-making on Wednesdays, and so on.

At first I was terrified that Mrs. Walker would ask me to do some pioneer chore with which I was unfamiliar. But after watching her or one of the girls, I caught on to the knack of soap-making and candle-dipping. There were other more specialized arts which I knew nothing about, such as using the spinning wheel which sat in the corner of the parlor. Lacy and her mother, however, did most of the clothing production— washing and dyeing the wool, carding it, and spinning it into yarn. Then there was the handwork. I hadn't the faintest idea how to maneuver the wooden pegs, or bobbins, used to embroider lace, or how to create the delicate patterns of such old-fashioned arts as tatting and netting.

Other things took some getting used to, as well. I could not get accustomed to sleeping on a straw-filled mattress. And I felt most indelicate about using the chamber pot which boldly sat in the bedroom. I preferred the outhouse, which at least I'd had some experience using when I'd been camping with my family.

The Walkers grew or produced nearly everything they used. They were very frugal; nothing was wasted. After I had been there a week, Mr. Walker butchered a hog. The meat was salted down and stored, the fat used to make lard, bits of meat were scraped off the bones to turn into sausage, and even the meat from the hog's head was boiled and used to make headcheese. The feet were put into a barrel of brine to pickle. The pig's tail was considered a treat when roasted over the coals in the stove, as I learned when Lacy and Marinda argued over who should have the pleasure of eating it.

I discovered that the farm served as its own little community, meeting most all of its own needs. What was not produced on the farm was obtained by barter. Surplus farm produce was traded for items the Walkers could not raise themselves, although those items were few in number. The family grew almost all of their own food—vegetables, fruits, grains, meats from their animals, and milk and butter from their cow. The root cellar, located next to the house, was filled with potatoes, carrots, beets, turnips, cabbages, and squash. Onions were braided together into long ropes and hung from the ceiling beside wreaths of red peppers. Apples were stored in bins. Barrels containing salted fish, mutton, and hams were stacked in the pantry, along with freshly made cheese and butter. What could not be stored for the winter was bottled, smoked, dried, or pickled. Mrs. Walker grew her own herbs on a little patch of garden in front of the house. She tended the garden herself, tenderly cultivating each plant.

The Walkers made most of their own clothing, and wore it until it was nearly threadbare. The girls had only three or four outfits apiece, which were well cared for and carefully stored in the large trunk in their room when not being worn. The shoes were high-topped, either laced or buttoned. It took ever so long to do up the shoes. How I missed my comfortable, lightweight tennis shoes and thin ankle socks.

So many aspects of my life were completely altered, right down to the principles of simple hygiene. Underclothing was not changed for days at a time. No one owned a toothbrush. One bath a week was considered entirely adequate. I became quite adept at finding surreptitious ways to wash a bit more often, but it wasn't easy. Water was a precious commodity. Even the Saturday night bath water, filmy with soap and scum, was not wasted. After everyone had bathed in the big metal tub, Mr. Walker hauled the bath water outside and dumped it onto the garden.

Most days followed the same routine. We were up early for breakfast and morning chores, then there was butter to be churned, mattresses to be aired, or furniture to be polished. Food preparation took the biggest share of any single day. All of the girls helped Mrs. Walker with the meals, including me. Breakfast usually consisted of oatmeal mush, sprinkled with brown sugar made from the sap of the backyard box elder tree, and milk. Some kind of meat accompanied it, and eggs or potatoes. Lunch, which the Walkers called dinner, was the main meal of the day. It was most often an oven meal of roasted meat, gravy, boiled potatoes, bread, and fruit for dessert. Sometimes we ate boiled raisin cake for dessert, which I particularly enjoyed, or homemade ice cream, or small cookies Mrs. Walker called Welsh cakes. A light supper at night might consist of soup, cold leftovers, cheese, or bread and milk.

Mrs. Walker was an excellent cook and skilled in the use of damper, draft, and poker in cooking on her wood-burning stove. From her, I learned how to feed the kitchen stove the correct amount of wood so that the fire inside burned neither too hot nor too low. Temperature was gauged by feel. What was hot enough for baking bread was too hot for custard, and not hot enough for pie crust. Those lessons were not learned, however, without incident. On more than one occasion I burned my fingers on the hot stove, failing to appreciate the warmth it generated.

Sunday was always a welcome break from routine. Although I had scarcely enjoyed this day at home, now I looked forward to it simply because it was a reprieve from the unending chores. Only the most necessary tasks were performed on the Sabbath. The day was devoted to worship, scripture reading, and attendance at meetings. The meetings were held in a small adobe building a few miles from the Walker farm. To my surprise, I learned that Mr. Walker was the bishop of our ward. Sometimes during the week, folks from the ward came visiting. On such occasions, the brooms and plows were put away and all enjoyed a few hours of relaxation and conversation. Occasionally the Walker family drove into town with the horse and wagon to do some shopping or attend a special function, but these excursions were rare. Most of the time was spent on the farm.

One warm September afternoon, Lacy and I were seated at the kitchen table shelling fresh peas from the garden. The house was stifling, and I longed for the modern convenience of air conditioning. The sweat collected along my forehead until it dripped into my eyes. I wiped my face with a corner of my apron.

"How do you stand this heat?" I asked Lacy irritably.

"What choice do we have?" she replied with a shrug of her shoulders.

"What choice?" I repeated. "Where I come from, our homes are cooled with refrigerated air or swamp coolers. Of course, I prefer the refrigerated air because the temperature can be more precisely controlled, but it's more expensive to operate than a swamp cooler."

Too late I realized my mistake. Lacy was staring at me as if I'd lost my marbles.

"What in the world are you babbling about?" she exclaimed.

When I made no reply, she gave me a disparaging look.

"Stop complaining, will you?" she said, scowling. "You talk as if none of this has ever happened to you before."

I stared at her, debating whether I should truthfully answer the comment put to me. I had tried several times to make Lacy and the others understand that I was not one of them. But they could not, or would not, comprehend what I was trying to tell them. Lacy had scoffed at me, Thomas refused to discuss the subject at all, and the younger children couldn't grasp what I was talking about. On one occasion I had tried to explain my predicament to Mrs. Walker. She listened, and then consternation flooded her eyes. She felt my forehead, asked if I were feeling ill, and advised me to lie down for the remainder of the afternoon. I decided not to bring up the matter with her again, for it caused her obvious distress. As for Mr. Walker, I didn't dare broach the topic. His gruff countenance was enough to dissuade me from uttering a word.

Now, as I stared at Lacy, I decided against making any reply. I went on shelling the peas in my bowl, saying nothing more. After a moment's silence, she continued in a conversational tone. "When we're through here, I'm going upstairs to do up my hair. May I borrow your blue calico to wear tonight?"

I knew which dress she referred to, as I had seen it carefully folded in the trunk. It was a dark blue color, covered all over with a feathery pattern in lighter blue. But I didn't know why she wanted to wear it. The dress was a Sunday best.

"Are you going somewhere special?" I asked.

She hooked up one blonde eyebrow and eyed me with impatience. "Of course not, you ninny. Have you forgotten that it's Silas's regular night to pay a call?" She heaved a great sigh at my obvious stupidity. "You wouldn't let me borrow the dress last time, you know. You promised you'd let me wear it if I took your turn at churning the cream. Which I did," she added coldly.

"Of course you can borrow it," I answered. "You may wear it whenever you wish."

She looked at me in surprise. "Well, aren't we gracious," she said in a sarcastic tone.

I ignored the comment. "Tell me about Silas," I said, genuinely interested.

"What could I possibly tell you that you don't already know?"

"Pretend I've never met him," I persisted, "and tell me what he's like."

"You certainly enjoy playing the queerest games," she said, shaking her head. "All right. You know there's no one I like talking about more than Silas Beecher. He's wonderful. Dreamy. When he looks at me with those dark eyes, my knees turn to jelly." She paused, a silly half-grin on her face.

"What else?"

"Oh, you know," she sighed.

The rest was probably better left unsaid. I was soon to have the opportunity of meeting Mr. Dreamy Eyes myself anyway. I could wait. I finished shelling my share of the peas and put the bowl on the table.

"Which dress are you going to wear?" Lacy asked suddenly from her chair across the table.

"What?"

"This evening. Which dress will you wear?"

"To visit with Silas?" I asked in confusion.

"Of course not," she answered, making a face. "For your visit with Horace."

"Horace?"

"Horace Baumgarten. Your one and only true love," she answered, perfectly straight-faced.

I smothered a giggle. Why would I want to be in love with someone named Horace Baumgarten? "Oh, of course," I replied airily. "Horace. How could I have forgotten about dear old Horace?"

The giggle refused to be suppressed. I burst into laughter. The whole scenario was hysterical. Here I was supposed to be in love with a boy named Horace Baumgarten, when *I* wasn't even who I was supposed to be! The whole situation struck me as unbelievably funny. I laughed until the tears ran down my cheeks.

Lacy stared wide-eyed at me. When she spoke, her voice was a hoarse whisper. "You must be crazy, Katharine. I've never seen you act like this before."

"I've never experienced this before. Believe me," I said, gasping with laughter.

"I'm going to speak to Mother about you," Lacy warned darkly.

Her comment had a sobering effect. I didn't want to confront Mrs. Walker with any more explanations.

"I'm sorry," I replied, trying to control the mirth that still threatened to spill out of me. "It must be the heat." I clamped a hand over my mouth to staunch the laughter.

Lacy gave me another long, threatening look and then turned back to the peas in her lap.

Still chuckling to myself, I left the kitchen and climbed the stairs toward my room.

As it turned out, Mr. Dreamy Eyes was all eyes and nothing more. I had never met a duller person in my life. His conversation was limited to monosyllables and meaningless gestures. In all fairness to Lacy, he was nice looking—in an unusual sort of way. He had brown wavy hair, large brown eyes, and a thin nose. But his hair kept falling into his eyes, forcing him to constantly brush it back again onto his forehead. And he seemed to have some difficulty with his breathing. Every few minutes he snorted noisily from his nose, which at first greatly disconcerted me as I could not identify the source of the sound. I thought one of the Walkers' hogs had gotten loose in the house.

If Silas was one step removed from the Neanderthal Man, Horace Baumgarten was only slightly more interesting. I couldn't imagine what the real Katharine Walker, wherever she had disappeared to, found likable about him. He was the most ungainly figure I had ever encountered. Tall and gangly as a scarecrow, he bore a remarkable resemblance to my mental picture of Icabod Crane, the character in the story of the Headless Horseman. His face was long and horse-like, his neck scrawny, and his legs and arms dangled from his body. When he sat upon the couch in the Walkers' parlor, he was a tangle of long, lean body parts.

Horace, however, was obviously in love with Katharine Walker, for he kept staring at me all evening with a worshipful gaze. There was no doubt in his mind that I was "his" Katharine. Like every one else, Horace mistook me for who he thought I was. He made reference to conversations and activities we had apparently enjoyed together, and he talked freely of friends or acquaintances we had in common.

Lacy seemed to be having an immensely good time. She giggled and prattled through the entire visit, peeping surreptitiously in Silas's direction every few seconds. I had to admit she did look attractive in the dark blue cotton dress, in spite of the fact that the seams bulged noticeably against her plump figure. The contrast of blue against her yellow hair was very pretty. She had it pulled back into a chignon, with three ringlets hanging down the back. Her cheeks shone with color—either from the excitement of Silas's visit or from the effort of holding in her breath so she didn't split the seams of the dress.

It was a grueling evening for me, however. I had to pretend I was acquainted with the people and places Lacy and the young men discussed; and what was even worse, I had to act as if I were enjoying the visit. For once, I welcomed the sight of Mr. Walker. He stepped into the parlor at precisely nine o'clock in the evening and stood in the center of the room with his timepiece in his hand, staring pointedly at Silas and Horace. They instantly rose to their feet, murmured a hasty good-bye, clamped on their hats, and left the house. I was so relieved I could have hugged Mr. Walker. Almost.

CHAPTER FIVE

THE SUN WAS AN ORANGE BALL of fire sinking into the west, leaving behind a sky of flaming color. I sat in the back of the wagon between Jesse and Marinda, enjoying the ride into town. Thomas, seated near the front, was engrossed in conversation with Mr. and Mrs. Walker, while Lacy sat apart in a corner, careful not to muss her best calico. Tonight she wore her hair in long ringlets, with the hair on her crown parted in the center and combed smooth. Her honey-colored curls glistened in the light of the gas lamps along the roadside, and her blue eyes sparkled. She had even managed to sneak some color on her cheeks, though not enough so Mrs. Walker would notice. The green leaf-patterned dress she wore took on a deeper shade in the fading light.

Thomas looked well groomed in his black trousers, white starched shirt and black coat. He wore a plain silk cravat tied neatly at his neck. His boots, too, were cleaned and polished. Thomas was not particularly handsome, but he had his good points. His eyes were small, though of a rich shade of blue. His hair was thick and curled slightly at his neck. He had a slight build, but at the same time he was lithe and nimble. He was an excellent horseman, too. I had watched him break a new horse Mr. Walker had purchased; though the animal was wild and untamed, Thomas had had it saddle-broken in short order. He could be stubborn and pig-headed, as I had learned; but on the whole, I rather liked him.

I glanced down at the plum-colored print I wore, smoothing the wrinkles out of the skirt with the palm of my hand. The dress felt soft and comfortable to the touch. It was the same dress I had found myself wearing on the day I "arrived," if I could thus describe my abrupt entrance into the 1870s. I had been confused and frightened that day; but now, as I sat in the wagon in Katharine Walker's Sunday best dress, those thoughts were far from my mind. I was enjoying the feel of the cool breeze on my face, the whisper of wind through my hair.

I felt a twinge of anticipation ripple through me. The evening ahead promised to be interesting. Mr. Walker had announced at breakfast that he intended to take us all to the theater. Everyone had worked quickly to complete the day's chores so we would be ready to go after dinner. We changed into our best clothes and climbed into the wagon. Mr. Walker selected a large, ripe watermelon from the garden and put it into the wagon beside us. My mouth watered just thinking of that juicy melon; I could hardly wait to eat a big slice of it. I supposed we would cut into it on our way home, as a sort of after-theater treat.

The wagon bounced and jostled along the rutted road. My body and mind slowly relaxed as I watched the sights along the roadside. The closer we got to town, the more congested the road became, and the homes and buildings began to crowd one another. We passed a saddle and harness shop, and across the street a building housing an iron works. There was a millinery shop, a dry goods store, and a tailoring establishment further on. On either side of the road ran a wide ditch, or trench, filled with running water. I knew the water was used to irrigate crops and trees, for I had seen Mr. Walker divert the water from the ditch that ran along his farm.

The Playhouse came upon us suddenly as we approached State Street and First South. It was an imposing structure, much larger than any of the other buildings I had seen, and its beauty and symmetry took me by surprise. Built in the classical Greek style, it had a flight of broad steps leading to the main entrance where two Doric columns flanked the carved doors. The roof was hipped with a promenade on top and several chimneys. In front of the building, four handsome gas lamps radiated a smoldering light.

I couldn't take my eyes off the Playhouse as Mr. Walker parked the wagon and all of us climbed down. Hundreds of people were hurrying to enter the theater, and many of them carried items such as baskets of fruit or sacks of potatoes. I even saw one man carrying a live chicken under his arm. Mr. Walker took his watermelon from the back of the wagon and we joined the throng headed for the building. At the door a fellow was taking tickets, and in lieu of tickets—as I now discovered—he also took wheat, potatoes, and chickens. I saw a large ham stacked in a crate beside the door, with a honeycomb leaning next to it. Mr. Walker gave him our watermelon, and the doorman reached into his crate and handed Walker a cantaloupe in change!

I would have been stunned by this bartering for tickets had my attention not been arrested by the loveliness of the interior of the Playhouse. It was most elegant. The stage was large and spanned by two columns on either side. I counted three balconies, or galleries, in addition to the main floor seating. The boxes in the gallery were beautifully crafted with lacy filigree. Even the ceilings were elaborately decorated. The theater was so spacious that I guessed it could seat close to 1,500 people. I didn't have long to study the building, however, because shortly after we took our seats the performance began. First a prayer was offered, and then the curtain rose on a painted backdrop of a roaring locomotive just as the orchestra burst into a rousing overture.

The play that evening had been advertised as an "unparalleled attraction." Written by a local actor, John Lindsay, it was entitled *Under One Flag or Love and War*. Mr. Lindsay played in the title role, and Miss Nellie Colebrook appeared as the heroine. I was intently interested as the play began. It was very different from any play I had ever seen. Although it was meant to be a serious drama, I frequently found myself snickering under my breath at the prosy dialogue and lofty euphemisms delivered by the players. It reminded me of a melodrama I had once seen at the university.

The play was performed in five acts. Long before the final act I was squirming in my seat. The play was entirely too long and slow-moving to suit my modern taste for fast-paced, action-packed productions. As part of the fourth act, Mr. George Mecars, appearing as "Roving Bill," executed a series of trick shots with his rifle. I watched, fascinated by the novelty, while he shot the corks from three whiskey bottles, snuffed out a candle, knocked an egg from the bowl of a pipe held in an actor's mouth, shot an apple from the top of a bottle with his rifle held upside down, and—my favorite— while lying on his back with his rifle held upside down, Mr. Mecars shot the top off a lamp chimney.

Incidental to the fifth, and mercifully the final act, was a rousing chorus of singers who performed several patriotic war songs dating from the Civil War, I supposed, which included "Just Before the Battle" and "Battle Cry of Freedom." The pieces were quite exhilarating and sung with great fervor; nevertheless, I was relieved when the orchestra sounded the final drum roll.

I was exhausted by the time we filed out of the theater. The play had begun at 7:30 and it was now nearly 10:00. I yawned as I made my way through the crowd exiting the building. As we started out, I caught sight of Horace Baumgarten. He raised his hand in greeting and then shouldered his way through the crowd toward me, a lopsided smile on his face. I groaned. The last thing I wanted was a conversation with lanky Icabod Crane. He made his way resolutely toward us and was soon at my side.

"Good evening, Sister Walker," he said enthusiastically.

"Evening, Ica—uh, Brother Baumgarten," I replied.

"Did you enjoy the performance?"

"It was interesting."

"Yes, indeed. Brother Lindsay is quite a playwright. Did you know tonight was the first time his new play has ever been presented on stage? I thought he and the other players did remarkably well, didn't you?" Icabod gushed.

"Quite," I answered, anxious to be on my way. Mr. Walker and the other family members were a few steps ahead of me, moving toward the door.

"I believe Mr. Lindsay is one of my favorite dramatic actors," he went on. "I saw him perform here last winter in *Hamlet*. Did you see the play?"

"No, I'm afraid I wasn't around for that one."

"Oh, it was wonderful. Mr. Lindsay gave a sterling performance as Hamlet, and if I recall correctly, Mr. Foster played the king and Mr. Emery had the part of Laertes, and . . ."

"I really must hurry along," I interrupted. I started forward as briskly as I could, hoping to lose Icabod in the throng. But he persisted in sticking by my side.

"Following the presentation of *Hamlet*, the hilarious farce *The Trials of Tompkins* was presented. I confess I have never laughed quite so hard as I did over the amusing antics of Timotheous Tompkins. You're familiar with the farce, no doubt . . ."

"Excuse me," I fairly shouted. I saw an opening through the crowd and dashed ahead. I continued to push my way forward until I reached the front entrance. The rest of the family was somewhere ahead of me, lost in the throng.

The door was nearly within my reach when I saw him. He was just passing through the entrance to the outside. I saw the dull glimmer of the iron key hanging from his vest pocket and caught a glimpse of his craggy face and piercing eyes. My body began to tremble uncontrollably. I cried out to him, but the old man with the key failed to hear me. He disappeared through the door and was lost to my sight.

Desperately I pushed my way to the entrance, but there were so many people still in the Playhouse that I could make little headway. My heart was thumping in my throat and my legs felt like lead weights. Still I pressed forward, my breath coming in ragged gasps. I had to catch him, talk to him, before he disappeared altogether. At last I pushed myself through the theater door, quickly scanning the road and grounds ahead. It was some seconds before I caught sight of the old man, just stepping into a buggy.

"Wait!" I cried.

I raced toward his carriage, bumping into several people in my haste. A child darted out of my path, narrowly escaping being bowled over by my charge across the lawn. The old man was seated in his buggy now, collecting his reins. I gathered my long skirts up in my hand and tried to run faster, but they tangled around my legs and prevented me from getting much speed. I waved an arm in the air, shouting "Wait! Please wait for me!"

If the old man heard me, he gave no indication of it. He shook the reins and the horse surged forward just as I reached the curb of the street. I thought about running after the buggy, but just as quickly discarded the idea. I could never catch the prancing horse. My heart was beating so wildly that it took several moments to catch my breath enough to move. When I turned around, people were staring at me.

I shot a final glance at the departing buggy, sighed, and started back in the direction of the theater to wait for the Walkers. I should have felt embarrassed, considering the disapproving glances I got from the people standing nearby, but I wasn't. I didn't care what they thought about me. All I could concentrate on was the fact that I had again missed an opportunity to speak to the old man with the key.

The sight of the old man brought a flood of memories, and my heart ached with loneliness and frustration. I missed my parents, my friends, my job. Everyone would be wondering what had become of me. My parents must be frantic by this time; I pictured them talking with the police about their missing daughter. Mom would be struggling to hold back her tears, and Dad would be torn with worry. The time for their trip to California would have come and gone by now. I wondered if they had gone ahead without me, and felt a tug of remorse because I hadn't wanted to go with them. I thought about my sporty Mustang parked on the curb near the Church Office Building. The windshield was probably littered with parking tickets by this time, I realized grimly. My stomach began to ache and my head pounded. I slowly walked across the lawn, my head bowed in despair.

A few moments later I located the Walkers, and together we climbed into the farm wagon for the trip home. I thought about the watermelon Mr. Walker had brought to the theater and how much I had been looking forward to eating it; but now I was glad it was gone, for I could not have taken a bite. My stomach felt as if I had swallowed a wheelbarrow full of rocks.

The Walkers talked eagerly about the play, discussing its qualities and virtues. I listened half-heartedly, mumbling a comment or two. Mr. Walker reminded us how Brother Brigham had taught that every pure enjoyment was from heaven; and when the Saints came together in righteousness, they would be benefited and refreshed in their entertainments. He added that Brother Brigham often counseled that those players on the stage should ever be as humble and righteous as if they were on missions preaching the gospel. No impure thoughts should be inspired there, and no impure words expressed. I briefly considered Brother Brigham's words. He certainly would have abhorred the loose and lurid standards of modern-day entertainment.

My thoughts turned morosely to the predicament at hand. I analyzed my options. I could do nothing and stay with the Walkers indefinitely. I could wait until some twist of fate whisked me back to the twentieth century. Or I could actively search for the old man with the key and get him to tell me how to get back home. I settled on the last. It was what I knew I must do all along—but the problem was how to go about it. I needed help in finding the mysterious old man. I quickly ran through a mental list of all those I had met who might be able to help—the Walkers, Silas Beecher, Horace Baumgarten—I suddenly frowned. The thought of Horace accompanying me on such a quest was almost more than I could bear. No, Thomas was the best possibility; and in reality, he was not much of a possibility. I had to find a way of making Thomas understand enough to help me. I pondered that problem the rest of the way home.

The following morning, I worked quickly to complete my chores so I could talk with Thomas. He spent most of the day in the fields, however, cutting hay with Mr. Walker. They grew hay, barley, and other grains in the large field behind the house. Most of the grain was harvested now, but some still remained in the field, and Walker was anxious to get it cut and stored in the barn before the first frost. Although the days were still hot, the nights were beginning to cool off, and soon autumn would be nipping at the air.

I waited impatiently for the hour when Thomas would come inside for the noon meal, but instead Mrs. Walker sent Marinda to the fields with a lunch basket for the men so they wouldn't have to leave their work. Finally, I could stand the waiting no longer. I slipped out of the house and walked briskly toward the fields, brown now and barren from harvesting. I caught sight of Thomas atop the hay wagon, reining the big work horses toward a stack of piled hay. I watched as Mr. Walker pitched forksful of hay onto the wagon while Thomas held the horses steady. When the hay was heaped onto the wagon, Thomas clucked his tongue and the horses plodded toward the barn. I moved around to the side of the barn and waited. In a moment, Thomas drew up and jumped down from the wagon. He grabbed a pitchfork and proceeded to pitch the hay into the barn.

I stepped to his side and watched him silently for a moment or two. His face and forearms were streaked with sweat. The old felt hat he wore was soiled. His boots were covered with dust from the fields, and stray bits of hay clung to their heels. The hay flew from his fork into the barn; he scowled in concentration as he worked, quickly and rhythmically.

I glanced over my shoulder. No one else was about. I drew a deep breath.

"Thomas?"

His pitchfork paused, poised in his hand. He turned and glanced at me. "I didn't hear you come," he said. He scooped another load of loose hay with his fork and tossed it into the barn. Then he leaned on the long wooden handle of the fork and wiped his forehead with his sleeve. "Whew, it's hot. How about bringing me a drink from the pump?"

I obediently walked to the pump located not far from the barn and worked the handle until a stream of water ran into the dipper I held under the faucet. I carried the dipper over to Thomas. He took a long drink from it and then poured the rest over his head, letting the water run down his face and onto his shirt.

"Thanks." He wiped a hand across his face and set to work again with the pitchfork.

"Thomas, I must have a word with you. I need your help," I said earnestly.

"What is it?" He kept pitching the hay without breaking stride.

"Could you please stop that for a minute and listen to me?"

He frowned and reluctantly put down the fork. "What is it, Katharine? Be quick about it, Father is waiting in the field for me."

"I'm looking for someone. A man . . ." I paused, drawing a halting breath. "He's an elderly man, not too tall, with gray balding hair and strange piercing eyes. He carries a black iron key on a chain from his vest pocket—a rather large, ornately-turned black key. Have you seen anyone like that?" I asked anxiously.

"Why do you want to find him?" Thomas returned, his eyes narrowing suspiciously.

"I think he can help me get back to my own time. To my own life. I'm not Katharine Walker," I said quietly.

Thomas stared at me for several seconds, saying nothing. I bit my lip waiting for his reply, hoping he wouldn't scoff and turn away.

"Why do you think this man can help you?" he finally asked. His voice echoed disbelief.

I breathed more easily now. At least Thomas was listening. "Because he was in the cemetery when I suddenly found myself present at Brigham Young's graveside service. One minute I was leading my normal life in the 1990s, and the next moment I found myself plunked in the middle of 1877. Somehow, I think the old man has something to do with it. I was speaking to him just before the whole thing happened."

"The 1990s?" Thomas repeated, one brow hooking up in amusement.

"Yes, Thomas. The 1990s. Electricity. Nuclear bombs. Microwave ovens."

Thomas's jaw slowly fell open.

"I need your help in finding the old man. I haven't the slightest idea where to look for him. Will you help me, Thomas? Please?" I begged.

Thomas stepped back a pace, as if he were suddenly afraid of me. But his face retained its skeptical expression.

"I don't believe any of this, Katharine," he said finally.

I was prepared for his rebuttal. "If I could prove it to you—that I'm not from your century—then would you help me?" I asked evenly.

His eyes grew wary. "How can you prove that?"

"Give me your promise first. If I convince you that I'm telling the truth, will you promise to help me find the old man with the key?"

Thomas shifted on his feet, and I could hear him breathing in the stillness of the long afternoon shadows. "I'm listening to what you have to say," he hedged.

"Very well. Would you believe me if I told you of a way to milk Elsie using a machine instead of by hand?"

"Using a machine?" he repeated, his brows coming together in a frown.

"Yes. You know, a machine like your pump over there."

Thomas's eyes darted to the pump standing near the barn, and then back to me.

"Where I come from, most cows are milked by machines run with electricity. Electricity runs all our machines, from milk machines to computers. You're going to love it in a few years, Thomas. Electric lights, electric washing machines, electric stoves—it makes life so much easier. Since you don't have electricity yet, though, we'll have to make do with what we have."

Thomas looked puzzled, then angry. "Look here," he began sternly.

"Let me finish," I interrupted. "We don't absolutely need electricity to run a milking machine. We can do it on the same principle as a water pump. You can place cups over the cow's teats and suction out the milk with an ordinary pump, creating a vacuum. The machine will do the work for you. It will save you a lot of time." I smiled, pleased with my dissertation. I didn't know how it could fail to persuade him.

Thomas glowered at me. "That's nothing new. And besides, it doesn't work. It's been tried before and found to be damaging to a cow's teats. It makes them bleed." He started to pick up his pitchfork.

"Wait, Thomas. That's because they used a continuous sucking action instead of an intermittent one, like a calf sucks."

He paused, glancing up at me.

"If you used suction cups with soft rubber lining, you could pump air through the airline so that it squeezes the cups together and then suck the air out again, pulling the rubber linings and creating the vacuum. Then you have a pulsating, or intermittent, sucking action that's a more natural motion on the cow's teats."

Thomas laid the pitchfork down and stared at me. "How do you know that?" he asked in a hoarse whisper.

I stared calmly back at him.

He tried to say something more, but couldn't. His voice got lost somewhere in his throat.

"Will you help me find the old man?" I asked softly.

Just then Mr. Walker appeared at the open barn door. "Thomas? What's keeping you, boy? I'm waiting for that hay wagon."

Mr. Walker looked from Thomas to me. I turned my head so he wouldn't see the emotions on my face. Thomas gave me a last quick stare, then grabbed his pitchfork and started toward the hay wagon.

I began to panic inside. If Thomas didn't agree to help me now, he probably never would. "Thomas!" I cried out.

He turned and looked back at me. His face was flushed. "I'm going into town tomorrow to take our tithing into the Tithing Office. You can go with me if Mother doesn't need you at home. We'll look then." With that, he swung up into the hay wagon and lashed the horses with the reins.

I clapped my hands together. I would have shouted with joy and danced a jig right there on the spot if I could have done so unobserved. Instead, I swallowed my delight and walked primly back to the house.

The rest of the day seemed to last forever. It was hot inside the house and the chores were endless. When we had finished with our regular work, Lacy and I peeled a bushel of peaches for bottling and helped Mrs. Walker cook them up on the wood-burning stove. The kitchen was so warm and close that I nearly fainted. I had not gotten used to the layers of clothing I was required to wear. The numerous petticoats and long, heavy skirts were almost more than I could tolerate in the summer heat. I yearned for the cool comfort of shorts and a T-shirt. How I missed the freedom of leather-strapped sandals and the luxury of relaxing in a patio chair with an icy cold soda pop to drink.

Thomas avoided any conversation with me that evening, refusing even to look me in the eye. I knew he was thinking about the things I had told him, and I knew that he was unsure of what to make of me. It was like Thomas to keep his peace when something perturbed him.

When at last I fell into bed that night, I was exhausted and discouraged. Even with Thomas's help, there was no guarantee that we would be able to find the mysterious old man with the key. And if we did succeed in locating him, there was always the possibility that he could not help me return home. I refused to dwell on that, but the thought lurked in my subconscious, teasing and tormenting me. I had fitful dreams during the night about cows trotting down freeways and milking machines hooked up to automobiles. It was a relief when the first slanted rays of morning peeped through my window.

CHAPTER SIX

I AWOKE EARLY, eager for our trip into town. It took every ounce of patience I possessed to sit still during breakfast and morning prayers. I hoped Thomas would introduce the subject of taking me into town with him while the family was still assembled around the breakfast table, but he didn't. I hurried through my chores, wondering if Thomas was doing the same. The day wore on, however, and Thomas did not come in from his work in the fields. I began to grow uneasy, fearing he had changed his mind about going. Every few minutes I glanced out the kitchen window or stepped outside the house to see if he was still at work in the hay field.

At last, in the late afternoon, he came indoors. He went to the kitchen pump to wash his hands and face. I handed him a towel.

"Are we ready to go yet?" I whispered.

He looked at me a long time before answering. "Just because I've agreed to take you with me doesn't mean I believe the things you said."

"That's all right, Thomas, as long as you're willing to help me," I replied.

"Ask Mother if you can come along. I'll meet you in the wagon as soon as I get the tithing loaded."

Twenty minutes later, Thomas and I were on the road heading north toward the center of town, with five big burlap sacks filled with grain in the back of the wagon for a tithe.

Thomas sat stony and silent, the reins taut in his hands. I looked sideways at him.

"Thomas, I really appreciate this. Maybe, if we're lucky, we'll see the old man in town. If not, we can ask about him. Where do you think we should start looking?"

"We're not looking anywhere until I've delivered this load of grain," Thomas growled.

"Of course. But after that, Thomas, where then?"

Thomas darted a glance at me. His expression was dark. "I don't know. We'll see."

That was good enough for the moment. I tried to relax and enjoy the trip. The hay wagon bumped and jostled over the rugged road. I thought about the network of freeways I was accustomed to traveling and fast, air-conditioned cars. The reality of their existence seemed almost impossible on this rutted country road.

"Tell me about the city, Thomas. How many people live in Salt Lake now?" I asked curiously.

Thomas gave me a searing glance. "You know the answer to that as well as I do."

"Pretend I don't know the answer. Come on, Thomas. Humor me." I smiled brightly at him, but he only scowled in return.

When he continued to sit silently, I nudged him in the ribs.

"All right. All right. But just to pass the time. Counting new settlers and the growing number of non-Mormons, the last population figure I heard was about 20,000 people."

I tried to imagine 20,000 people—not very many, compared to the numbers with which I was familiar. The entire population could have been seated in the Delta Center arena.

"A lot of non-Mormons, huh?" I replied, after thinking further about his answer.

"Yeah. The completion of the transcontinental railroad has brought a lot of people in."

"I guess some non-Mormons have set up successful businesses, haven't they?"

"You mean like the Auerbach brothers? Yes, they've done well. Frederick Auerbach came to the valley about thirteen years ago, after he and his brothers had operated stores in California and Nevada mining towns. The Walker brothers, too, have been successful with their store." Thomas frowned slightly. "I guess you can't really call Joseph Walker a gentile. He was a member of the Church, but he's pretty much aligned himself with the non-Mormons in town."

I wondered if Joseph Walker had felt himself fettered by the standards of the Church, like I had. I suddenly flushed at the thought. Sitting next to Thomas, whose faith was steadfast, I felt like a renegade Mormon too, and was strangely embarrassed by it.

"I guess the last few years have brought some changes," Thomas continued in a thoughtful tone. "The Church leaders used to be the leaders of the community, as well. Now it seems that leadership has passed to a group of businessmen, and most of them aren't members of the Church."

"But many of them are," I suggested, urging him to go on.

"Yes, of course. Many of the wealthy and powerful men have made their fortunes in merchandising, railroading, banking, and mining. Like William Jennings, for example."

"William Jennings?"

"Don't try to pretend you've never heard of William Jennings. Father had him out to the house last winter."

"I'm sorry," I said lamely, shrugging my shoulders.

Thomas heaved a very loud and pointed sigh. "William Jennings is probably the wealthiest man in the valley. He's involved in more industries than anyone else."

"How did he make his money?" I asked, genuinely interested.

"From what I recall hearing Father say, when Jennings came to the valley he entered the meat business. He soon expanded into tanning and leatherwork, using the hides of the cattle he butchered. Then he started a dry goods store and later built the Eagle Emporium on East Temple Street. I think he's also involved in banking, smelting, and railroading."

"That is impressive."

Thomas nodded.

"You haven't mentioned anything about these men being involved in politics. Are they?" I asked, thinking about the commercial ventures that political leaders of my own day were often engaged in.

"Some are. I wouldn't be surprised to see Jennings run for mayor some day."

"Who is the mayor, Thomas?"

"Feramore Little. And in case you've forgotten, George Emery is the territorial governor."

"That's right. Utah is still a territory, isn't it? Do you anticipate statehood in the near future, Thomas?" I asked, curious to hear his thoughts on the matter.

Thomas pondered the question. "No, I don't think so. The Union won't have us so long as we're practicing polygamy. And we'll never give up that principle until the Lord directs us to, even if it means not having statehood."

I said nothing for several minutes. Thomas's strong support for the principle of polygamy caught me off balance. I would have liked to record his views for Professor Bowen to read.

"Have I answered all your questions now?" Thomas asked.

"For the moment."

We rode in silence for some time. Soon the homes and places of business began to grow thick around us. Thomas snapped the reins and the horse broke into a brisk trot. I became absorbed in studying the buildings around us. Most of them were homes, built of adobe or brick, until we reached about Second South. Thomas was traveling up Main Street, which he called East Temple Street, it being the major business and commercial street. On the corner of Main and Second South stood a one-story adobe building with the name "Walker Bros." painted on the front. I craned my neck to look at the building as Thomas drove by. The establishment was advertising dry goods, clothing, hats, groceries, and miners' supplies on a billboard in front of the store. I wondered if the Walker brothers were also involved in banking. In my mind's eye I saw the towering Walker Bank building of my own day, which is—or would be—located in that same vicinity.

All along Main Street, stores and shops nestled against each other. A mercantile called S.P. Teasdel dealt in gentlemen's clothing. Barratt Bros. sold furniture, house goods, and feathers. Next door to Barratt Bros. stood Wells Fargo & Co. As we approached the corner of First South, a prominent three-story building caught my eye.

"What building is that, Thomas?" I asked, pointing.

Thomas looked in the direction I indicated. "That's William S. Godbe's exchange building where he houses his drugstore. Godbe is one of the apostate merchants I was telling you about. A few years back we had an economic crisis here in town. Maybe you remember," he said pointedly. "The westbound freighters were charging excessive prices for goods being shipped in. Also, more gentile merchants were setting up stores and charging high prices. To ease the problem, President Young and some of the other brethren set up a cooperative store and encouraged small Mormon merchants to combine their goods and join them."

"Zion's Cooperative Mercantile Institution. Right?"

"That's right. I see you haven't forgotten everything." Thomas frowned and then continued. "Z.C.M.I. opened in the Eagle Emporium. Prices were lower than at gentile establishments, and consequently some of the gentile merchants were driven out of business. Godbe and some of the other apostates and non-Mormons put up a fuss about the co-op, and Godbe broke completely with the Church at that time, leading others away with him. Godbe, Walker, Auerbach, and some of the others managed to hang on, and when the railroad came in 1869, bringing in more non-Mormons, their mercantiles prospered. The mining boom of the '60s helped, too."

I tried to remember what I knew about the early mining in Utah, but I didn't know much. "What about the mining,

Thomas? How much has it influenced the economy?"

"A lot. Both gold and silver were discovered in the west mountains in 1864, and also thirty miles east of here at Parley's Park. The wealth from mining increased the money supply and boosted trade. The first banks were founded to serve the mining companies."

"Are the Walker brothers involved in banking?"

"Yes, they have a small bank in connection with their mercantile. Why?"

"I was just wondering," I replied. I considered telling Thomas about the Walkers' future prosperity and expansion in banking, but thought better of it. Now was no time to get his hackles up with my insights into the next century.

"There, across the street, is Jennings's Eagle Emporium," Thomas said, nodding his head.

I looked at the two-story stone building. A wooden eagle with wings spread was perched over the main entrance. Four pilasters were spaced along the front of the building, and pediments topped the windows on the ground floor. The roof, too, formed a pediment, with the word "Emporium" carved in the center.

But it wasn't the Emporium that held my attention. Right next to it, on the corner of the street, stood something that brought a lump to my throat.

"Oh, look, Thomas! The old clock," I cried.

"You mean the town clock? Yes, that was erected about four or five years ago. It's driven with four large springs which have to be wound every few days." Thomas nodded knowingly.

"The old clock," I murmured, clasping my hands together. The sight of a familiar object filled me with emotion, and I could feel tears springing to my eyes. Amidst a maze of strange buildings and foreign names, there sat that solid old clock, just as I remembered it. The large orb with a clock face on four sides, attached to a slender column secured in a stone base, seemed an anchor to me in a sea of confusion. My eyes feasted on its ornamental bronze detail. How often I had walked down Main Street past the old clock without giving it a second glance. Now I wanted to jump down from the wagon and wrap my arms around it. But a moment later we were past it, moving ahead up Main Street.

The buildings squatted one beside another, a conglomeration of adobe and brick with false facades. Men and women dressed in plain homespun were going about their business in the stores and shops, or visiting on the streets. Dust churned in the air from the constant motion of horses and wagons. I felt as if I were part of a TV western Mom had left on the air too long. I almost expected to see Laura Ingalls come racing around the corner, braids flying. Telegraph poles lined one side of Main Street. They reminded me of the telephone poles that used to dot the street when I was a little girl.

As we made our way up Main Street toward South Temple, the buildings clustered even closer together. One shop in particular caught my attention. The storefront sign read "F. Auerbach & Bro." I smiled to myself. This little two-story brick mercantile was the forerunner of a major department store that would grace the corner of Third South and State Street. I recalled shopping at Auerbach's with my mother as a child. I could still see the jewelry and watches lined up in their glass cases on the main floor, and the mezzanine where I liked to sit at the counter with Mother, eating a cream cheese sandwich. When Auerbach's went out of business, Mom's disappointment was keen.

Around the corner of Main Street and First South I spotted a large building with the name of "H. Dinwoodey Furniture Co." painted on the side. I thought of the lovely Queen Anne chair my parents had recently purchased from Dinwoodey's, the one Mom wouldn't let me set anything on. Farther up Main Street we passed Zions Savings Bank & Trust Co., and a few doors north of that loomed the big three-story Z.C.M.I building. Thomas pointed to it as we passed in the wagon, but his gesture wasn't necessary, for I was already studying the architecture of the building and thinking about what he had told me concerning the co-op. It was not much different from the Z.C.M.I. store I was familiar with, except that it was smaller and lacked the pediment centered on the roof. The rows of windows, separated by cast-iron Corinthian columns, were the same. I remembered reading that parts of the original cast-iron facade were used in remodeling the store when it was enlarged and expanded in 1976.

I stared at the historic building until Thomas nudged my shoulder, directing my attention to a two-story sandstone and adobe building sitting on the southwest corner of South Temple and Main Street.

"That's the Council House. It was one of the first public buildings erected in town. It's used as a general council house for the brethren, but it also houses the public library. The territorial legislature used to meet there as well."

I scrutinized the building as Thomas told me about it. It was a square structure with rectangular windows, a hipped roof, and a cupola on top. The bottom floor was constructed of reddish sandstone, and the second story of adobe. I recognized this building as one I had noticed while driving home with the Walkers after Brigham Young's graveside service. It occupied the site of the future Deseret News building.

We crossed South Temple and pulled into the yard of the Deseret Store and Tithing Office, located on the spot later to house the grand Hotel Utah. The tithing office, and indeed the entire block, was surrounded by a high wall. The store consisted of a two-story adobe building with a single-story addition in the back. The name was printed in large letters on the front and side, and underneath it read, "HOME MANUFACTURES."

I waited in the wagon while Thomas unloaded the sacks of grain and took them inside. I hoped he would inquire about the old man with the key while he was there. The afternoon was hot; perspiration gathered along my brow. Even though it was nearing the end of September, the temperature continued to be uncomfortably warm. I brushed away a fly buzzing around my head and retied the strings of my bonnet.

I watched as more men drove up in their wagons. One carried a wire cage full of chickens. Another brought a gunny sack filled with vegetables. As I watched them, I considered the tithes they were bringing to the storehouse. One-tenth of their increase, whether it was in cash, cows, chickens, or cantaloupe, was reserved in obedience to the commandment of tithing. I thought about these people and the long hours they labored in their fields and shops. It was a sacrifice to give a tenth, but they willingly and obediently made that sacrifice.

I considered my own adherence to the law. It had been several years since I had paid a tithe—more years than I cared to recall. The money I earned belonged to me, I had reasoned; why should I give it to a church which was already wealthy? But seeing these men carrying part of their livelihood into the Tithing Office sent a pang of guilt shooting through me. Suddenly I felt embarrassed to be sitting in plain sight where everyone could see, with my conscience scolding me. A couple of the men tipped their hats as they walked by. I felt like slinking under the wagon. I hoped Thomas would hurry with his business so we could drive away.

A few moments later he came out of the building. He climbed up in the wagon and took the reins. "Gid up," he directed, giving the reins a shake. He said nothing more as he turned the horse and wagon around and headed toward the street. I waited for him to tell me if he had learned anything about the man with the key, but he sat stonelike in the seat of the wagon, the reins tight in his hands.

"Did you make any inquiries?" I finally blurted out.

Thomas gave me a quick glance. "I asked a couple of the brethren in the Tithing Office. No one knew the man you described," he replied coldly.

My heart sank. I slumped down in the seat of the wagon. "What do we do now?"

"I think this whole thing is a wild goose chase, Katharine. You ought to forget about it."

"I can't, Thomas. What I've told you is the truth. I'm not making it up."

We sat in silence as he reined the horse around the corner and started back down Main Street. As we rounded the corner of South Temple, I glanced over at the temple block. The temple itself was only partially constructed; the domed Tabernacle dominated the block. In the northwest corner stood a two-story adobe building flanked by two one-story wings. That had to be the Endowment House. I knew such a house was built on Temple Square in which marriages were performed prior to the completion of the temple. On the southwest corner of the temple lot, a simple adobe building was being torn down. Workmen were removing the adobe bricks and carting them away. I supposed the building was being dismantled to make way for the Assembly Hall, which would rise on that spot.

I should have been awed by the historic significance of what I was seeing, but all I could think about was finding the old man with the key so I could get back home.

"Couldn't we try looking somewhere else?" I asked Thomas. "Someplace where people commonly go—a mercantile or a bank, perhaps?"

He groaned.

"Please, Thomas."

"Oh, all right. We'll try the Eagle Emporium," he answered curtly.

Thomas guided the horse down Main Street until we reached William Jennings's store. He pulled up alongside the building, jumped down from the wagon, and threw the reins over the hitching post. I let myself down from the wagon seat, and together we went inside the mercantile.

Upon entering, we found ourselves in the dry goods department. A large window facing the street displayed a variety of items—ribbon, cuffs and collars, woolen knit goods, bolts of cloth, and "the new cork corset, made to dispense with whalebone or cane supports," as the boldly-painted sign in the window proclaimed.

I followed Thomas through the dry goods section to the shoe room, where an assortment of ladies' and children's footwear was on display. To the rear were the grocery and hardware departments. Thomas glanced about and then strode over to an old gentleman wearing spectacles and a straw hat who was examining fishing tackle. I stayed where I was while Thomas spoke to him. I saw the old man shake his head and say something in reply. Thomas thanked him and moved on to another acquaintance.

Each person Thomas spoke to gave him the same negative reply. I couldn't bear to watch any longer. I turned my attention to the goods on display, hoping to take my mind off my worries. I looked at the glassware, crockery, tinware, firearms, and tools arranged on the counters and open shelves. To my left were men's and boys' clothing. In the opposite direction sat half a dozen big iron cooking stoves, very much like the one the Walkers had in their kitchen.

I walked around the store a bit, examining the tubs, brooms, bacon, cheese, and candies. There were boxes of canned goods and barrels containing flour, salt, and sugar. The prices were incredibly low compared to what I was used to. I browsed through the stacks of metal containers filled with coffee, spices, baking soda, and so on. The containers had quaint pictures printed on them that made me smile.

"You wait here while I go upstairs," Thomas hissed in my ear. "I know a couple of the clerks who work in the wholesale department. I'll ask them about your mystery man."

"Okay," I answered meekly.

I watched as Thomas threaded his way through the store to the back staircase and disappeared from sight. I sighed and tapped my foot impatiently. People milled about me, inspecting goods and choosing the articles they wished to purchase. It appeared that Jennings did a brisk business. I started to wander around, looking first at one article and then another. Spotting the ladies' department, I went in that direction. On one table was a stack of lovely shawls. I picked one up and looked it over. It was a pale blue wool with fringe all around the edges. The sign on the table announced, "Ladies' shawls from sixty cents upward."

On another counter were bolts of cloth, with prints starting at seven cents per yard. Dress goods varied from ten to twelve-and-a-half cents per yard. Silk parasols, $1.25 each. With the money I had earned from Professor Bowen, I could have had my pick of anything in the store. Maybe I ought to buy several items and take them back with me. My friend, Terri, would get a real kick out of one of these parasols. And I'll bet Mom would love having an old-fashioned shawl, and Dad . . . What was I thinking?! Had I gone completely berserk? I could no more take these things back with me to the twentieth century than I could escape my imprisonment here in 1877. I might be confined here for the rest of my life! That thought set me trembling.

I put the blue shawl back on the table. My hands were shaking so badly that I almost upset the whole pile of shawls. I wished Thomas would hurry. I scanned the room for a glimpse of him. It was some minutes before he spotted me and came to my side.

"I told you to stay put," he said irritably. "I've been looking all over the mercantile for you."

"I'm sorry, Thomas. Did you find out anything?"

"Nothing. No one seems to know the old man. Come on, let's go. Father will be expecting us back."

Thomas took my elbow and steered me out of the Emporium. He helped me into the wagon, climbed in himself, and a moment later we were bumping and bouncing down Main Street toward home.

My mind and body were numb. I didn't feel the deep ruts in the road or the hot sun beating down on my back. Thomas sat silently next to me, his eyes trained on the road. It was some time before I could even collect my thoughts. My conscious mind refused to accept the fact that I might never return to my home and family. There had to be some alternative—some solution. I let my thoughts meander along paths of their own, not trying to make sense out of any of it.

It took nearly thirty minutes to get home. By the time Thomas pulled into the yard, the twisting and turning paths of my thoughts had gradually merged, arriving at a common ground. All my instincts told me that this whole episode was not real. I was either imagining it, or dreaming it, or a little of both. The old man with the key did not exist. Thomas Walker did not exist. Eventually I would awaken from whatever sleep possessed me, and everything would be back to normal. I simply must be patient until that happened.

I walked wordlessly into the house while Thomas put the horse and wagon away. Mrs. Walker was in the kitchen, stirring a pot of steaming soup over the stove.

"I'm glad you're back," she said without looking up from her cooking. "I need your help with supper. Could you please hand me that plate of sliced carrots?"

I obediently picked up the plate from the counter and handed it to her.

"Thank you." She glanced at me as she took the plate from my hand. "Katharine, are you feeling unwell? You're awfully pale," she said, putting a hand on my forehead. "And you're clammy to the touch."

She quickly scraped the pieces of carrot into the pot and covered it with a lid. Then she set the plate aside.

"Are you ill?" she asked again.

"No, just a little tired," I answered. "It was a long, hot ride into town."

Mrs. Walker peered intently into my face. "I want you to lie down until dinner. But first I'm going to give you a dose of this."

She walked into the pantry, opened the cupboard, and removed a quart bottle filled with dark green liquid. Then she poured out a spoonful of it. "Open up," she said firmly, holding the spoon to my lips.

The liquid had green specks floating in it and looked exceedingly disagreeable. I backed away. "What is it?" I asked nervously.

She thrust the spoon toward me. "Don't try to dilly-dally with me, young lady. A good dose of clover tea always does the trick. You'll feel better in no time. Open your mouth."

I reluctantly parted my lips. Mrs. Walker pushed the spoon against my teeth and the liquid slid down my throat.

"Ugh! That's the most horrible thing I've ever tasted," I cried.

Mrs. Walker gave me a satisfied look. "The more bitter it tastes, the better it is for you." She replaced the stopper and put the jar back in the cupboard.

I had never tasted anything so awful. The tea was so bitter that my eyes watered and even my nose stung. I couldn't unpucker my mouth. If none of this was real, the clover tea gave a remarkably convincing imitation.

CHAPTER SEVEN

Over the next few days, Thomas and his father spent their afternoons at the temple block helping to tear down the old tabernacle. That simple adobe building had been one of the first erected in Salt Lake City, serving as a meeting hall for the Saints. It was the same building I had seen being dismantled the day Thomas and I went into town. Mr. Walker told us the brethren were preserving the triangular piece of carved pine, crafted into a rising sun, which had graced the east end of the building. I sensed that Mr. Walker felt a bit melancholy over the destruction of the building, for at dinner that evening he reminisced about his early experiences inside the tabernacle and the discourses he had heard from Brother Brigham at that pulpit.

The next evening Mr. Walker returned from town with a large package tied in brown paper and string under his arm. After dinner he called all of us together.

"I enjoyed a few words with Brother C. R. Savage yesterday at the temple block. He mentioned that he had some fine photographs of our late prophet and president at his gallery of art. I stopped by Savage's Gallery this afternoon and purchased this," Mr. Walker informed us. He carefully untied the string from around the package and removed the paper.

Mrs. Walker gasped. "Oh, Henry, it's lovely." She took the portrait from her husband's hands and held it up for us to see.

The Walker children murmured their approval as Mr. Walker nodded with satisfaction. The object of such interest was a photograph of Brigham Young mounted in an oval frame measuring about twelve inches by fourteen inches. I studied it curiously. The portrait looked like it had been taken of Young while in his late forties. The president was clean-shaven and of sober expression. His hair was longish, hanging past his collar, and brushed off his forehead. He wore a white shirt, white vest, and black coat. A black cravat, embellished with a white floral pattern, was tied around his neck. His hands were loosely folded at his waist. The face, in particular, arrested my attention. It was stern, yet at the same time, kind. The eyes expressed a sense of determination and the mouth suggested courage and resolve.

"I think it's a fine likeness," Mr. Walker was saying.

"It is indeed," Mrs. Walker agreed.

Mr. Walker took the portrait and walked into the parlor with it. The rest of us trailed after him. He went to the wall opposite from where the couch sat and held the picture up in a conspicuous spot on the wall.

"I think I'll hang it here," he commented.

"A very good place," Mrs. Walker concurred.

"Thomas, fetch me my hammer and nails."

Thomas promptly did as he was told, and a moment later Mr. Walker had the portrait secured to the wall.

I stepped back several paces and studied it. Brother Brigham had been a handsome man, broad-chested with sturdy shoulders. His features reminded me of Burt Lancaster, an actor I had once seen in a video my mother brought home. This particular portrait of Brigham Young I had never seen before. Brother Brigham gazed steadfastly down at me, his eyes boring into mine. I shrank back slightly under that frank, intent stare. The portrait made me feel uncomfortable, as if Brother Brigham could see all the way into my heart.

"I shall tell Brother Savage that we are very much pleased with the portrait," Mr. Walker said, hooking his thumbs into his vest pockets. "I want you children to remember Brother Brigham and the great man he was. I want you to tell your children and your grandchildren about him, that he might live in the hearts of the people. I can truly say that I have never met a finer example of a man in my life. Not only was he a prophet, a colonizer, a community leader and a successful businessman, he was a pragmatist who could equally inspire the Saints to raise a mighty temple to their God as well as advise a farmer on the most favorable time to plant his crops. Though honored and revered by men, he was ever submissive to the will of God, giving all glory and praise to Him whom he served. I once heard Brother Brigham say that he did not have anything to do with the Saints being led to this valley; that it was the providence of the Almighty, for he, Brigham, never could have devised such a plan."

Mr. Walker closed his eyes for a moment, as if remembering the words that fell from Brother Brigham's lips. Then he continued in a quiet voice, "'We have been thrown like a stone from a sling, and we have lodged in this goodly place just where the Lord wants his people to gather.' I can recall Brother Brigham saying that at a conference in the old tabernacle as if it were yesterday. And I was only seventeen years old."

No one said anything. All eyes were on Brigham Young's portrait, as if he, instead of Mr. Walker, were speaking to us. My skin prickled, so intense was the feeling in the room.

"Brother Brigham loved the Saints," Walker went on. "Even when the valley grew in large numbers and he was pressured with the affairs of administration, he still continued to set aside time each day to listen to the cares of the people. He was quick to judge, yet always sensitive and tender. He was idealistic, but also practical. It was Brother Brigham who led out in the development of agriculture and business enterprise. He conceived of the idea of damming the mountain streams for irrigation. He had canals, roads, and bridges built. He directed a string of colonies from Salt Lake City to the Pacific. In the midst of all of his sweeping plans, he never lost sight of the individual. He provided work for the unemployed, shelter for the homeless, and comfort for the widow and orphan."

Walker paused, glancing at each of us in turn. I felt the sincerity of his words burn into my soul as his gaze rested on me for an instant.

"After my mother died, I had the primary responsibility of caring for my younger brothers and sisters. Brother Brigham knew I would need assistance. He personally located a family for us to stay with until we were able to construct a home of our own, and he saw to it that I had employment. He sent me to work in the canyon where the men were building a dam across one of the streams. Damming the swift mountain creek was no easy task, although I can remember on one occasion help came in an unexpected manner."

Walker paused and smiled to himself. "The stream was full of beaver. When they understood we were building a dam, they pitched in to help. During the night they'd cut willows into three-foot to four-foot lengths, weave them into the dam, and cover it up with mud. We worked during the day, and the beavers operated at night. They were a great help to us."

"Now we will do as Brother Brigham so often urged," Mr. Walker pronounced with a sudden vigor that made me jump. "We will cease to be idle and be about our labors. As you know, General Conference is little more than a week away. Thomas, I'd like you to clean the leather on the carriage so it will be ready for us to drive into town. Lacy, you and Katharine are to help your mother prepare for company coming in for the conference."

"Yes, Father," replied Lacy. Her words were obedient enough, but her expression and attitude clearly conveyed that she resented the extra work created by having guests in the house.

"Tomorrow will be soon enough to start our tasks. For now we'll read from the holy scriptures, say our prayers, and then off to bed with you," Walker said.

When we were through with our family worship, Thomas and the other children filed out of the parlor. I followed behind.

"Wait a minute, Katharine. I'd like to talk to you," Mrs. Walker said, touching my shoulder.

"Yes?"

"You haven't looked well the past few days. You're still pale, and I've noticed you're eating poorly."

"Oh, I feel fine. Honest," I replied hurriedly. I didn't want Mrs. Walker reaching for her clover tea again. "Really, I'm fine."

Mrs. Walker looked at me closely. "Perhaps you just need a rest, then, or a change of scenery. How would you like to go with your father and Thomas to visit Aunt Lizzy when conference is over?"

"Aunt Lizzy?"

"Yes, perhaps the trip to Provo would do you good. Give you a chance to rest for a day or two."

"Provo?" I repeated.

"It's been a long time since you've been down to Provo, hasn't it? Marinda and Lacy can take over your chores for a few weeks. You go and enjoy yourself."

The thought of traveling to Provo filled me with excitement. I had driven down in my Mustang with Terri several times to meet fellows or attend dances on the BYU campus.

"I would like that," I replied eagerly.

"All right. I'll speak to your father about it." Mrs. Walker kissed my cheek. "You run along to bed now."

Our houseguests began arriving the following Tuesday. Mrs. Walker, Lacy, Marinda and I had spent days in the kitchen baking cakes and breads, boiling potatoes, preparing meats and putting up preserves. The cupboards in the pantry were filled to overflowing and the root cellar was stuffed with foods that needed to say cool. Not only had we prepared an abundance of food, but we had cleaned the house from end to end. I aired the tick mattresses, swept the ashes from the fireplace hearths, and churned a barrel full of butter. By Tuesday night I was worn out. One family from Brigham City had come earlier in the day to stay with us over the four days of the conference. The parents were fairly young, already with a brood of children. They were given our room—mine, Lacy's and Marinda's—to use while we girls took temporary quarters out on the back lawn.

Three families in all stayed with us. Some slept in their wagons parked next to the house, others occupied Thomas's and Jesse's room. The house bulged with guests. Mr. and Mrs. Walker calmly went about the business of seeing to their guests' comfort. For myself, I felt run ragged with cooking, cleaning, and entertaining a houseful of people in addition to my regular chores.

General Conference began on Thursday with a priesthood meeting at 10:00 a.m. in the tabernacle. In the afternoon a general session was held. Meetings took place the next day and again on Saturday and Sunday. I was required to attend the meetings along with everyone else. The weather was unusually hot for October, and I sat in the tabernacle with perspiration dripping off my face. My clothes stuck to my body and my underarms were sopping wet. In spite of my physical discomfort and the lengthy meetings, I was interested in what was transpiring in the tabernacle. At the Saturday morning meeting, John Taylor was sustained as the president of the Quorum of the Twelve Apostles and as Trustee-in-Trust for the Church. Two counselors to the Twelve were also named, John W. Young and Daniel H. Wells. Others were sustained in various positions—Albert Carrington as president of the Perpetual Emigrating Fund, Orson Pratt as Historian, Angus M. Cannon as president of the Salt Lake Stake of Zion.

Later in the meeting, a long list of names were announced as missionaries to labor in the field. Many were called to work in the Scandinavian countries, although some were designated to serve in the States—Wisconsin, Michigan, and New Mexico. I knew through my study of Church history that in the early days of the Church missionaries were often called at conference time from the pulpit, without prior knowledge of their assignments. I had heard Mr. Walker relate his experience as a young man being called up out of the congregation with an assignment to serve as a missionary to Canada. The assignment had come as a complete surprise to him. I wondered if these newly called missionaries were experiencing the same thing.

The most fascinating thing about this conference for me was seeing prominent leaders of the nineteenth-century Church. I stared into the faces of John Taylor, George Q. Cannon, Orson Hyde, Lorenzo Snow, and others. Their messages to the congregation, too, were interesting in an historical sense. When the conference was over, I thought deeply about the things I had heard and seen. The conference activities and speakers seemed so real that I had a hard time convincing myself that they were all figments of my imagination or products of my dreams.

Two days after the conference adjourned, Mr. Walker began preparations for his trip to Provo. When Lacy found out that I was going, she made such a fuss about staying behind that Mrs. Walker agreed to let her accompany us. At first Mr. Walker was reluctant to take all three of the older children, fearing it would leave too great a burden on his wife while we were gone. But Mrs. Walker assured him she could manage with Marinda's and Jesse's help.

Three days later we set out. The day was sunny and a gentle breeze fanned our faces. We bounced along the road in an open wagon filled with provisions, blankets, and a bedroll for each of us. Mr. Walker's two roan draft horses walked at a steady pace, and he did not urge them to hurry. I slowly began to realize that it was going to take more than one day to reach Provo.

I settled back against a clump of straw to watch the scenery pass by. It wasn't long before we had left the farms and homes behind and nothing was in front of us for miles except open ground. September had left her brush stroke on the mountains, painting them in vibrant hues of orange, gold, and red. Billowing clouds cast shadows across the jagged slopes, creating an ever-changing picture on the mountainside. I picked out a girl's face with long flowing hair, a sailboat, and a slinky cat. As we drew abreast of towering Mt. Olympus, I recalled the evening I had spent in Terri's bedroom, listening to her new rock tape and gazing out her window at the mountain. The memory brought with it a torrent of homesick feelings, and I felt tears spring to my eyes. I dashed them away with the back of my hand before Lacy, who was sitting across from me in the wagon, could see my sadness and question me as to the reason.

That Lacy would question me, I had no doubt. She had been talking nearly non-stop ever since we left the farm. She moved from subject to subject like a bird wheels in flight, with a seemingly endless store of observations, opinions, and probing questions. For the last half hour she'd complained about missing Silas Beecher's company. She had been enumerating his sterling qualities, and now she leaned back on her elbows in the straw and breathed a long, mournful sigh.

"Oh, I don't know how I shall survive without seeing him," she moaned.

"Perhaps you'll find someone in Provo to take your mind off him," I answered brusquely.

She straightened up in indignation. "What a thing to say! Do you think I'd betray Silas while I'm away for a mere few weeks?"

"It did occur to me."

She sniffed disdainfully. "I'm not surprised. You certainly have treated Horace disgracefully."

"I have not. I've always been polite," I retaliated.

"You've broken his heart!" Lacy cried. "You refuse to see him, and if he does manage to spend a few moments with you, you behave rudely."

She was right about the first two arguments, but I didn't think I was guilty of the last. "When have I ever behaved rudely with Horace?" I asked.

"Just the other night. When he came to see you, you told him that his feelings for you were an illusion."

That was true. I had said that. But I was being honest, not rude. "Let's not argue over Horace," I sighed. "And I apologize for questioning your loyalty to Silas."

"I should think so," Lacy replied firmly.

We both sat in silence for some time after that. Finally, Lacy spoke in a cautious voice. "Do you really think there might be some interesting young men at the ranch?"

I shrugged my shoulders, smiling to myself at Lacy's sudden interest.

"The ranch hands Father usually hires are rough, ill-mannered, and bad smelling." Lacy wrinkled her nose. "But perhaps you're right. Perhaps there will be one or two strong young shearers who stayed on."

Shearers? Why would Mr. Walker hire shearers? I wondered. For the first time I thought about just where it was in Provo we were going. I had assumed Aunt Lizzy and her husband ran a farm, like Mr. Walker's. But Lacy had mentioned a ranch, and shearers. The only kind of ranch I knew about was a cattle ranch. And why would cattle ranchers need shearers? Maybe there was something about the business of cattle ranching I knew nothing about.

"You can rest assured that if there are any young men about the place, Lacy will find them," Thomas interjected from his place on the wagon seat. He had been riding up front with his father since we left that morning, and for the most part had been engaged in conversation with Mr. Walker.

Lacy stuck out her tongue at him. Thomas grinned back, which made Lacy all the more huffy.

Mr. Walker clucked to the horses as we started up a hilly incline. The matched pair of strawberry roans picked up their pace, pulling the wagon bumping and creaking after them.

Mr. Walker turned his head to glance at us. "You young women may not be aware of the fact that I have always been selective about the hands I hire—and about whom I allow my daughters to keep company with." He gave us a meaningful look. "I learned early on how to judge the calibre of a man."

Lacy fidgeted on her seat of straw, knowing a story with a pointed moral was forthcoming.

"It was our second year in the valley," Mr. Walker began. "Although I was only fifteen, I was old enough to recognize trouble when I saw the gold seekers streaming into Salt Lake City on their way to California. We were already short on rations. With so many Saints coming into the valley, food was scarce. When the California miners began arriving about mid-July, Brother Brigham and the other leaders were concerned that they would stay for the winter, thereby straining our already meager supplies."

"The situation was relieved somewhat when Brother Jefferson Hunt agreed to guide the gold miners over the southern route to California before the snows fell. Many of the miners went, but several stayed behind for the winter. A few of those gold seekers who remained professed to embrace the gospel and submitted to baptism. Some married Mormon girls. When spring came, most of those girls found themselves abandoned by their 'Mormon' husbands who left for the gold fields with the first thaw."

Although I couldn't see Mr. Walker's face as his back was to me, I plainly heard the scorn in his voice.

"'Winter Saints,'" he said contemptuously. "That's what we called 'em. I didn't need any more lesson than that to teach me the importance of determining a man's character before you put your trust in him. It's a thing I want you girls—and you too, Thomas—to always remember."

Thomas nodded, his old felt hat dipping up and down on his head.

I thought about what Mr. Walker had said. I began to understand why these Mormons were so suspicious and cautious of those outside their faith. Those "winter Saints" had taken unfair advantage of the Mormons' shelter, food, and human kindness, and turned their trust to mistrust. That mistrust would color Mormon motives for years to come.

We traveled all that day. At dusk we stopped near Point of the Mountain, between Salt Lake and Provo, to eat and spread out our bedrolls. Thomas built a fire while Lacy and I stirred up some johnnycake. The evening meal was plain and simple, but there is something about eating simple fare cooked over an open fire, under a canopy of stars, that transforms a meal into something very special indeed.

After we'd had our fill and prepared camp for the night, we sat around the campfire talking. That is to say, the Walkers talked while I listened. I leaned back on both elbows, stretching my legs to the fire, and drank in the night. The sky was milky with stars, and a butter-yellow moon hung balanced overhead. I could easily pick out the Big Dipper, and its companion the Little Dipper, in the star-streaked sky. I had never seen the stars so bright or so plentiful. I supposed it was because there were no electric lights from the city or pollution to cloud the view. I sat still, listening, looking, in what seemed a vacuum of time and space.

Before long the conversation around the campfire slowed to a sleepy pace. Thomas, who was sitting next to me, yawned, stretched, then pulled his hat down over his eyes.

Mr. Walker took a stick and stirred the tired embers with it, then he directed Lacy and me to our beds. My "bed" was a quilt spread over the straw in the wagon, with another quilt on top to cover me. Although the day had been warm, the night air was nippy. I hadn't noticed how chilly it had grown while we sat beside the fire, until I settled into my bed of straw. I hoped one quilt would be enough to keep me warm.

Lacy crawled into the wagon beside me, pulling most of the blanket along with her. I sighed and snuggled closer to her. If I was going to stay warm, I would have to make do with a portion of the quilt and Lacy's body heat. Lacy yawned noisily and promptly drifted off to sleep. I lay awake for some time, looking at the sky and thinking. It was perfectly quiet around me except for the soft crackle of the fire and the comforting voice of a cricket. My thoughts dwelt on the Walkers—their devotion to the gospel and their example of family solidarity and unity. And in some crazy, indescribable way I felt, for the first time, content to be one of them.

We arrived in the Provo valley shortly before dark the next day. The peaks of Mt. Timpanogos were aglow with the last dying rays of sunlight. Mr. Walker directed the horses toward a broad meadow, beyond which lay a hollow where Aunt Lizzy's house snugly rested.

As we pulled into the yard, three young boys came racing out of the house toward the wagon, shouting and laughing as they ran. They danced up and down while Mr. Walker reined the horses to a stop and jumped down from the wagon seat. He gave each of the boys a big bear-hug and started toward the house with them.

As I stepped from the wagon, I looked around curiously at my surroundings. Aunt Lizzy's house appeared to be the only house in the area. It sat like a contented child in its mother's lap nestled in that little hollow, with four big elm trees to shade and protect it. The house itself looked very much like the Walkers' home, only smaller. It was painted the same ocher color and had the same gabled roof, wide porch, and narrow windows. A stand of hollyhocks grew beside the porch, their sturdy stocks and red friendly faces offering a hearty welcome.

I followed Thomas and Lacy inside. A large woman, tall and plump, stood just inside the door. She and Walker greeted each other with an embrace. Her brown hair was tucked up into a bun and she wore a crisp, clean apron over her woolen dress. She looked to be somewhat younger than Mrs. Walker, but not as pretty.

"How are you, Aunt Lizzy?" asked Thomas, as he gave her an affectionate hug.

"Well, Thomas. I'm well. My, look how tall you've grown!" Aunt Lizzy clapped her hands together in delight. "And Lacy and Katharine—how fine you both look."

I wasn't the least bit surprised when Aunt Lizzy hugged and kissed me right along with everyone else, as if she'd always known me.

"It's nice to see you, Aunt Lizzy," I murmured.

"Well, now," Mr. Walker said in a booming voice. "Let's get that wagon unloaded. Might even be able to find a little something for you children in the wagon if we look hard enough." Mr. Walker ran his hand over the youngest boy's brown, curly head, rumpling his hair. The little boy squealed and raced toward the door.

"Come on, Thomas, we'll help you unload that old wagon," the eldest boy offered.

I smiled in spite of myself. They were cute boys; none of them could have been much older than Jesse. Thomas took two boys by the hand and walked with them out to the wagon. The youngest boy, who had been waiting impatiently beside the door, yelped with glee.

"I believe Rachel sent along a jar or two of her gooseberry jam, Lizzy," Mr. Walker said, putting a hand on Aunt Lizzy's shoulder.

"She knows how much the boys and I love her jam. I've never seen gooseberries grow so big and juicy as they do under Rachel's care."

"Aunt Lizzy, would you mind if I rinsed off some of this dust?" asked Lacy, rubbing her hands together. "I'm covered with it."

"You and Katharine go out to the pump and splash some water on your faces and hands while I warm supper for you. You must be starved. The boys and the ranch hands have already eaten, so we can have ourselves a quiet, cozy meal together."

In the time it took for us to clean up, Aunt Lizzy had supper on the table. I was ravenous after two days on the road eating from a campfire. Aunt Lizzy had cooked mutton, fried potatoes, squash, and biscuits. It pained me to admit she was not the cook Mrs. Walker was, especially considering the fact that I was so hungry. The mutton was tough, the biscuits soggy in the center, and the squash hard as tacks. The potatoes dripped with grease. No one else seemed to mind the food or give any indication of disappointment in it. So I grasped my fork firmly in hand and set to work.

Conversation at the table ran thick and fast, with everyone trying to catch up on one another's news. As I listened, I was able to pluck the names of Aunt Lizzy's boys from the conversation. Emmett was the oldest boy's name, followed by Thorpe and Reuben. I was curious about the fact that no mention was made of Aunt Lizzy's husband. I had looked for him to come in when we sat down to dinner, and when he failed to appear I assumed he was away. But now I feared the poor man was dead and forgotten, as no one made reference to him.

After supper was finished and the dishes put away, everyone assembled in Aunt Lizzy's parlor. Where Rachel Walker's parlor was decorated in greens and pinks, Aunt Lizzy's was mostly done in earth tones. I guessed she was accustomed to living close to nature, her house sitting as it was, snuggled in the hollow. Aunt Lizzy asked a lot of questions about Brother Brigham's funeral and the conference we'd just attended in Salt Lake. Mr. Walker gave her a full account, leaving nothing out.

I knew it was time for bed even before Mr. Walker had to remind us. My trail-weary body ached and pained with every movement. I longed for the feel of a firm mattress against my back and a down pillow for my head, but I knew a lumpy straw tick was all I could expect.

Even while I was thinking about my comfortable support mattress and fine mahogany bed back home, Walker rose from his chair and made preparations to retire. Aunt Lizzy followed suit. She kissed each one of us good-night, then waited while Mr. Walker gave us final instructions.

"You children may stay up ten minutes more if you wish," Walker said in a tired voice. "Don't neglect your prayers, and each of you read a passage of scripture before you sleep. I shall see you all at daybreak."

With that, Walker took one of the lighted lamps from the table and followed Aunt Lizzy into the bedroom which adjoined the parlor. He shut the door behind them.

I was shocked by his action. What was he doing in Aunt Lizzy's bedroom? And behind a closed door, too? The thoughts that sprang to my mind were appalling. I frantically looked at the others to gauge their reactions, but they were completely unruffled, as if nothing out of the ordinary had occurred.

I grimly watched the closed bedroom door, trying to form some excuse for Walker's extraordinary behavior. When the strip of light under the bedroom door suddenly vanished, I was aghast. I flamed with indignation. How dare Walker treat his family with such flagrant contempt? I couldn't even imagine what Mrs. Walker would have said had she known her husband was cavorting with another woman! Such a scoundrel he was, and pretending to be so pious and . . . then it struck me. It was what everyone else in the family knew, of course, and accepted as a fact of life—the reason I had not seen Aunt Lizzy's "husband" at the dinner table. Aunt Lizzy was Walker's plural wife! The idea was certainly unsettling. It would take some getting used to. I shook my head in bewilderment. I wondered if I would ever cease to be amazed by these nineteenth-century Mormons.

"That's it, everybody. Bedtime." Thomas's voice boomed in my ears. Aunt Lizzy's boys moaned and pleaded for a few minutes more, but Thomas was immovable. "You heard Father. Let's go. Now."

I lay in bed that night thinking about the principle of polygamy and its application to the Walkers. I remembered how Professor Bowen wanted me to search polygamist diaries in order to ferret out all the negative comments I could find. But here was an example of the principle right under my nose, and I hadn't heard or seen anything that suggested disharmony, jealousy, or envy. Walker's children seemed to be well-adjusted and happy. Aunt Lizzy didn't strike me as particularly downtrodden.

If she was jealous of Rachel Walker, she hid her feelings well. She had seemed to be genuinely appreciative for Rachel Walker's gift of gooseberry jam. And what of Rachel? Would she have sent the gift if there were ill feelings? I didn't think so. If the Walkers were a typical polygamist family, then I marveled at how well the Saints handled what had to be a difficult principle to live.

CHAPTER EIGHT

IT WASN'T UNTIL THE NEXT AFTERNOON that I discovered just what kind of ranch Walker and Aunt Lizzy ran. I had long since realized that if I wanted to learn about my surroundings without raising eyebrows, I had to do a little exploration on my own. I couldn't get away until late in the afternoon, after my chores in the house were completed, and it took some cleverness on my part to slip out of the house without rousing Lacy's curiosity about where I was going. I made my escape while she sat writing a long, rambling letter to Silas.

Slipping out the back door unnoticed, I walked quickly past the vegetable garden, through the orchard, and toward the big brown barn which sat some distance from the house. At the side of the barn were located a number of low-fenced pens.

I smelled the sheep before I actually saw them. The oily, musty odor of wool assaulted my nostrils. As I approached the pens, three sheep came out of the enclosed portion of their pen and trotted over to me. One nudged his nose up to the fence and bawled plaintively. A sheep ranch. I should have known that from Lacy's comments about the shearers. There didn't seem to be any more sheep about other than the few in the pen. And these sheep looked very different from any I'd ever seen. Of course, my field of experience was not broad—I'd only seen a handful of sheep before in my life—but every one of them had been pure white. These sheep had black faces, tails, and legs. Even their wool was tinged with black. I bent down to study the sheep who was standing closest to the fence. He was a silly looking creature, with floppy black ears too large for his head, a narrow muzzle, and eyes that encased a black, bar-shaped pupil. I reached out tentatively to pet his wooly head.

"Baa-aa-aa."

Startled by the sound, I jerked back reflexively, ramming my hand against the pen in the process. The rough wood fence scraped away a layer of skin on the back of my hand.

I uttered a string of words that would have brought the wrath of the whole Walker clan down on my head had they heard me. The sheep bawled again, as if denying his implication in the crime. I blew on my injured hand in a senseless effort to staunch the pain.

"Better let me have a look at that hand."

I jumped at the unexpected sound of a man's voice, coming from behind and to my left. As I whirled around to see who had spoken, a young man dressed in work clothes and a rumpled felt hat was striding toward me.

I instinctively hid my hand behind my back.

"Come on, let me see it," the young man directed. "It might need attention." He had stopped next to me by this time, and was reaching for my hand.

Like a guilty child I held it out for him to see.

He took my hand in his own work-roughened ones and looked at it closely. "If you clean up that scrape and bandage it, I think we'll be able to save your hand."

I looked up sharply into his face. His expression was sober, but his eyes danced.

I snatched my hand away. "I'll be just fine, thank you," I said in a scathing tone.

"That's good. I wouldn't want anything to happen to you before we had a chance to meet. I'm one of the ranch hands here. My name's Caleb Hollister. My friends call me Cabe."

"How do you do, Mr. Hollister." I emphasized the last two words of my sentence.

Caleb Hollister's face broke into a grin. I thought it was the most obnoxious grin I'd ever encountered.

"I didn't catch your name," he said, letting the words trail off into a question mark.

"I didn't give it to you. It's Katharine, but you may call me Miss Walker." I smiled with smug satisfaction at my quick come-back.

"Katharine, huh?" He paused, drawing a hand across his chin. "I don't think that quite suits you. I believe I'll call you Kate." Again, that impudent grin. He was certainly impertinent; I thoroughly disliked him.

"You may not call me Kate. I hate being called Kate. Hopefully, I can avoid having you talk to me at all."

I turned on my heel, ready to leave, when he lightly touched my arm and said, "Say, Kate, I'm afraid your hand is bleeding. You can use my handkerchief until you get to the house if you wish."

I glanced down at my injured hand. Though I hated to give him the satisfaction of responding, to my dismay I found a bloody trail running down my fingers. He already had his handkerchief out of his pocket and extended to me.

I ignored the proffered handkerchief and wiped the blood from my hand onto my freshly-laundered apron.

My snub didn't seem to ruffle him. He put the handkerchief back in his pocket. "Vicious animals, those sheep," he remarked solemn-faced.

I turned my back on him and quickly walked to the house. I felt his eyes following me, and I had no doubt he wore that awful grin. I walked briskly without once turning around to look back at him. My hand was hurting and still bleeding. I took the corner of my apron and pressed it tightly against the injury. Blood seeped through the fabric. *I'll never be able to get the blood out of this apron*, I thought. *It'll leave a miserable stain.* His fault. I frowned as I thought of Caleb Hollister's impudent manner. I knew it was irrational thinking, but still I placed the blame for the spreading stain on my apron squarely upon him.

Disgusted, I strode into the house. Lacy didn't even look up from her letter-writing. I took an old cloth from the closet and went outside to the pump, washed the scrape on my hand, and bandaged it with the cloth. Then I set about scrubbing the blood stains out of my apron.

For the rest of the afternoon I helped Aunt Lizzy in the kitchen. She chatted easily as we worked, asking me about my activities in Salt Lake and kidding me about the boyfriends she was certain I had by the dozen. Where Rachel Walker was reserved and quiet by nature, Aunt Lizzy was quite the opposite. She laughed and chattered as if we were the closest of friends. Her open, friendly manner did much to put me at ease. I gathered that she'd been married to Mr. Walker for about twelve years, and spent nearly all that time on the sheep ranch in Provo, going only occasionally to Salt Lake City to visit. Her life on the ranch apparently suited her, for I could not detect a hint of dissatisfaction with her lot.

"I guess you're anxious to see Abby again," she said in the course of our conversation.

"Abby?"

"Abby and the rest of the sheep will be coming down from pasture in the next day or so. She's full grown now. You'll hardly recognize her, Katharine."

"I'm sure that's true."

"You won't mind that she's not a lamb anymore? My, how you loved that little lamb." She smiled and patted my hand.

"Well, I guess Abby and I will have to get reacquainted," I said lamely.

"Did you know we birthed thirty-four lambs this spring? Only lost three of them, too. Your father was real pleased to hear that." She smiled to herself and began humming a spritely tune.

I peeled the potatoes for supper, although my sore hand made it cumbersome, and put them in a pot of water on the stove to boil. Aunt Lizzy had to prepare a mountain of food, enough to feed the family plus the ranch hands. By six o'clock the hands started shuffling into the yard to wash at the pump. I hoped Caleb Hollister would not be among them. It wouldn't hurt my feelings if he dropped off the edge of the world. But I wasn't so lucky. From the corner of my eye, I saw him file into the kitchen with the rest of the men. I kept my back to him, busy at the stove.

When Mr. Walker and the rest of the family came inside, we all took our seats at the table. I managed to sit as far away from Caleb as I could. After Walker pronounced a blessing on the food, the next few minutes were taken up with passing the plates of food from hand to hand. There were three ranch workers at the table with us. The one sitting next to me was a grizzled old man with stubble on his chin and hair streaked with gray. As he took the bowl of potatoes from my hand, he nodded and grunted, "Thank ye, Miss Walker."

The other ranch hand was much younger, probably in his thirties. He was tall and lank, and his work clothes fit poorly on his lean frame. Mostly he kept silent throughout supper, speaking only when others specifically addressed him. I got the impression he was the sort who preferred to keep to himself.

At the far end of the table sat Caleb. I couldn't help glancing at him a time or two, but only when I was sure he wasn't looking in my general direction. He wore the same clothes he'd had on earlier, minus the hat, of course. No hats were allowed at the dinner table. Without his hat I was able to get a better view of his face, although my assessment was accomplished in short, surreptitious glances. Caleb's hair was darker than I had at first thought, and rather long, hanging well over his collar. His eyes were hazel, his nose prominent but well proportioned, and his mouth not unattractive—when he wasn't sporting that infuriating grin. His eyes caught mine once, quite by accident. He flashed me a smile which I pretended not to see.

Mr. Walker introduced the ranch workers to Thomas, Lacy and me. "You all know Virgil Gustafson," he said, indicating the elderly man sitting next to me. "This is Gus's sixth year as foreman on the ranch, isn't it, Gus?"

Gus nodded in acknowledgement, then forked another piece of boiled potato into his mouth. It was a small mouth, I noticed, and puckered around the edges like an old brown apricot.

"These two young men are shearers. They hired on at shearing time and have agreed to stay through the fall to help us out on the ranch. This is Luke Satterfield"—the ranch hand merely glanced up from his plate—"and Cabe Hollister."

Caleb reached across the table to shake hands with Thomas.

"That's my son, Thomas," Walker told him, "and my daughter, Lacy."

"How do you do, Miss Walker," Caleb replied, rising slightly from his chair.

Lacy blushed a bright pink, and murmured a hello.

"And this is my daughter, Katharine," Walker finished.

"Miss Walker and I have already met. It's nice to see you again, Miss Walker."

I could have wrung his neck for that! Lacy's head snapped around to look at me, and Aunt Lizzy's face registered surprise. Caleb could easily have said "hello," or "nice to make your acquaintance," or anything else but what he had said. Now I would have to field a dozen questions as to where and how I had met him. I was sure he had answered as he did just to goad me. I was so angry that I scarcely acknowledged his greeting.

The conversation at the table revolved around the sheep and work on the ranch. Mr. Walker and Thomas had spent the day inspecting the ranch and being brought up to date on conditions in general. That topic of conversation didn't cease at the table. Walker and the hired hands discussed particular problems they faced with the sheep, and jobs which needed attention on the ranch.

Because of the nature of the conversation, the ladies said little. I was glad of that, for I was still fuming and did not feel kindly disposed toward polite chatter. I kept my eyes away from Caleb during the remainder of the meal, and when it was over I avoided any contact with him as he made his way out of the house.

I could tell Lacy was dying to question me. She cornered me right after the dishes were washed and put away.

"Katharine, why didn't you tell me?"

"Tell you what?" I replied, trying to forestall the inevitable.

"That you'd met him? Met Cabe Hollister. We've only been here one day and you've already made the acquaintance of the most handsome man on the ranch," she breathed.

"Handsome? I wouldn't choose that word to describe him. Excuse me, Lacy, I have chores to do." I tried to walk past her, but she put a hand roughly on my arm.

"How did you meet him? Tell me all the glorious details," she said, panting.

"There's nothing to tell. He just happened to be there when I walked outside the house. That's all." I inched my bandaged hand into the folds of my skirt.

"Well, what did he say to you?" she persisted.

"Nothing. Just hello. For heaven's sake, Lacy," I said in exasperation.

"Oh, Katharine. He's the most handsome man I've ever seen. Did you notice his eyes? As deep and green as the sea." She sighed, closing her eyes part way as if in a trance.

"Now how would you know? You've never seen the sea," I retorted.

"And his hair—the color of sleek chestnuts." She closed her eyes completely this time.

"That's disgusting." I moved past her while her eyes were still shut, and started up the stairs.

"Katharine, wait a minute!" She hurried to my side. "Will you introduce me properly to him? I mean, so I can talk with him?"

"You'll have no trouble getting him to talk. You can trust me on that." I scowled and briskly climbed the stairs.

The routine at Aunt Lizzy's house was not much different than at the Walkers' home in Salt Lake—one unending round of cooking, cleaning, mending, scrubbing. In addition to that, it was harvest time and Lacy and I were faced with preserving bushels of fruit and vegetables. The very next day Aunt Lizzy brought out her empty fruit jars from the cellar and directed Lacy and me to the peach orchard.

"I'll ask one of the ranch hands to pick the top branches for you," she said, handing each of us a bucket.

I peered up at the branches, heavy with fruit. "We might as well get started," I sighed.

Lacy and I had been picking for about half an hour when Caleb Hollister appeared, carrying a long wooden ladder. Lacy sucked in her breath sharply when she saw him.

"What luck," she breathed into my ear excitedly. "Just look who's going to help us with the peaches."

"Yeah, what luck."

"Now don't forget, you promised to help me engage him in conversation."

I rolled my eyes heavenward. "Great," I muttered.

"Hello. I understand you can use some help here." Caleb strode over to us, the long ladder swinging easily in his grasp.

"Thank you, Mr. Hollister. We didn't know how we were going to reach those peaches on top," Lacy answered in a sugary voice.

I scowled darkly. "Harump."

"Excuse me, did you say something, Miss Walker?" Caleb asked, turning to me. I saw a twinkle spring into his eyes.

"I merely said 'good-day,' Mr. Hollister."

"Oh. For a moment, I thought you might be repeating a phrase you used at the sheep pens the other day," he said with an innocent expression.

I felt my face glow with embarrassment. I hoped he hadn't heard the profane words I'd spoken when I hurt my hand on the fence. Though it should not have bothered me that he had, for some reason it did. Lacy, hearing his comment, gave me a puzzled look.

Caleb didn't wait for a reply. Instead he leaned the ladder against the peach tree, took the bucket Lacy so willingly handed him, and climbed up the rungs.

"Do be careful up there," Lacy cooed.

I went back to my picking while Lacy stood gazing up into the tree top. When my bucket was filled, I carefully dumped the ripe fruit into a bushel basket Aunt Lizzy had provided for us. The peaches were round and firm, just right for bottling. I picked one up from the basket, cradling the fuzzy skin in my hand. It recalled to mind the plump peaches my mother preserved every fall—late Albertas, like these. The memory brought a swift pain with it. I hadn't thought of Mom and Dad for some days, and the remembrance made my heart ache.

The snap of a twig overhead drew my attention back to the present. Caleb was standing on the bottom rung of the ladder, his eyes on my face. I turned away, not wanting him to witness my private misery.

"I'll take that for you," offered Lacy sweetly. She grasped the bucket filled with peaches from Caleb's hand and added them to the ones already in the bushel basket.

Caleb stepped down from the ladder. "Is something the matter?" he asked me in a quiet voice.

Lacy, bent over the bushel basket, didn't hear his question or my murmured reply.

"No." I shook my head. "I'm fine."

He searched my face a moment longer before taking the ladder and moving on to the next tree.

Caleb helped us pick for over an hour, until we had filled the bushel basket several times over. I discovered he wasn't quite as abominable as I had first believed. His manner was easy and he amused us with his quick, dry wit. Lacy fawned over him something dreadful. She kept nudging me when he wasn't watching, wiggling her brows and heaving great meaningful sighs. Perhaps she'd been right in calling him handsome. But she was mistaken about one thing. His eyes were not the color of the sea. I had seen the ocean and it could not compare with the shade of Caleb Hollister's eyes. They were a deep vibrant hazel, with flecks of brown that turned to tawny yellow in the sunlight. His hair was dark brown, accented with tones of reddish-gold which gave it a rich appearance. His brows were dark and full, and his jaw firm. I could begin to understand why his presence sent Lacy into shivers of ecstasy.

When we'd picked as much fruit as we could preserve in two days' time, Caleb put the ladder under his arm and prepared to return to his other chores. First, however, he turned to Lacy and said, "Miss Walker, do you think I could trouble you for a glass of lemonade? My throat is about as dry and dusty as an old bone."

"It'd be no trouble at all," Lacy bubbled. "You just stay right here and I'll bring you a glass." She trotted off, jubilant over her assignment.

Finding myself alone with Caleb made me acutely uncomfortable. My ill feelings for him had not lessened appreciably in spite of the cordial hour we had spent. I shifted my weight uneasily from one foot to the other.

He apparently sensed my discomfiture. "Miss Walker, I think I owe you an apology for the way I behaved yesterday," he said. "It seems we got off on the wrong foot to begin with, for which I accept the blame. I hope you'll forgive me."

I studied his face, trying to tell if he was in earnest or merely toying with me again. He looked genuinely contrite.

"Well, perhaps I did bristle a bit prematurely."

"Perhaps a bit," he returned, a gentle smile coming to his lips.

"However," I continued briskly, "I did hope you'd have the decency to avoid dredging up the matter of my misguided choice of words while at the sheep pen."

Caleb's smile widened. "I apologize for that, too."

I nodded with the air of a haughty ruler who has just heard a plea for mercy from his subject. "Then perhaps we can proceed on more cordial terms," I said in a condescending tone.

"I'd like that, Kate."

"Don't call me Kate," I said between clenched teeth.

Just then Lacy returned with a tall glass of watery lemonade. She handed it to Caleb with great ceremony. He thanked her, then gulped down the juice. Smacking his lips appreciatively, he handed Lacy the empty glass. Then he hoisted the basket of peaches and walked with us back to the house. Lacy managed to stay near his side while we walked—much like a puppy dog, I thought with disgust.

We started peeling and bottling the peaches as soon as Caleb had set them on the table and returned to his chores. Aunt Lizzy, Lacy and I worked the rest of the afternoon, and when we were through, row after row of golden peaches sat gleaming on the counter. Although I was exhausted from the work, I couldn't help feeling a certain pride as I surveyed those filled jars.

After dinner, the family retreated to the front porch to escape the heat of the kitchen. With cooking peaches all afternoon and then preparing a hot supper, the kitchen was like a furnace. Although the air was growing cool, we didn't mind. It felt refreshing on our flushed faces and perspiring bodies. Mr. Walker and Thomas took up the newspaper, intent on reading it before the sun withdrew its light. The younger boys played tag on the porch steps, while Lacy and I rested the best we could while trying to avoid their running feet.

Aunt Lizzy had brought a ladies' magazine outside with her. She thumbed purposefully through it until she located what she apparently was searching for. I peered over her shoulder. On the right side of the page was a picture of Queen Victoria of England in all her regalia, with her children around her. I knew Aunt Lizzy was very much interested in Queen Victoria and the British royalty. She knew the names of the royal family by heart. Whenever she read something about them in the papers, she would clap her hands in delight or solemnly shake her head, depending on the fortunes of the royals. I glanced at the picture again. Prince Albert had died in 1861; in his prime he'd been a handsome looking man, but alas, the queen was beginning to look matronly. Aunt Lizzy studied the picture and the accompanying article with great attention.

I sighed and leaned my back against the porch step. Every muscle in my body ached. If there was anything I had gained from my nineteenth-century experience, it was an appreciation for the stamina of the pioneers. My body still hadn't gotten used to the demanding labor required of these women.

Emmett and Thorpe soon tired of their game of tag and wandered back into the house. Reuben plunked himself down beside me on the step, planting his chin in his hands.

"What ya doin'?" he asked in a conversational tone.

"Resting," I said emphatically.

"I ain't tired," he returned.

"That's because you're a child," I informed him.

He nodded solemnly, accepting the point on fact.

I looked over at him. His brown hair hung in his eyes and a dried streak of vanilla custard from dinner clung to his chin. When I first came to Aunt Lizzy's home, all three of her boys had seemed to blend into one whole. But as I got to know them, each took on his own distinctive personality. The oldest, Emmett, was quiet and serious-minded. Thorpe was a tease and could be a real pain in the neck. I liked Reuben the best. Although he was the youngest, he seemed to possess enormous good sense, and was charming and sweet in his own way.

"How old are you, Reuben?" I asked him. "You look to be about Jesse's age."

"Naw, I'm bigger than Jesse. He's only seven. I'm eight," Reuben replied, throwing out his chest.

"Is that right?"

"Ah huh. And I'm stronger, too. I can wrassle our big old sow to the ground."

"You can?" I said with feigned awe. What I really wanted to ask was why in the world he would want to wrestle some foul-smelling pig.

"You know what?" he continued in a confidential whisper.

"No. What?"

"I found a cave in the rocks out past the pasture. It's a pirate cave, I'll bet. Might even be some pirate gold hidden in there. It's a real good place to hide a treasure."

I put a hand to my mouth just in time to cover a long, lazy yawn. "I've never heard of pirates coming to Provo. Don't they mostly raid ships out on the ocean, and stuff like that?"

"Sure they do. But they got to have a place to bury their treasure. A cave is a fine place to bury stolen treasure."

Before I could comment further, the sound of the gate swinging open caught my attention. Mr. Walker put away his paper and stood up expectantly.

"Evenin', Bishop Walker," a short, stocky man said as he approached the porch. I couldn't make out the features of his face in the failing light, but I could hear the anxiety in his voice.

"Hello, Brother Gambit. What brings you out here this time of night?"

"My best plow horse got herself caught in some baling wire. She's cut up pretty bad. I come to ask if you might take a look at her in the morning."

"No need to wait til morning, Brother Gambit," Mr. Walker replied, starting down the porch steps. "Sounds like she needs attention right now."

"Well, I surely would appreciate it," the man named Gambit answered.

"You want me to come with you, Pa?" asked Thomas.

"No, son, you get some sleep. We've a big day tomorrow."

I knew Walker was weary from his day's work. He and Thomas had both labored on the ranch since sunup. But I'd come to learn that when people needed help, Walker was the first to lend a hand. It didn't matter if he was tired, hungry, or busy with his own affairs. He'd drop whatever he was doing to go to a neighbor's aid. Mr. Walker was a great one for preaching, but his example spoke the best sermon.

Aunt Lizzy fetched her husband his hat while Walker saddled a horse for the trip to Mr. Gambit's place. I had no idea where Gambit lived, but I was certain it must be some distance away. Gambit climbed on the horse behind Mr. Walker and they rode off, stirring up a cloud of dust.

CHAPTER NINE

THE NEXT MORNING I awoke early. I quickly dressed and went downstairs. Aunt Lizzy was already heating the stove to start breakfast. She asked me to go out to the milk house to fetch a pail of milk for the griddle cakes. With the milk pail swinging in my hand, I walked the short distance to the little adobe structure built partially underground to keep milk, eggs, and cheese cool. The air was crisp and clean smelling. Even though it was nearly mid-October, it still smelled like summer. Indian summer, this kind of weather was called. It reminded me of Indians, too. I imagined Indian braves racing their painted ponies over the meadows, their long black hair glistening in the early morning light. Tucked away in the hollow as we were, it wasn't hard to picture bare-chested braves gazing down from the ridges onto the Walkers' cozy house. I hoped they were friendly Indians.

When I reached the milk house, I found Thomas and Caleb Hollister standing nearby, deep in conversation. Caleb's sleeves were rolled to his elbows and he carried a bucket of feed. When Thomas saw me, he nodded in greeting. I walked over to them.

"You're out and about early," Thomas said.

"Aunt Lizzy asked me to get some milk for breakfast."

"Breakfast sounds awfully good to me," Caleb commented, flashing me a smile.

I smiled slightly in return.

"Your brother was just telling me about Mr. Gambit's mare. Apparently, Mr. Gambit and your father were able to pull her through," Caleb said.

"Oh? The horse will be all right, then?"

"You know Father," Thomas answered. "There's nothing he admires more than a fine horse. He nursed that mare all night long. Didn't get home until a few hours ago."

I knew precisely what Thomas meant. Mr. Walker was an excellent judge of horseflesh and he appreciated a prime animal. When I had first come to stay with the Walkers, I knew next to nothing about horses. I'd never had any experience with them. But I soon learned that a man's horse is a vital part of his livelihood. A good horse is critical to work on the farm or the ranch. Mr. Walker owned two draft horses to help with the heavy work on the farm in Salt Lake. They were strong, powerful animals—blocky in body, broad in the shoulders and thighs, thick-muscled legs, and big feet. Walker's horses were a matched pair, of a breed called Percheron. They were a handsome shade of reddish-gray, with white hairs intermixed throughout their coats.

The Percherons were a spirited pair. Their stride was quick and their temperament lively. When we first got to Provo, I made the mistake of calling the big chestnut work horse in Aunt Lizzy's barn a Percheron. Thomas quickly corrected me. It was not a Percheron, he said, but a Belgian. He told me that Belgians are stockier than Percherons and have gentler dispositions. For myself, I could not see much difference between the two breeds of horses; but if the Belgian was calmer and gentler, I suspected that was the reason Walker chose him for Aunt Lizzy and the smaller boys to use here at the ranch.

For ordinary riding, Walker had his own horse. It was a beautiful, sleek saddle horse, coal black with a white blaze on his forehead and four white socks. He called the horse Crow, and he rode it when he went into town without the wagon or on short errands. He hitched Crow to the carriage when he and

Rachel went for a drive, and I knew he was not above racing the horse now and again against those of his neighbors.

The Walkers kept another horse on the farm in Salt Lake, a mare named Queen of Sheba. This horse did not belong exclusively to Thomas, but he rode it more than the other family members. Sheba was a dark chestnut color, with a black mane and tail. She was much smaller and lighter than the draft horses.

"I'm glad to hear Mr. Gambit's horse is mending," I commented.

"You can bet that mare wouldn't have pulled through without Father's skill and patience. He told me this morning that she'd gotten all tripped up in the wire, thrashed about and went down on her front knees. Her legs and underbody are cut up, and her knees are bruised and swollen," Thomas reported.

I pictured the horse rearing and thrashing to free herself of the wire caught around her legs. It wasn't a pretty scene. I blanked it out of my mind.

"Well, I'd better be getting that milk for Aunt Lizzy," I said.

Caleb set aside the bucket of feed he'd been holding and said, "Let me get that milk for you, Miss Walker."

He took the metal pail from my hand without waiting for my reply and disappeared into the milk house. A moment later he returned with the pail filled and frothing over the rim. I reached out to take the pail from him.

"Please. Allow me," he said, sweeping his free arm wide in a gallant gesture.

I shrugged and started back toward the house. Caleb's stride matched my own.

"You know, I've never been to the Great Salt Lake City," Caleb began conversationally. "Have you always lived there, Kate?"

I sighed loudly. No matter how often I reminded him, he still persisted in calling me Kate. "Yes. Always," I replied irritably.

"Have you ever attended the university there?" he asked.

"The University of Utah? Yes, I graduated from there. Although I attended BYU my first semester—at my parents' request," I added, remembering their gentle but insistent urging that I attend the Church school.

Caleb looked puzzled. "University of Utah? Do you mean the Deseret University? I've never heard it called by any other name."

"Yes," I said quickly. "The University of Deseret. Just a slip of the tongue. Sorry." I quickened my pace, but Caleb lengthened his stride accordingly.

"What's that other place you mentioned?" he asked after a moment's silence. "Is that another school?"

"Well, not exactly. At least not yet."

Caleb paused for an instant, apparently trying to figure out what I meant. Then he shook his head and caught up to me.

"I think after next spring's shearing I'll have enough money saved to start at the university. It's been an ambition of mine for as long as I can remember."

I glanced at Caleb's face. He wore a thoughtful expression. I wondered why he was bothering to tell me all of this.

"What topic do you want to study?" I asked idly, not particularly interested in his reply.

"Law," he answered, without a moment's hesitation. "I'd like to be involved in the process of achieving statehood for the territory. I think a man with legal training could be an asset in that endeavor."

I was surprised by his lofty aspirations. I had supposed he was content with his work as a shearer. "You should pursue your goal," I answered. "I think the study of law is a commendable choice."

He brightened noticeably at my response.

"I don't think Thomas is optimistic, however, about the possibility of the territory coming into the Union very soon. We had a discussion on that point not long ago," I commented.

"Perhaps Thomas looks at it from a different angle than I do," Caleb replied. "Many farmers believe the Saints will be better off economically if we retain territorial status."

"Perhaps," I agreed.

"Is Thomas intent on farming? I wondered if he might have an interest in soldiering."

"Soldiering? Do you mean a military career? No, I don't think so. Why do you ask?"

"Your parents must have admired Colonel Thomas Kane very much to have named their son after him."

I had never considered that. It made me curious to know if Mr. Walker was acquainted with Kane; perhaps he could even tell me about the man. That would be something to put in my research notes. I wondered if Professor Bowen had located my notes on Thomas Kane yet.

We'd reached the house by this time. Caleb opened the back door for me, then he followed me inside and put the pail of milk on the table.

"Morning, Brother Hollister," Aunt Lizzy greeted him. "I hope you're hungry. We've griddle cakes, potatoes, and eggs enough to feed a battalion."

"I'm sure I can manage my fair share, Mrs. Walker," he laughed.

A few moments later the rest of the family and hired hands came in for breakfast. Luke Satterfield slid wordlessly into his chair, keeping his eyes on his plate. I hadn't had two words with the lanky shearer; he did his work and kept to himself. The older man, Gus, was more friendly, but he wasn't one to waste words, either.

"Mornin', Miss Walker," he said to me, removing his broad-brimmed felt hat and stuffing it between his knees. Gus's voice was rough and grainy, like sandpaper.

When Mr. Walker took his seat at the table, I noticed immediately the heavy dark circles ringing his eyes. He'd gotten little sleep, yet he was up with the rest of the hands, ready to start a full day's work.

From their talk at the table, I learned that the men were going out to the pastures to gather the sheep and bring them back to the ranch for the winter. This task apparently would take more than one day, and most of the conversation revolved around their preparations. Gus, as ranch foreman, would remain behind, readying the pens and making other necessary arrangements for the sheep. Luke Satterfield and Caleb would accompany Thomas and Mr. Walker to the pastures.

There was much bustling about after breakfast. Even the younger boys were put to work running last-minute errands. By noon, everything was in readiness. I stood on the porch watching the men mount up. Caleb swung into his saddle with the ease of a man born to it. He sat tall and erect astride his horse, the reins resting loosely in his hands. Watching him, I thought how natural he would look sitting, instead, behind the wheel of a shiny red Porsche. The confident posture, the casually styled hair, and the hint of arrogance about his mouth all contributed to the image in my mind. The picture brought a smile to my lips. At that precise moment, Caleb's gaze collided with mine. He flashed me a grin and reined his horse over to the porch where I was standing.

"You take care while we're gone, Kate. When I get back, I want to hear more about that university."

I smiled in spite of myself. "I might just tell you."

Caleb nodded. "I'll look forward to it."

He touched his heels to the horse's ribs and quickly rejoined the others. A few moments later they rode off amidst a chorus of shouts and whistles, heading southeast toward the high pastures.

I felt a slight tinge of disappointment over Caleb's departure. It was not that I particularly enjoyed his company. Indeed, he could irritate me faster than anyone I had met. But he was someone I could talk to—someone who had not been previously acquainted with Katharine Walker, and I needed that. I sighed and turned to go inside the house.

"Oh, how I shall miss seeing him," Lacy whispered in my ear. She had come to my side without my noticing it. "He's positively the most handsome man I've ever seen."

My eyes narrowed with evil intent. "More handsome than Silas?" I asked wickedly.

Lacy opened her mouth in protest, her eyes wide with indignation. "Of course not! How dare you suggest such a thing?"

I looked at her with an accusing eye. "You just said—"

"I know what I said," she broke in huffily. "But I meant aside from *Silas* he was the most handsome. Really, Katharine!"

"Oh, I see. For an instant I thought you had forgotten about Silas. How silly of me." I had to hide my grin behind my hand as I walked into the house. Lacy followed behind me, a testy expression on her face.

Lacy, Aunt Lizzy and I spent the rest of the day bottling more fruit. When we finished with that, it was time to start dinner. I hoped the household chores would lighten with the men gone, but Aunt Lizzy had other ideas. With fewer meals to prepare, she informed us, there was time for a little extra housecleaning. Over the next two days we scrubbed floors and walls, aired the mattresses, polished the wood trim on the fireplaces, and cleaned the pantry cupboards. Satisfied with our work in the house, Aunt Lizzy sent us outside to scrub the milk house floor, sweep out the barn, and put fresh straw in the chicken coop.

By the third day my hands were rubbed raw and the tips of my fingers were cracked and bleeding. I was feeling more than a little antagonistic about my circumstances. I could hear Mr. Walker's words ringing in my ears: "Idleness is the devil's workshop, Brother Brigham used to say." Well, neither Brother Brigham nor Mr. Walker would find room to fault us on that score.

I rubbed my sore hands with some foul-smelling ointment Aunt Lizzy provided for that purpose, and walked outside into the October sunshine. The air had a bite in it now, although the sky was a cloudless blue. As I walked, stretching the cramped and tired muscles in my legs, a breeze came up and seized a cluster of fallen leaves, sending them sailing about my legs. Overhead, brown-edged leaves pulled loose from their moorings and fluttered to the ground. They crunched under my feet as I went along with no specific direction in mind. The color on the mountainsides was a brilliant blend of greens, reds, and yellows, a vivid patchwork quilt draping the mountains' hills and valleys.

At length I found myself near the sheep pens. The three lone lambs who inhabited the pens baaed plaintively as I approached. For an instant I felt sorry for them. They had not been allowed the freedom of roaming the pastures like their fellows, for they had to be hand-fed. I watched them for a few moments. They put their muzzles to the fence, crowding one another in their efforts to reach me. When they realized I had no food for them, they lost interest and went back to munching the grain in their troughs.

I had learned a fair amount about sheep raising since coming to the ranch. I knew these lambs were orphans. Lambs without mothers, like these in the pen, must be hand-fed milk from a bottle. When they are ready, they can begin to eat a little mush and then grass and alfalfa grown on the farm. An orphaned lamb is not part of the regular flock, for he can't take care of himself. He stays on the ranch all summer while the rest of the sheep graze in the high pastures.

I didn't know how many sheep Walker kept on his ranch, but I knew he raised them for their meat as well as their wool. I learned that the fleece off one sheep yields about ten pounds of wool, enough to make several suits of clothes. In the spring the shearers come to the ranch. These men are professionals, going from ranch to ranch throughout the shearing season. A good shearer can clip a fleece in about twelve minutes. He uses hand clippers that have big, flat blades and look like a large pair of scissors. The wool is cut so that it comes off all in one piece, then it is rolled up and tied with a cord into a tight bundle and taken to market.

Sheep ranching is not easy. The shepherd must always be on guard against predators or other wild animals which may frighten and separate the flock. A flock of sheep might bolt in a lightning storm or at any sudden noise. When a sheep becomes separated from the flock, it is very vulnerable. It may become lost or attacked by animals. Sheep also fall prey to sickness and disease. They often suffer from worm parasites, or sheep scab which is caused by mites and ticks. Foot rot and sore mouth are common conditions, as well. I admired the Walkers' skill and constant care in looking after their sheep.

I wandered away from the pens and walked toward the barn. It felt good to be out of the house and relax for a few minutes. I kicked at the pebbles along the dirt path, enjoying the feel of the sun on my back and the breeze whispering through my hair. Consequently, it was a moment before I realized that I was being watched. Virgil Gustafson's squinty old eyes peered out at me from beneath bushy gray brows as he sat on a barrel beside the barn, a length of cut willow in his hand. I blushed, even though I wasn't sure why I should feel embarrassed. I suppose I felt like the guilty child who has just been caught neglecting her chores.

"Afternoon, Miss Walker," Gus said in his gravelly voice. "Saw you comin' a piece back. Did you want somethin' in particular?"

I blushed a second time. "No. Actually, I was just sneaking a moment's rest."

"I can understand that. It'd take more than a moment to rest these old bones, though, I can tell you." Gus's puckered mouth split into a smile.

I took a few steps toward him. "What are you making out of that willow, Mr. Gustafson?" I asked curiously. He had cut and peeled the skin off several strips of willow which lay in a pile at his feet, and was working with his knife on another.

"Your aunt mentioned she'd like a wicker chair to set out on her porch. Figured I might as well make myself useful. Got a little time on my hands til your pa and the others get back from the meadows." Gus's knife skillfully stripped away the skin from the willow branch he held in his hand. He didn't miss a stroke as he talked.

I watched in silence while he worked. I should have been impressed by the skill needed to produce such hand-crafted items, but, strangely, all I could think about was the speed and efficiency of factory-produced furniture. My mind went back again to the wing chair my mother had purchased at Dinwoodey's. It was one of several identical pieces, differentiated only by the color and pattern of its fabric. I hugged my arms against my body. The breeze had picked up, putting a definite chill in the air.

"Mr. Walker, uh, that is my father, seems to put a good deal of trust in your judgment. Have you always worked on a sheep ranch?" I asked.

Gus chuckled, a deep throaty rumble. "I guess you could say I've done a little bit of most everything. Sheep ranching, cattle ranching, breaking broncs, mending fences." Gus looked up at me, squinting in the sun.

"That's an impressive list. I gather you've worked in other places than Provo."

"Yep. I was born in the East, but I came west as soon as I could sit on a horse without fallin' off. I've seen a few places, that's for sure."

"I envy you. I've seen very few places and never lived more than sixty miles from Salt Lake."

"The Great Salt Lake City is not a bad town," Gus replied, working his knife.

"Maybe not, but I'd like to live someplace else for a while. The east coast might be exciting. It would give me a different point of view. Broaden my outlook." I stared past Gus's shoulder, imagining myself dressed in a slinky sequined dress and partying the night away at some magnificent hotel in New York City.

"Mostly I've found it don't make a lot of difference where a person lives. It's how he lives that counts for something."

Gus's words ignited a flash of anger inside me. I thought of the fences and hedges designed to keep me within the bounds of Church teachings. "Even if a person is forced to accept values he doesn't agree with?" I asked more sharply than I intended.

Gus was quiet for several seconds. Then he drew a raspy breath. "I can't recall ever hearin' that values and morals are

118

forced onto a person. Those things can be planted by others, but the growing is somethin' one has to do all on his own."

I glanced up quickly at the old man's face. His eyes were on his work, but I sensed he'd picked his words with care. I shivered suddenly in the brisk air. However carefully Gus had chosen his words, I preferred to ignore his message. What I was thinking about was Gus's remark concerning Salt Lake. I wondered how much time he'd spent there, and if by any chance he knew of the old man with the watch and key. I asked him about it.

"What did you say this feller looks like?" Gus asked.

"He's an older man, with gray hair and strange, piercing eyes. Not too tall, and kind of thin. He carries a fancy gold watch in his vest pocket, and from the chain hangs a black iron key. He keeps the key in plain sight. Do you know anyone like that?" I asked hopefully.

Gus stroked his grizzled chin a few times, squinting off into the distance. "Can't say as I've ever met him," he said slowly.

My heart sank in disappointment.

"But I've heard tell of him."

"You have?" I cried excitedly. "Do you know how I can get in touch with him? I really need to talk to him."

Gus said nothing for some moments. I was on pins and needles waiting for his reply. He continued to stare into the distance wordlessly, then fixed his weathered gray eyes on me. "I suspect, Miss Walker, that you'll find him when your heart is right."

I stared open-mouthed, trying to comprehend what Gus had said. It made no sense. His answer was gibberish in my ears. "What are you talking about?" I finally managed to blurt out.

Gus looked at me with a calm and even gaze. Then he went back to shaping the willow in his hand. I waited for him to say something more, to clarify his answer, but he continued to work the supple young willow without speaking.

I didn't know what to make of him. Maybe he'd misunderstood my query. Or perhaps he was just a bit eccentric. I considered questioning him again, but decided against it.

"I guess I'd better be getting back to the house. Aunt Lizzy will be wondering where I am," I mumbled.

Gus nodded, his eyes still on the slim piece of willow in his hands.

"It was nice to talk with you, Mr. Gustafson. And good luck with that chair." I turned and strode away. I could feel the old man's eyes on my back. I quickened my pace until I was well out of his sight.

CHAPTER TEN

THE MEN RETURNED the following afternoon. We heard the bawling of the sheep in the distance. Thomas came first, whooping and hollering like an Indian and riding his horse at top speed. He raced up to the sheep pens, threw open the gates, then galloped back toward the herd, waving his hat at us in greeting. We had come out onto the porch—the boys, Aunt Lizzy, Lacy and I—when we first heard the sheep approaching. A few moments later we saw a great white moving cloud, sweeping down off the hillside toward us. I was astonished at the number of sheep in the flock. There must have been over three hundred of them, their white woolly bodies being carried along on a jumble of black spindly legs and hoofed feet. Two big brown and white collies kept pace with the flock, darting and dodging among the sheep to keep them moving along.

Thomas and two other hired hands rode swiftly out in front of the flock. They stopped their horses at either end of the pens, ready to direct the sheep inside. It seemed to me that the sheep needed no directing. They turned into the gates without any urging from the men on horseback or the collies. In a short time the rows of pens were filled with bleating, milling sheep. Thomas and the hands slammed the gates shut. Mr. Walker and Caleb had been at the rear of the flock. Walker trotted his horse down the row of pens, making certain the sheep were secured.

Caleb sat astride his horse, holding a scrawny-looking sheep in the crook of one arm.

Aunt Lizzy clapped her hands in delight. "It does look like everything went well," she exclaimed. "Come, girls, let's get supper on for the men."

I reluctantly followed her inside. I would much rather have gone over to the pens with the younger boys to talk with Thomas and the others about their trip. Through the kitchen window, I kept track of what was going on outside.

When Thomas came in for supper, he was fairly bursting with enthusiasm. Even though his face was streaked with dust and grime, his clothing dirty, and his eyes ringed with tired circles, his smile was bright. Aunt Lizzy hugged and kissed him, then motioned for him to sit down at the table. The other men, including the foreman, Gus, filed inside and took their places. I had avoided Gus as much as possible after our last conversation together. At that time I'd had the distinct feeling that he knew something I did not about the reason I was here, and it made me feel uncomfortable around him. He paid little heed to me at the moment, however, as his attention was focused on the men who had just returned.

After they had eaten their fill, Walker and the others proceeded to give a full report of their time spent in the high pastures rounding up the sheep. Apparently, all had gone well. They had gathered every sheep save one who had gotten tangled in a thicket of brambles and wore himself to death trying to escape the sharp thorns hooked in his fleece. One or two were sickly, but that was to be expected, and Walker was confident he could nurse them back to health. The sheep I had seen Caleb carrying under his arm was the weakest of the flock, barely able to walk. Walker charged Reuben with the task of caring for that particular sheep, seeing that it was fed and protected.

Thomas had evidently enjoyed the excursion and respite from work on the ranch. He eagerly told us about rounding up the strays and related a few humorous incidents which had taken place. Lacy and I were introduced to the hands who had been with the sheep all summer at the meadows. Both men were married and appeared to be in their late thirties. They were a ragged pair, and smelled of sweat and damp wool. They brought to mind Lacy's earlier comment about the ranch hands her father hired.

Caleb was quieter than the others, letting them share their experiences and stories before he added anything. I thought he looked tired and worn, as all the men did, but I detected a certain contained excitement in his demeanor. I had opportunity to notice it because Caleb's eyes kept returning to mine. I wondered if Thomas had told him about my "strange" behavior in wanting to locate the old man with the key. There would have been ample time while on the trip for Thomas and Caleb to have many chats together. If some of those conversations were about me, then surely Caleb would not fail to tease me about it.

I returned Caleb's gaze coolly. His smile widened into an impudent grin. I felt a surge of irritation rise inside me. I had looked forward to his return in a perverse sort of way, but the moment he was back he succeeded in annoying me. I frowned and kept my eyes on my plate.

When at last the talking was through, the men rose to check on the sheep and finish last-minute chores before dark. The three younger boys disappeared with the men. Lacy and I cleared the dishes and tidied the kitchen while Aunt Lizzy hummed cheerfully as she went about her work.

When the chores for the evening were finished, I decided to go outside to see how Reuben was coming along with his little woolly charge. He had been back and forth all evening from the house to the barn, heating milk to give to the sick ewe and getting blankets and other items he needed to care for her. Through habit, I grabbed my poke bonnet from the peg beside the kitchen door before leaving the house. I tied the ends loosely under my chin and let the bonnet hang down my back.

The night air was cold. I shivered as I walked the short distance to the barn. In the darkness I could see the inky outlines of the sheep in their pens and hear their bleating. They seemed to be restless, milling about and nuzzling one another. Both collies lay resting beside the pens. One raised his head to watch me as I passed. His tail thumped the ground in friendly greeting. The black sky was nearly moonless and the stars were hidden by gray wisps of clouds.

I pushed open the barn door. A circle of light illuminated one corner of the barn where Reuben sat on a bunched pile of straw, stroking the sick sheep. He lifted the lantern when I entered so I could see better.

"How's she doing, Reuben?" I asked, peering down into the sheep's narrow black face.

"Not so good. She won't eat anything. I've tried to bottle feed her some milk, but she won't take it." He rubbed the sheep's woolly back, a worried frown on his face.

I knelt down beside him. "She's awfully thin, isn't she?"

"Awfully."

I reached out and hesitantly touched her fleece, stroking it for a moment. When I pulled my hand away, it was oily where I had touched her. I self-consciously wiped my hand across my apron.

We sat in silence for several minutes, our eyes on the ewe.

"Don't you think you ought to come inside now?" I finally asked gently. "It's getting cold."

Reuben shook his head. His brown hair shimmered golden in the light from the lantern. "I'm gonna stay right here till she gets better."

"Well, you can't stay out all night. Go inside now, and you can come back first thing in the morning."

"No."

A tremor passed over his body. I took one of the blankets he had brought out for the ewe and tucked it around him. He shivered again, drawing the blanket tighter about him, all the while keeping his eyes glued to the sheep.

I was about to insist that he come inside when the barn door opened. Caleb Hollister stood silhouetted in the entrance, the pale light of the moon behind his shoulders. He strode inside, shutting the door quietly behind him. He didn't say anything, just walked over to the sheep lying on its bed of straw and bent down to study her. He lifted her head into the lantern's light and examined the sheep's eyes.

"Has she eaten anything yet?" he asked Reuben.

Reuben shook his head sorrowfully.

Caleb gently lowered the animal's head, patted it, and stood watching her for a few seconds more. I kept waiting for him to notice me, but he acted as if there was no one else in the world except Reuben and that sheep. Finally he turned, smiled absently at me, and sat down on the straw next to Reuben.

"Do you think she'll make it?" Reuben asked him in a quivering voice.

Caleb hunched his shoulders. "I don't know. We'll do all we can for her. Here, hand me that bottle of milk."

Reuben gave him a thick-glassed jar with a rubber nipple attached on top. Caleb pried the sheep's jaws apart and put the nipple between its teeth. He tilted the sheep's head back and held the bottle up so the milk would flow into the sheep's throat. The ewe struggled feebly against the nipple. Most of the milk ran out her mouth, but I thought I saw her swallow a bit of it.

Caleb gave the bottle back to Reuben. "We'll try feeding her every hour or so."

I cast about in my mind for something I might say or do to assist, but my knowledge of sheep was infinitesimal compared to Caleb's and Reuben's. I sat quietly on the straw, watching the sheep with them. The animal was certainly pathetic looking. Her fleece was ragged and her body thin. Her yellow eyes were gray in the shadows. She bleated mournfully as she tried to gather enough strength to stand on her wobbly feet. Caleb put an arm around the sheep and laid her firmly, yet gently, back down on the straw.

"What you need is rest, little one," he said in a reassuring voice. "Time enough to get up and run when you're well."

I watched Caleb soothe and comfort the sheep. His strong brown hands calmed the sick animal with every pass over its head and every scratch between its ears. It was plain to see that Caleb was experienced when it came to animals. His touch was firm yet gentle, resolute yet patient.

Reuben shifted his position on the straw and stifled a yawn. I reached over and put my arm around him. He cuddled close, leaning his head against me. I was surprised by the soft feel of his hair against my cheek. He yawned again, openly this time.

"Close your eyes, Reuben, and rest. I'll wake you when it's time to feed the sheep again," I said quietly.

Reuben's blue eyes were heavy, but he refused to give in to sleep—afraid, I supposed, that the sheep might need him.

Caleb leaned over and rumbled his hair. "You and the sheep both need your rest," Caleb said, smiling. Reuben grinned back at him.

The sheep had calmed now. Her eyes were closing and her breathing growing more rhythmic. I felt my own eyes getting heavy.

"Don't you fall asleep on me, too," Caleb said, grinning at me.

"Did I look like I was about to?"

"If you count the fact that your head was nodding."

"Sorry. All that talk about sleep was getting to me, I guess," I replied, smiling.

"Perhaps you can manage to stay awake by telling me more about that university you spoke of. YBU, was it?" he asked, trying to remember the initials correctly.

I chuckled aloud. "BYU. It stands for Brigham Young University."

"Here in Provo?" he asked. "Do you mean Brigham Young Academy?"

"Yes, that's the one." I yawned. I was so tired I didn't care whether the slight change in name aroused his curiosity or not.

"Why did you call it Brigham Young University?" he asked after a moment's pause. "And why do you call the school in Salt

126

Lake City by a different name, too?"

"You wouldn't believe me if I told you," I replied, stifling another yawn.

"How about giving me a try?"

I looked up into his face. He was completely serious.

Reuben sighed against my shoulder and his head drooped. I gently laid his head on my lap, pulling the blanket up around his chin. His eyes were closed. He opened them for a moment, then his eyelids sagged closed again.

"Well?" Caleb was looking at me earnestly.

"Well, what?"

"Why the change in name? Is it just recent?"

I considered my answer. "It hasn't happened yet as far as you're concerned. For me, it's past history."

He stared at me without saying a word for what had to be a full minute. Then he broke into a low chuckle. "You're a very mysterious young woman, Kate Walker. Mysterious, but quite delightful. Well, it doesn't matter about the name, really. The point is, how did you like your experience at the university? Did you feel like you received a good education?"

I thought about my years of schooling. I had enjoyed my classes for the most part, and considered myself well prepared in my field. "Yes," I answered truthfully. "I feel good about the education I received. I majored in history. Originally I wanted to become an archaeologist. I'm terribly interested in old things. After I graduated I had hoped to get employment at a site where archaeological work was being carried on. Some place like the Custer battlefield in Montana. After the fire there, the battlefield was an historian's dream. Artifacts were laid bare that had been buried in the tall grass for over a hundred years." I stopped suddenly, seeing the look of confusion on Caleb's face.

"A fire? On the battlefield?" he repeated questioningly. "Are you speaking of Colonel George Armstrong Custer and his company of men who were wiped out on the Little Big Horn last year? I've never heard of a fire. That place is a national cemetery."

"Of course. You're absolutely right. Sometimes I tend to ramble on," I said hurriedly. "About the university in Salt Lake—I think you'd like it. I hope you'll be able to attend."

Reuben stirred in my lap, murmuring in his sleep. I brushed his hair off his brow, trying to gather my thoughts.

"Kate?"

"Yes?" I answered too hastily. I was afraid of his questions. With every word, I seemed to be blundering worse than before.

"Do I make you nervous for some reason? I apologize if that's the case." Caleb was smiling, but his eyes were solemn.

"No. Of course not. Certainly not," I lied.

"I'm relieved to hear you say that. I was hoping we could be friends. While I was up in the meadows with the sheep, I was thinking about what you had said to me. About pursuing my goal of studying law. Actually, I was discouraged about it, feeling I might never get the opportunity to go to school. But what you've said about the University of Utah has encouraged me. I've decided to enroll at Deseret University and pursue my legal training."

His mixed references to the University of Utah and Deseret University amused me, but I didn't dare smile. He was in perfect earnest. "I'm glad I was able to help," I said. "I think you've made a wise choice."

"You're absolutely right, Kate."

I saw the enthusiasm in his eyes. They shone in the feeble light thrown from the lantern; the flecks of gold gleamed in their hazel depths. Even in the half-darkness of the barn, Caleb Hollister's eyes spun their spell on me.

I jumped as the ewe suddenly woke, bleating mournfully. Caleb took the bottle of milk and fed it again to the sheep. This time she swallowed more of it. Caleb talked encouragingly to her, coaxing her to eat. After he'd persuaded the sheep to take all she would, he stood up, brushing away the straw clinging to his trousers. I carefully lowered Reuben's head onto the straw and straightened the blanket around him.

"I don't think Aunt Lizzy will let Reuben spend the night out here in the barn, but he surely seems to have his heart set on it," I said in a whisper to avoid waking the sleeping child.

Caleb held his hand out to me. I took it and he helped me to my feet. I thought he kept hold of my hand a little longer than necessary once I was standing.

"Shh," he murmured, nodding toward Reuben.

We tiptoed out of the barn and began walking toward the house. I slipped my bonnet up on my head and retied the ends. The sky had cleared in patches, and through one of the gaps the moon shone clearly. It lighted the path back to the house with a soft glow. The dogs, who had been resting beside the pens, rose to their feet and padded along behind us.

"Will you be checking on the ewe any more tonight?" I asked Caleb.

"Yes. I'll go back in a few minutes and try to feed her some more. Perhaps I can get her to eat a bit of bran mush."

"You really care about that ragged little sheep, don't you?" I asked him tonelessly.

"I guess that one little sheep is about the most important thing to me there is at the moment," he replied after a pause.

His answer ruffled me. I could understand that nursing the sheep back to health was important to Mr. Walker as a practical matter in running his sheep business. I could understand a child's attachment to a sick animal. I could even understand the loyalty of a hired hand. But I thought Caleb's devotion bordered on the absurd. There were many things vastly more important than saving the life of one insignificant sheep. Complex and ponderous world problems faced us. The threat of global war loomed ever closer. It was narrow-minded and naive to place the value of one sheep above the concerns of a world beset with troubles.

Before I even realized what I was saying, I heard myself blurting out, "Do you mean to tell me all you have to worry about is one skinny, sick sheep? What about the formidable problems of pollution? Nuclear disarmament? World hunger?" I ranted. "Haven't you seen those destitute, spindly-legged

129

African children all over your television screen? How can you compare those kinds of problems to one measly sheep?"

Caleb's jaw dropped and he stared open-mouthed at me. "I don't understand what you're talking about," he finally managed to answer.

"Nothing. Never mind," I mumbled, quickening my pace. I was anxious to get to the house and away from him.

I hadn't gone five paces when I froze in my tracks, the skin on my arms prickling. "What was that sound?" I gasped. The noise had come from the hills to the east, distant yet frighteningly near. It sounded like ghostly wailing, and it sent shivers along my spine.

"Coyotes. They know we've brought the sheep back down from the meadows."

The howl sounded again, and then another joined in a haunting chorus. I involuntarily clutched Caleb's arm.

He patted my hand reassuringly. "Don't worry. They won't leave the hills. Not yet, at least."

"Not yet?" I repeated, the words sticking in my dry throat. "What do you mean not yet?"

"The coyotes are always watching the flocks, waiting to catch a sick lamb, or perhaps one who has become separated from the others. When we bring the flock down from the pastures, the coyotes follow. They'll become bolder as the winter sets in and food becomes scarce. On more than one occasion I've had to chase a hungry coyote out of the sheep pens."

I glanced over in the direction of the pens. The sheep were clearly nervous, pacing about and bawling loudly. The collies, too, stood alert. Their ears were pricked up and their noses sniffed the air. I wanted to let go of Caleb's arm, but my fingers refused to loosen their grip.

"Why don't the sheep ranchers trap the coyotes and kill them?" I knew the question was irrational even before I asked it, but the coyotes' eerie howl had sent all reason fleeing from my mind.

Caleb laughed. "That's like asking why we don't get rid of all roses because they have thorns."

By this time we had reached the house. I disengaged my hand from Caleb's arm and managed to regain some shred of dignity. "I suppose I'm not quite used to country living yet," I said stiffly. I straightened my apron and deliberately lifted my nose in the air.

"I think I have you figured out, Kate," replied Caleb in a teasing tone of voice. "Outwardly you're properly genteel, but I'd wager underneath that prim bonnet lurks a lioness." He chuckled, his hazel eyes glistening in the moonlight. "A lioness in lamb's clothing."

I sniffed in disdain. "A very imaginative thought, Mr. Hollister."

"Please. Call me Cabe," he returned, grinning broadly.

He took my hand, bowed from the waist, and watching me with laughing eyes, gallantly pressed my hand to his lips and kissed it.

I snatched my hand away. "Good-night, Mr. Hollister."

CHAPTER ELEVEN

Y OU MUST BE TIRED this morning, Katharine."
I fumbled with the blue and white calico dress, struggling to
pull it over my head. When I finally managed to get it on properly, I glanced over at Lacy. She was still in her petticoats,
standing in the middle of the room, watching me.

"What did you say?" I asked, knowing very well what she had
said and what she had meant.

"Those late night strolls must make it difficult to get up in
the morning." Her face was expressionless, but her eyes flashed.

"I wasn't on a stroll, Lacy. I had been at the barn checking on
Reuben. Caleb Hollister was there, feeding the sick ewe. When
he finished he simply walked me to the house. That's all."

Lacy's eyes narrowed.

When I had returned to the house last evening, it was later
than usual. I thought Lacy was asleep. She was in bed with the
candle out, but apparently she had only pretended to be
sleeping. She must have watched Caleb and me from the
window of the bedroom. She must have seen Caleb kiss my
hand and interpreted it to be something it was not. Well, if
Lacy was nosy enough to spy on me, then I'd go ahead and let
her think what she wanted to.

I quickly finished dressing, and without giving Lacy another
glance left the room and hurried downstairs. Aunt Lizzy already
had breakfast nearly prepared.

"Did Reuben come in to bed last night?" I asked her, giving the eggs a stir.

"No. He insisted on staying with the ewe. Your father and I decided it would be all right to let him spend the night in the barn. He's just washing up now for breakfast."

Even before she finished the sentence, Reuben came bounding into the kitchen, slamming the back door behind him.

"Katharine! Guess what?"

"What, Reuben?" I bent down to his size and looked intently into his face.

"The ewe is eating! Cabe stayed up with me all night and we got the sheep eating on her own."

"That's wonderful, Reuben." I kissed the top of his head and smiled. "I'm really glad."

"Cabe says she's going to be all right now."

Reuben bounced over to his mother and hugged her waist. "I'm hungry, Ma. How long till breakfast?"

"If you set the plates on the table for me, Reuben, we can eat all the quicker," she answered him.

Reuben and I busied ourselves in the kitchen until the rest of the family and the ranch hands appeared for breakfast. When Caleb came into the kitchen and saw me, he smiled wearily. He looked tired and his clothing was wrinkled. A few wisps of straw still clung to his shirt sleeves.

"Oh, Cabe, it was so good of you to help Reuben with that poor little sheep last night," Lacy purred next to my ear. She stood at my side, giving Caleb a syrupy smile. "Why don't you sit down at the table and let me dish you up some food? You look exhausted."

Caleb allowed Lacy to dish him a heaping plate of eggs and biscuits. Then, filling a plate for herself, she sat down in the chair next to his. She kept up a constant chatter while Caleb ate, showering him with attention.

Her behavior disgusted me. I didn't know if she was cosying up to Caleb because she liked him, or because she was trying to make me feel jealous. In either case, she was making a fool of herself. I saw Aunt Lizzy sending her disapproving signals, but she refused to heed them. By the time the meal was over, I felt completely embarrassed for her. I kept my eyes on my plate when Caleb rose from his chair and excused himself from the table.

After he'd gone, Lacy flashed me a triumphant stare across the kitchen table.

"You've just behaved like an idiot, Lacy," I whispered.

"Oh, really? We'll see about that." She tossed her head and looked at me defiantly.

I stood up from my chair. "May I be excused now, Aunt Lizzy?"

"Of course, dear. Uh, Lacy, dear, I'd like a word with you before you leave."

I gave Lacy a scathing "I told you so" look and left the room.

The morning passed quickly. As I attended to my chores, I thought about my conversation with Caleb the night before. I must have sounded like a lunatic, going on as I did about twentieth-century problems. If Thomas and Caleb had discussed my peculiar behavior while they were away with the sheep, last night would have been a perfect time for Caleb to comment on it. But he hadn't. In all of our discussions, he had never hinted that some of my comments were rather bizarre by his standards. I wondered about that and why he accepted me without question. To my surprise, I found myself looking forward to talking with him again.

At noon Thomas came into the house. He passed me on the stairs as he was going up and I was coming down.

"Hi, Thomas," I said, touching his arm. "What are you up to?"

"Came in to change my clothes. Pa asked me to go into town to pick up a few supplies." He took another step up the stairs and then paused, turned and looked at me. "Do you want to come with me? I won't be long. I need to be back shortly."

A mental picture flashed through my mind of the city of

Provo as I knew it. The modern department stores, corner gasoline stations, fast-food places—none of them would be there. When I thought about the void that should have been the BYU campus, it was more than I could bear. "No, Thomas, I don't think so. Thanks for asking, anyway."

He shrugged. "Maybe I'll ask Cabe to go with me, then."

"Thomas?"

"Yeah?"

"What do you think of Caleb? I mean, do you like him?"

"If you want a glowing report, then you should ask Lacy. She's totally smitten with him. Or haven't you noticed?" Thomas said almost snidely.

"I don't care what Lacy thinks. I want to know what you think about him."

"Why?" Thomas asked suspiciously.

"Well, I value your opinion."

"Come on, Katharine. You never ask my opinion about anything unless you have something up your sleeve."

"That's not true," I protested. "I respect your thinking very much."

Thomas turned and started up the stairs again.

"Wait! I mean it, Thomas. I'd like your opinion."

Thomas sighed with impatience. "He's all right, I guess."

"Does he seem genuine to you? Do you think he says what he believes, or is he more interested in making an impression?"

Thomas looked puzzled for an instant. "I don't think he puts on airs. Cabe says what he means. I think he's direct and honest. Why?"

"Oh, I don't know. Sometimes I can't tell if he's serious or just having fun at my expense."

"Well, I think if Cabe is serious about something in particular, you won't have any difficulty in knowing it. Now, is there anything else you want to discuss, or can I go change my clothes?"

"Thanks, Thomas. And thanks for the invitation into town."

"Sure," Thomas muttered as he climbed the stairs.

When I reached the bottom step and walked into the kitchen, I found Reuben just coming in the back door.

"How's your sheep this afternoon, Reuben?" I asked brightly.

"She's gonna be fine. Want to come see her?"

"Not right now, but maybe . . ."

"Come on, Katharine. I was just going to take out some more milk for her. Come with me. You see if you think she's better. Please."

The pleading look in his eye won me over. "All right. But just for a minute. I promised Aunt Lizzy I'd help her in the parlor."

Reuben grabbed a pint bottle of milk from the icebox in the pantry and gestured for me to follow him. It was a lovely afternoon. The sky was a clear blue without a trace of clouds. Yellow leaves swirled around my feet in the autumn breeze. I filled my lungs with the crisp October air and blew it out slowly.

One of the collies bounded to Reuben's side as we neared the sheep pens. The dog jumped up on him, licking his face.

"Down, Buck. Get down, boy," Reuben said to the collie. He rubbed the dog's head affectionately.

The sheep in the pens bawled as we passed by. I suddenly remembered something Aunt Lizzy had said when we first arrived at her home.

"Wait a minute, Reuben," I said, grabbing hold of his arm. "Do you know which sheep is Abigail?"

"Abby? Sure. I'll find her for you."

Reuben climbed over the rail of the pen nearest us and started wading among the sheep, bending down over one and then another for a closer look. A few seconds later, waist-deep in sheep, he called out to me. "Here she is, Katharine!"

He picked up one of the sheep in his arms and carried it over to the railing. The sheep struggled to escape, squirming and kicking like a child in the midst of a tantrum. Reuben held the struggling animal out for me to see. It looked no different than any of the other sheep as far as I could determine; perhaps a little scrubbier, if anything. I wondered why the real Katharine

Walker felt so attached to it.

"Is she a favorite of yours?"

Caleb's voice came unexpectedly to my ear. I turned to see him walking toward us from the barn.

"Hi, Cabe," Reuben said cheerfully. "Katharine wanted to see her sheep that Papa gave her the last time she was here."

Caleb strode over to the pens and stopped only inches from me. He reached out and patted the sheep. "What's her name?"

"It's Abigail," I said quickly. "She's not really my favorite. It's just that . . ."

At that moment Aunt Lizzy called from the porch. "Reuben? Reuben, come here, please."

Reuben put on an exasperated look. He dumped the sheep into Caleb's arms. "I have to go. Ma's calling me." He ran off, with the collie chasing after him.

Caleb wrestled with the sheep, trying to get all four legs tucked under his arm. I chuckled at the picture.

"I suppose you think this is easy," Caleb grunted, lifting his chin just in time to miss a blow from a flailing hoof.

"I thought you went into town with Thomas," I replied, grinning.

"He invited me to go, but I couldn't get away. I had a few chores to finish up. So this is Abigail?" he asked, nodding at the sheep which was now folded securely in his arms.

"I guess so." I glanced at the scraggly little beast and wrinkled my nose. "I thought sheep were supposed to be all white. Not like these with black faces and black feet. She doesn't really look like the lamb I imagined following Mary to school one day."

Caleb chuckled and set the sheep back on the ground inside the pen. It quickly scooted into the midst of the flock. "Mary's lamb was probably a Merino. Merinos have white, fine wool, white faces and legs. They're very popular for their fine fleeces in the sheep-raising countries of Europe and in the Northeast, where your nursery rhyme about Mary's lamb originated. Our sheep here are Suffolk. The breed came originally from

England, but they are raised here in the West for their wool as well as their meat. Suffolks have coarser wool than the Merinos, and they're smaller in size."

"Suffolk or Merino, they're not the smartest creatures, are they?" I commented, watching Abigail bumbling about the pen, bumping and jostling the other sheep.

"Sheep aren't as dull-witted as some other animals. Take turkeys, for instance," Caleb replied.

"Turkeys?"

"A turkey can drown in a rainstorm. Some turkeys will stand looking up at the rain with their mouths open without sense enough to know they're drowning in the rain water."

I gave Caleb a skeptical look. "Come on," I said, "you're kidding me."

"I'm not. Honestly. Compared to turkeys, sheep are quite intelligent."

I smiled. "If sheep are so smart, why do they senselessly follow one another about?"

"That's the way with sheep," Caleb answered simply.

I thought about his reply and frowned. "Witless as sheep," I muttered, suddenly thinking of Professor Bowen's penciled message in the margin of his notes on the Mormons.

"I didn't catch what you said," Caleb responded, bending his head closer to mine.

"Someone I once knew made the comment that Mormons are as witless as sheep." I thought my statement would repel Caleb, knowing his allegiance to the Church, but he merely nodded his head and thought a moment before speaking.

"In some ways we are like sheep," he said quietly. "Sheep are guileless, gentle, and obedient. They tend to band together, are easy to direct, and heed the call of the shepherd. A lot like the Saints."

His answer surprised me. I had never thought of the comparison in exactly that way.

"The sheep's obedience is something we would do well to

imitate. As you were saying earlier, sheep tend to follow one another, and that's the very thing that makes herding a large number of sheep possible. It enables the shepherd to protect his flock. The sheep learn to trust and obey the shepherd, much as we place our trust in the Good Shepherd."

Caleb's eyes were gentle as he looked into my face. I stood staring at him, hanging on his words.

"In the scriptures, Christ is often compared with a shepherd. And the similarities fit on many levels. I think my favorite parable is the one found in John, chapter 10. Do you remember it, Kate? 'He goeth before them, and the sheep follow him; for they know his voice.'"

At that moment I became acutely aware that I was not familiar with the parable Caleb quoted from—not with that parable or any other. It had been years since I had read the scriptures, and longer than that since I had given them any serious thought. I yearned to discuss this particular verse of scripture with Caleb, but I couldn't because I had no under-standing of it. I determined right then and there that I would not let the sun set without reading the parable in John.

A sudden gust of wind came up, scattering a pile of dead leaves clustered against the fence post. Before I realized what he was doing, Caleb had reached a hand toward my hair. I started at his touch.

"It's just a leaf," he said, smiling. He picked the dried brown leaf out of my hair and showed it to me. "As wary as a lioness, aren't you?" he said, still smiling.

I felt a little foolish at my reaction. "I know," I answered, trying to excuse myself. "A lioness in lamb's clothing."

Caleb laughed and threw the leaf into the wind. The breeze caught it and carried it away, tumbling and turning.

Dried, dead leaves swirled around our feet as we stood together beside the pen, watching the sheep. I felt dwarfed by Caleb's tall, sturdy frame. My head barely reached his shoulder. Caleb's touch had driven the more reverent feelings away, and I caught myself wondering what it would be like if Lacy's fantasies about Caleb and me were true.

"What are you pondering so earnestly?" Caleb asked, turning to look at me. "From your expression, it appears you're giving it some serious thought."

"It's nothing," I replied quickly. "Just the sheep. Reuben brought me out here to see the sick ewe in the barn. He says she's doing better."

I saw the flicker of a frown pass across Caleb's face.

"She is doing better, isn't she?" I asked in concern.

"We thought so. But I can't get her to eat anything this afternoon."

"And that's not a good sign, I take it?"

"No. Reuben doesn't know yet. When he left the barn this morning, she was doing all right."

"Oh, dear. Reuben will be awfully upset if anything happens to that sheep. He's become so attached to her."

"Yes, I know." Caleb passed a hand across his chin. "Let's not say anything about it to him yet. I'll try to feed her again in an hour or so."

"Well, I'd better be getting back to my chores. Keep me posted on the sheep's condition, will you?"

Caleb nodded.

He walked with me a few steps back to the house, then left to return to his own work. As I approached the house, I saw Gus on the back porch mending a section of wooden handrailing which had come loose. I drew a deep breath. I didn't wish to become involved in conversation with him if I could avoid it. Gus knew something about the old man with the key that he wasn't telling me, and that placed me in an awkward position.

I climbed the porch steps hoping Gus wouldn't see me. I'd nearly reached the top step when he straightened from his work.

"Afternoon, Miss Walker," he said.

"Good afternoon, Gus. How are you today?" I asked, trying to sound natural.

"Pretty fair. And yourself?"

"Oh, I'm just fine. Thank you." I didn't know why I felt I had to act as if I didn't have a care in the world.

"Nice day, isn't it?" Gus asked.

"Yes. A very nice day. It's good to see you, Gus," I said, reaching for the door.

Gus tipped his hat. I hurried through the door, but even as the door was closing I felt his eyes on me. Searching. Almost as if he were trying to read my heart.

It was nearly time for bed before I had a chance to sit down privately with Aunt Lizzy's book of scripture. I had some difficulty locating the verse Caleb had quoted from the book of John, but at last I found it. I had to read the chapter over twice before I could begin to make any sense out of it. It seemed the Savior was being questioned by a group of Pharisees, whom he answered in parable. He spoke about the sheep fold, an enclosure where the sheep were gathered at night for safekeeping. In the morning the shepherd came for his flock, calling the sheep by name. The sheep knew the shepherd's voice and willingly followed him. However, if a thief or stranger tried to call the sheep from the fold, the sheep became nervous and frightened, and refused to follow because they did not recognize his voice. Christ explained that he was the Good Shepherd who knew his sheep and would give his life for them.

When the Pharisees questioned Christ about his divinity, Christ replied that he had already explained to them, "but ye believe not, because ye are not of my sheep . . . My sheep hear my voice, and I know them, and they follow me; and I give unto them eternal life: and they shall never perish."

I snapped the book shut. My conscience burned with shame. Was I like the Pharisees—unbelieving, unhearing? Tears began to well up in my eyes. Did Christ know me by name? Was I one of his sheep? I knew the answer well enough. It lay like a stone in the pit of my stomach. I wanted to cough it up, spit it out. But I couldn't. It lay deep and cold inside me, accusing me with its very weight.

The tears spilled down my cheeks as I made my way to bed. I could plainly see the error of my ways—the pride I had felt in rebelling against my parents' teachings, the selfishness I had exhibited in doggedly pursuing my own path. Every tear that rolled down my face accused me, each sob stung me anew. I lay awake most of the night reviewing my life and actions. I was ashamed and tormented in both mind and spirit. I strived to determine what it was I should do to put my life back in order, to become one of his sheep. I thought about it until the moon nearly finished its ride across the sky. Finally I fell asleep, weighed down with sorrow and despair.

CHAPTER TWELVE

As SOON AS I WAS DRESSED the next morning, I went outside to look for Caleb. I had to talk with him, tell him about the wrestling of my spirit, seek his advice and comfort. It was later than the time I usually arose; I could tell that by the angle of the sun. It was also colder. The mild breeze from yesterday had become a brisk, chilling wind. The fallen leaves blew wildly about, cartwheeling in the turbulent air.

I hurried toward the barn, my body bent into the wind. I had left the house without a bonnet or shawl, and my skirts whipped against my legs as I walked. The wind pulled at my hair, tugging and blowing it about my face. When I reached the barn, I threw open the barn door. Caleb was inside; at his feet, lying on a bed of straw, was the ewe, still and lifeless.

He turned when he heard the door open. I saw immediately the sorrow etched on his face.

"Oh, no," I whispered hoarsely. I walked over to him, my eyes on the motionless sheep. "She's dead?"

Caleb nodded. "Reuben found her not more than ten minutes ago."

I stared down at the sheep. My own fierce needs evaporated, for the moment no longer important.

"Where's Reuben now?" I asked Caleb, my voice quivering.

"Isn't he in the house?"

"No. That is, I didn't see him before I came out."

Caleb's face took on a look of concern. "He was pretty upset. He ran out of the barn before I had a chance to say anything to him. Are you sure he's not inside?"

"Maybe I should go back to the house and look for him."

"I think that would be a good idea. He'll need someone to talk to. I'll go with you."

Together we left the barn and made our way back to the house. The wind tore at us, sending dust flying into our eyes. Mr. Walker and Aunt Lizzy were in the kitchen, finishing their breakfast.

"Is Reuben here?" I asked breathlessly.

Aunt Lizzy looked from me to Caleb. "No. He went out to the barn to tend his sheep and hasn't come back yet."

"The sheep's dead, Mrs. Walker," Caleb said quickly. "I got to the barn just as Reuben was running out."

Mr. Walker rose to his feet. "He hasn't been in here. Do you know where he might have gone, Katharine?"

By now Aunt Lizzy was on her feet, too.

"No. I went out to talk to Cabe, and he told me about Reuben. I don't know where he is."

Walker and Aunt Lizzy exchanged worried glances. Walker pulled his suspenders up onto his shoulders. "I'll look for him. He's probably somewhere just under our noses."

Walker strode out of the house and toward the sheep pens.

"I'll check the house," Aunt Lizzy stated. "Perhaps he came in the front door and we didn't see him."

"I'll help you," I added hastily. I glanced at Caleb. He nodded, telling me by his gesture that he would look for Reuben also.

Aunt Lizzy and I searched the house from top to bottom. Reuben was nowhere in sight. The other boys hadn't seen their brother all morning and Lacy, too, was at a loss as to where he might have gone. She advised me not to worry about him, that he'd show up sooner or later, but her words didn't do much to settle my mind. I was concerned about Reuben—I knew how much that sheep had meant to him.

By mid-afternoon we still hadn't found him. Aunt Lizzy alternated between feeling angry with him for disappearing and wringing her hands in worry. The day was becoming colder and gray clouds were moving in, threatening rain. If Reuben were somewhere outside, he would be cold and hungry. And soon it would be dark. I shivered as I thought of the eight-year-old boy outside, alone in the dark and cold.

With growing concern, Mr. Walker called the family and all the ranch hands together. He asked each of us if we had any idea where Reuben might be. I racked my brain, trying to think of some place a grieving boy might go to be alone with his sorrow. I knew of no such place. Walker suggested that we offer a prayer, asking our Father in Heaven to guide us in locating Reuben and to keep him safe until we found him. Walker himself was voice for the prayer. I squeezed my eyes tightly shut, concentrating on every word he uttered. My "amen" joined the chorus of others in sending our prayer heavenward.

After the prayer, Mr. Walker assigned each of us a place to look for Reuben. Mine was to check the bushes and shrubbery around the house. A small boy might squeeze between the bushes to hide his tears. I hurried outside. The hollyhocks were still in bloom, splashing color along the length of the house. Flowering bushes and shrubs made a network of greenery sufficient to conceal a child who may not wish to be found.

"Reuben? Reuben, where are you?" I called as I poked my head between the bushes. I checked behind every flower and shrub, calling Reuben's name. My hands became scratched from moving prickly bushes aside, and in my haste I failed to dodge a rose bush springing back into place. One of its thorns nicked my cheek.

After a thorough search, I was sure Reuben was not hiding behind the shrubbery. I could hear the others calling his name. I squinted up at the sky. The clouds were already turning a faint pink in the gathering dusk. My heart hammered in my chest, making it difficult to breathe. I had to summon every ounce of self-control to keep from panicking.

"Kate?"

I whirled around. Caleb was quickly coming to my side, taking long strides across the lawn.

"Any luck?" he asked huskily.

I shook my head. "I searched every inch of the yard. Where could he be, Cabe? And why doesn't he come home?"

Caleb made a quick scan overhead. "It'll be dark soon. I think he'd be here if he could."

"You think he's lost." My reply was a statement, not a question.

"Come on," Caleb said, grasping my hand and walking briskly away from the house.

"Where are we going?" I asked, taking running steps to keep up with him.

"We've searched everywhere on the farm. I don't think he's here. Let's go down toward the river."

"The river!" I cried in consternation. "You don't think . . ."

"I'm not thinking anything," he cut in hastily. "Let's check along the bank. Perhaps he's fallen asleep under a tree along the river bank. That's possible, isn't it?"

"Yes, of course. But surely by now . . ." My voice trailed off hopelessly.

We said nothing more as we half-ran, half-walked to the river. I had been to the river once before with Lacy to pick wildflowers that grew along the bank. The water had had the appearance of a gentle stream, flowing smoothly in its channel, serenely to the sea. But when I saw it this time, I was stunned. Its black waters looked ominous, threatening. The waters roiled and boiled over rocks and tree stumps. Broken branches that had fallen into the river had become claws, anxious to claim any unfortunate soul who stumbled too near.

I gripped Caleb's hand tighter. He led us along the bank, walking slowly, his eyes on the ground searching for telltale signs. We walked downstream for several yards, finding nothing suspicious.

"There's no sign that he was here," Caleb said finally. I thought his voice held a hint of relief. "Any suggestions where to look next?"

I bit my lip, thinking. "Maybe he headed toward the pasture lands."

"That's a good idea. Come on."

Caleb tightened his grip on my hand. We turned southwest toward the high pastures, walking as rapidly as we could. The wind had died down, making our passage easier, but the temperature had dropped dramatically over the last hour or so. In our hurry and concern, neither Caleb nor I had thought to put on coats. I shivered in spite of the brisk pace we were keeping.

"Are you cold?" asked Caleb.

"A little bit. I'll be all right."

Caleb paused, took both my hands in his, and rubbed them briskly. Then he ran his hands over my arms. The pressure of his strong hands brought the warmth back into my body. For an instant I felt like one of the sheep I had seen Caleb patting and stroking. It gave me the same feeling of comfort and reassurance that I had seen the sheep respond to.

"Does that help?" he asked.

"Yes, thank you."

Caleb took my hand and we started off again. "It's getting colder," he commented. "If we don't find Reuben soon, he's going to spend a miserable night."

I thought about how Reuben must feel, lost and shivering. The temperature could drop dramatically before morning came. If he were without shelter, the consequences would be very serious. The thought sent a stab of fear to my heart. We had to find him. Now. Before it was too late.

I closed my eyes and began a silent prayer. I prayed like I had never prayed before in my whole life. I had never wanted anything as badly as I wanted to find Reuben, safe and sound. I prayed fervently, almost frantically. I asked forgiveness of my sins. Then I promised God I would turn my life around, do whatever he wanted me to do, if he'd just help us find Reuben.

I don't suppose Caleb even knew I was praying. It didn't matter if he knew or not, but he didn't say anything until I was through. I was almost weak from praying so strenuously. I tripped on a rock in my path, lost my balance, and nearly fell. Caleb caught me, supporting me with his arm.

"Are you all right?" he asked, peering into my face.

I could feel tears gathering in the corners of my eyes. I didn't trust my voice to speak. I nodded silently.

"We'll find him," Caleb said in a determined voice.

We continued walking in the direction of the setting sun, our eyes scanning the landscape. Caleb called Reuben's name once or twice. The sky in front of us was tinged with red.

Suddenly, something Reuben told me not more than a week ago popped into my head. I hadn't remembered it until now, but it came abruptly into my mind and was crystal clear.

"Wait a minute!" I shouted.

Caleb halted in mid-stride. "What? What is it?"

"The pirates' cave!"

"The what?" Caleb asked, his brow wrinkling.

"The treasure cache hidden in the cave. Reuben told me that he found a cave he thought might have belonged to pirates. We had a discussion about why pirates would choose to cache their treasure in Provo—but that's beside the point. Caleb, I'll bet Reuben is at the cave."

"Where is this cave?"

"I don't know. But it has to be somewhere close. He evidently went there lots of times."

Caleb stood still, his hand on his chin. "The only caves I know of are in the canyon. It has to be there."

We looked at each other, excitement in our faces. In unison we turned in the opposite direction, east toward the canyon lands. We ran until I thought my lungs would burst, but still we ran on. The western sky was on fire now, and the sun nothing but a crimson disk slipping behind the mountain peak.

In spite of the cold night air, I was sweating. I ran a hand across my brow and brought it away, sticky with perspiration. At last the flat terrain gave way to rocky hills and rugged dirt paths. It was just light enough to make out small caverns in the rocky ledges of the canyon.

"Reuben! Reuben!"

"Reuben!"

We had looked inside of only four or five small caverns when we heard it.

"Here. I'm here!"

We froze in our tracks. "Reuben?" Caleb shouted, glancing from side to side.

"Over here."

This time the voice was weaker, but we were able to pick up the direction from which it came. Caleb dashed ahead and to the right, with me close on his heels.

He ducked inside one cavern, shook his head, and moved to another.

"Here he is," he cried out.

I pushed past him through the small opening. At first I could see nothing at all. It was pitch black inside the cave. But as my eyes adjusted to the darkness, I saw a shadow hunched up against the back wall of the cave, only a few feet from the entrance. I rushed over and folded Reuben in my arms.

"Oh, Reuben, thank heaven you're safe. We've been looking all over for you." Reuben's little body was ice cold in my arms. He hugged me and I heard a muffled sob rise in his throat.

"I hurt my leg. I can't move it. I think it's broken," he said in a hoarse voice.

By this time Caleb was at the boy's side, kneeling next to him. He murmured soothing words while he gently felt up and down both small legs.

"Ouch. It hurts there, Cabe. On my ankle," Reuben whimpered.

"It feels swollen, all right. How long have you been here in the cave, Reuben?" asked Caleb.

"I don't know. A long time. I was climbing up some rocks and fell. Not a long way, but I hurt my leg when I landed. I kind of dragged myself into this cave."

"Oh, Reuben, I'm sorry." I hugged him tighter, trying to give him some of my body warmth.

"I sure am glad to see you," he whispered.

"We're awfully glad to see you," I returned, giving him a squeeze.

"We need to get you out of here, young man," Caleb said. He stood up and walked to the entrance of the cave. I could see his silhouette in the light from the rising moon. He looked tall and broad-shouldered, almost completely filling the opening of the cave.

Reuben shivered in my arms. I rubbed his body briskly, trying to restore his circulation.

"Well, it's plain Reuben can't walk back, and I don't want to try to carry him in the dark. I might stumble and hurt his leg," Caleb said, coming back to us. "I think I'd better go back alone and get some help. Kate, can you stay here with Reuben until I return?" he asked me.

"Yes. We'll be fine, won't we Reuben?" I tried to sound enthusiastic, but I didn't enjoy the prospect of staying in this cave one minute longer than we had to.

"We'll be okay," Reuben mumbled.

"All right. The first thing I'm going to do is build a fire to warm you up, Reuben," Caleb said briskly. He strode outside the cave where I could hear him rustling around in the dark, searching for fallen branches and twigs.

"Katharine?" Reuben's voice trembled in my ear.

"Yes, Reuben?"

"My sick little sheep died."

My heart went out anew to the little boy cuddled in my lap. "I know, sweetheart. I'm so sorry about it."

Reuben didn't say anything more while we waited for Caleb

to return with the firewood. My teeth had begun to chatter from the cold. The cave was not deep, but the stone walls were cold and damp. Even though Reuben had on a wool flannel shirt, it was little protection against the cold. I squeezed him tight, warming both of us.

"This ought to keep you warm until I get back," Caleb said, dropping an armload of twigs and branches on the cave floor. He quickly arranged the sticks into a tepee shape, with the smaller pieces on the bottom. Then he lit it with a bit of flint and steel he always carried with him.

At first I didn't think the tiny sparks were going to ignite anything, but a moment later Caleb had a small flame going, and then a full-fledged fire. Reuben immediately scooted toward it, holding his hands near the flames.

Caleb selected a long, straight tree branch from the pile of wood he'd set aside from the fire.

"Let's have another look at that leg, Reuben, now that we have a little light." Caleb stooped down to study Reuben's injured leg. "We'll use this branch as a splint. That should give the leg some support and make it easier for you to travel. Kate, can I borrow your apron?"

I quickly untied the strings on the full-length apron I was wearing over my dress, took it off and gave it to Caleb. I didn't know what he wanted it for until I saw him carefully place the branch parallel with Reuben's leg. He folded the body of the apron into a long roll, with the strings extending on either end, and used it as a cord to tie the branch and the leg together. Reuben groaned when Caleb wrapped the apron around the area of his ankle.

It took only a few minutes to accomplish the job. "There," Caleb said. "That should do until we get you home."

"Thanks, Cabe," Reuben answered in a weak voice. He rubbed his leg, wincing with the pain.

"Now I'm going to get more wood so you'll have plenty to keep that fire going while I'm gone." He stepped out of the cave and into the black night. He was gone a little longer this time. When he returned, his arms were loaded. He set the sticks down on top of the heap he had gathered earlier.

"I shouldn't be gone long," he said quietly to me. "You'll take care of Kate for me, won't you Reuben?"

"Sure." Reuben tried to smile, but his lips were trembling from the cold and the pain in his leg.

"You're going to be fine," he said to the boy. "We'll have you home in your own bed inside of an hour. You've been a brave soldier, Reuben."

Reuben nodded.

I got up and followed Caleb to the cave entrance. It was cold away from the fire, and I shivered.

"You and Reuben stay by the fire and I'll hurry as fast as I can," Caleb said, looking intently into my face. His eyes were shadowed in darkness, but they seemed to burn with an intensity I had not seen in them before.

"Be careful," I cautioned. "You won't be able to see a thing in the dark. Don't trip and break your leg or we'll really be in a fix," I said, trying to sound upbeat.

Caleb took a step toward me. "You've been a brick through all of this. You're really something special, Kate, do you know that?"

He leaned closer, and before I could catch my breath his lips were against mine. He kissed me soundly, but with a gentleness and tenderness I had never experienced. I felt fire shoot through my veins. For an instant, I wondered if I had toppled into the flames Caleb had started inside the cave—I was dizzy enough for it to have happened. The fire inside me raged even after Caleb's kiss ended.

His fingers lingered on my cheek as he gazed steadfastly into my eyes. Then he turned and disappeared into the night.

My legs wobbled beneath me as I walked back inside the cave. Reuben looked up from the fire.

"Is he gone?" Reuben asked.

I nodded. I went over to Reuben and sat down next to him. I

had no need of the fire now, for my body still burned from Caleb's caress. I tried to recall the sequence of events that led up to his kiss, but my mind kept dwelling on the kiss, skipping over everything else. It was several seconds before I could concentrate on the situation at hand. I gathered Reuben in my arms and put my cheek next to his.

"Are you warmer now, Reuben?" I asked.

"Yes," he replied, nodding.

"Is your leg paining terribly?"

"Not so bad that I can't stand it."

Neither of us spoke for the next few seconds. Then Reuben asked, "How did you find me?"

I thought about the sudden stroke of inspiration I'd had, and I knew who was the Author of it. "I remembered you telling me about your pirate cave, Reuben. Is this the cave you were describing to me?"

"Yes. It's a terrific cave, isn't it? Only I don't think I'll come back here for a while," he added, a little crestfallen.

"It's a fine cave, Reuben. You came here after you found the sheep dead, didn't you?"

"Uh huh. I ran all the way here. It was a quiet place where I could be alone to think."

"Everyone needs a quiet place to think things over. You're lucky you have this cave. It was just unlucky that you fell on the rocks and got hurt."

Reuben was silent for a minute or two. "I thought my sheep was going to get better. She started to get better. Then she died."

"You took good care of her. You fed her, kept her warm, and did everything you could for her. She just heard the Shepherd's voice and followed him, that's all."

Reuben seemed to understand what I was saying. "You mean she's with all the other sheep who have died?"

"That's right. And I'll bet she's romping and jumping and having a grand time."

Reuben smiled and his voice held a trace of excitement in it.

"She's not lonely or sick now, is she, Katharine?"

"No, she's not. She's part of the Good Shepherd's flock, and you should be happy for her."

"I am happy for her." Reuben stared into the fire, a contented smile on his face.

I looked into the flames too, thinking of the lesson I had learned from the sheep. "May I also be numbered among his flock," I whispered softly.

Reuben snuggled against me, laying his head on my shoulder. "I bet all of you were worried about me," he said, covering his mouth to stifle a yawn.

"Worried? That's an understatement," I chuckled. "I know about a dozen people who are going to be awfully glad to see you. Do you know all the ranch hands were looking for you? Gus, Luke Satterfield, every one of them—not just Cabe."

Reuben didn't answer. I glanced down at him. His eyes were closed and his breathing even. I smiled and stroked his cheek. It was soft and warm under my fingertips. A sense of gratitude flooded through me. I murmured a silent prayer, thanking God for helping us find Reuben, and renewing my promise.

I sat looking into the fire for quite some time. Occasionally I threw on a stick or two to keep the fire bright. It was quiet here, like Reuben said, and I did a lot of thinking. I reviewed the events of the last several weeks since arriving so suddenly in the Walkers' time. I thought about the Walkers and how much they had come to mean to me. And I thought about Caleb. Had I been attracted to him all along and not admitted it to myself? The way Caleb had looked at me tonight—the way he had kissed me—kindled feelings I never suspected I possessed.

It had been about an hour since Caleb left when I heard the sounds of his return. I recognized his voice, and then Thomas's and Mr. Walker's as they approached the cave. I gently shook Reuben's shoulder.

"Wake up, Reuben. Your father's here. We're going to take you home."

154

Reuben sat up, rubbing his eyes. He looked a little dazed, as if he didn't know where he was or how he'd gotten there. I hugged him and kissed his cheek.

The next few minutes were tumultuous ones with exclamations of relief and joy, and hugs all around. Mr. Walker had brought several blankets. One of these he wrapped snugly around Reuben, and another he gave to me. I enveloped myself in it, grateful for its warmth and comfort. Caleb eyed me closely to make certain I was well taken care of.

Mr. Walker and Thomas laid a third blanket on the ground and lifted Reuben carefully onto it. Reuben moaned as he was moved. Caleb adjusted the boy's injured leg into as comfortable a position as possible. Walker and Thomas grasped each end of the blanket, and with Reuben couched in it started from the cave. Caleb stamped out the fire then reached for my hand, and we followed them out.

"Did you get along all right?" he asked softly when we were clear of the cave.

"Yes. Reuben fell asleep soon after you left."

He squeezed my hand. "We would never have found him tonight if it weren't for you, Kate."

I looked up into his face. His eyes wore the same intense expression I had noticed in them earlier.

Carefully, we picked our way home over the dark, rough ground. The men had brought lanterns with them, but their light only illuminated small patches of rocky earth. Caleb kicked a fallen limb out of our path. Another time he steered me clear of a clump of dry brush, all the while keeping tight hold of my hand.

Now that Reuben was safe and the ordeal nearly over, I realized how exhausted I was. All the emotional fervor of the day had taken its toll. Caleb seemed to sense my weariness. He put an arm around my waist and helped me along. When at last we sighted lights from the house, I must have felt as much relief as Reuben did.

A renewed round of hugs and kisses, mingled with happy tears, met us at the door. Aunt Lizzy made Reuben comfortable on the couch and brought him something to eat, then she dispatched Thomas for the doctor. Upon examination, the doctor determined that Reuben had broken his bone at the ankle. Aside from that, he seemed unharmed from his ordeal.

After the doctor left, I slipped away from the rest of the family, feeling a fierce need to unburden my soul. In the privacy of my room, I dropped to my knees and poured out my heart to God. I thanked him again for leading us to Reuben and expressed my gratitude for Reuben's safety and well-being. As I tried to express the thoughts which filled my heart, tears began to flow down my cheeks. In spite of my many scarlet sins, my rebelliousness, and my disregard for keeping the commandments, God had heard and answered my prayers. I felt profoundly humbled to know that he loved me. The remorse I suffered for my sins had been excruciating; but the knowledge that Christ provided a way for me to be forgiven filled me with hope and joy.

I arose from my knees just as Lacy entered the room. I hadn't heard her come up the stairs, and I was not yet completely composed. She immediately noticed my tear-stained cheeks.

She walked to the bed and flopped down on it. "You don't need to make a great show of piety for my benefit, Katharine," she said. "I'm not impressed by it."

Her words stung me. It hurt to have her misinterpret my feelings, especially now when I had experienced a spiritual awakening.

Lacy turned onto her side and gave me a scornful look. "Save your theatrics for Caleb," she said coldly.

"Lacy, if I could only explain things to you . . ."

She cut me off. "Why don't you start by explaining whether it was you or Caleb who found Reuben."

"Both of us," I answered, confused by the direction of her question.

"Both of you?" she repeated, lifting one blonde brow.

"Yes. We were both looking for Reuben, like everyone else."

"Isn't it convenient how you and Caleb happened to be together, looking in the same place." Her words were a mockery.

"You don't understand what I'm trying to tell you," I began in exasperation.

"I understand perfectly. You've done everything you can to make Caleb like you and dislike me," she said caustically.

"That's not true. But Caleb has nothing to do with what I want to explain to you. I've discovered it's the things of the spirit which are . . ."

Lacy jumped to her feet. Her blue eyes flashed with anger and her face was flushed. "Don't you start preaching to me, Katharine. Or making up excuses. I know you've been sneaking off with Caleb by yourself."

"I haven't been doing any such thing," I protested, taken aback by her accusation. "If you'll only listen to me . . ."

"Oh, I'm tired of listening to you," Lacy snapped. She turned away from me and wordlessly began to change into her night-clothes.

My shoulders sagged with disappointment. I had wanted to share a personal, spiritual insight with her and she'd been stubbornly unwilling to listen. All I'd accomplished was to fan the flames of contention between us.

By the time I started to slip out of my dress and into my long cotton nightgown, Lacy was already in bed with the covers pulled up around her ears. I climbed into the other bed on the opposite side of the room and lay, unmoving, under the blankets. The empty space between us seemed like a yawning canyon. I closed my eyes, trying to put the argument with Lacy out of my mind. The reverent feeling I'd experienced earlier was rapidly dissipating. With a sigh, I realized that this business of keeping on the straight and narrow path was not going to be easy.

CHAPTER THIRTEEN

THE FOLLOWING MORNING I was up early, helping to get breakfast on. As tired as I was the night before, I had enjoyed little sleep. It was a relief to get up, to busy my head and my hands. When the ranch hands came inside for breakfast, Caleb barely looked at me. He gulped down his food and quickly left the table to attend to his chores. I hurried through my breakfast too, unable to eat much of anything.

Lacy was sullen and quiet at the table. For the rest of the morning she went out of her way to avoid me. Once, while we were tidying up the kitchen, I caught her looking at me, anger smoldering in her eyes. But she didn't say anything, and for that I was grateful.

When my chores were completed, I went upstairs to wash my face and comb my hair. After I was through, I stared into the mirror fastened on the wall above the mahogany dresser. I saw the reflection of a young woman I hardly knew anymore. Her face was agreeable, but plain without the benefit of makeup. Her hair, parted in the center of her head and pulled back into a loose bun, gave her a prim appearance. Her cotton dress concealed her figure from neck to ankles. Was that image really me? Or had I, in fact, been transformed into Katharine Walker?

On impulse I shook my hair free, letting it fall its full length to my shoulders. I pinched a spot of color into my cheeks, and bit my lips until they turned red. I picked up the coarse tortoise-shell comb and attacked my hair with it, back-combing and fluffing it into the style I used to wear. Then I looked again into the mirror. The effect was ridiculous. My ratted hair was already sagging without the benefit of mousse or hairspray, and my cheeks looked splotchy where I had tortured them. The old-fashioned clothing I wore clashed grotesquely with the modern look I was trying to achieve.

I laughed disparagingly at this image of myself. Then I scooped up my plain brown hair and twisted it back into a bun. It went obediently into place. I smoothed out my dress with the palms of my hands, wrapped a shawl around my shoulders, and went downstairs.

I needed to get outside, and hoped the fresh air would clear my head. I walked through the kitchen undetected, opened the back door, and let myself out. The air outside was crisp and clear. All traces of the black clouds that yesterday had threatened rain were gone. I took a deep breath and let it out slowly. I allowed my feet to wander in their own direction while I tried to chase the worries from my mind.

The sheep were bleating loudly in their pens, and I found myself drawn toward them. I covered the distance from house to sheep pens in a few moments. The sheep were milling about, bumping into one another and baaing plaintively. I stood by the wooden railing of the pen and watched them. It seemed incredible that such ordinary animals could be the means of teaching me such extraordinary lessons. I thought about the scripture in the book of John that I had read two nights earlier. My commitment to cling to gospel principles had not slackened since then; in fact, it had increased in strength. As I looked at the sheep, I thought again of Professor Bowen and the book he was writing. If I ever got back to my own time, I vowed that I'd stand up to Professor Bowen—tell him that what he wanted to write about the Saints was biased and untrue. I would tell him so, even if it meant losing my job.

I was startled by the sound of footsteps on the hard, dirt-packed ground. I whirled around to see Caleb advancing toward me. My heart thumped crazily as he approached.

"I thought I might find you here," he said, stopping only inches from me.

"I was just watching the sheep," I mumbled. I clutched the top rail of the pen, feeling dizzy with him standing so close to me.

Caleb didn't reply, but I felt his eyes hard on me.

"I thought I might give Reuben that ewe of mine to keep."

"Do you mean Abby?" He put his hands on the railing next to mine.

"Yes, Abby. I know it won't take the place of the sheep he lost, but it might help to ease his grief."

"I think Reuben would be pleased." Caleb scraped the dirt with the toe of his boot. I could feel a restlessness in him as he stood beside me.

I pulled my shawl tighter around my shoulders, not because I was cold, but because Caleb's nearness sent shivers along my spine. The dried leaves on the ground stirred in a sudden gust of wind.

Caleb cleared his throat. "I wanted to talk to you, Kate," he said, his voice tight.

Whatever he wanted to say, I knew it was important to him. I tensed, gripping the top rail of the pen. "Yes?" My voice came out high and shrill sounding.

Caleb stirred the dirt with his boot. "About last night . . . I thought perhaps I should apologize for my bold behavior. That is, I'm not sorry I kissed you," his face flushed slightly, "I'm only sorry if I caught you unaware. I've had strong feelings for you for some time, though I knew you didn't share them."

I gulped and stared at the ground, unable to meet his intense gaze.

"You don't share them, do you?" he asked quietly.

My heart was beating so loudly I was sure he could hear it. I glanced up into his face. His mouth was tight and pale, and his eyes sought mine.

"Caleb, I . . ." I could get no farther. My voice drowned in the tumultuous emotions churning in my breast. Did this pounding of my heart mean that I cared for him? Even if I did, what would it matter? After all, this whole experience I was living was unreal—a dream. Cabe Hollister was not real. And I wasn't Katharine Walker.

"I thought that would be your answer," Caleb said stiffly.

"No, wait. You don't understand."

He had taken his hands off the rail and stood woodenly beside me. His face was carefully masked with a stoic expression.

I put my hand on his arm. "Cabe, if I told you about an experience I've had which seems completely impossible, would you believe me?"

A look of surprise crossed his face. "Of course."

I drew a deep breath. "It's beside the point how I feel about you. I'm not exactly the person you think I am." I watched his face, waiting to see what effect my words would have.

He didn't say anything for a few seconds. Then he reached for my hand. "Look, let's take a walk. Are you expected back at the house right away?"

"Not for a few minutes," I answered, my voice wavering. I let him curl his fingers around mine and followed him as he walked resolutely away from the sheep pens.

The warmth of his hand ignited the fire inside me all over again. It was all I could do to keep my breathing steady. We walked for several yards, with Caleb leading the way, in the direction of the river. I could feel the wind at my back, urging me along.

Caleb didn't say anything until the house was well out of sight. We cut across the alfalfa field and started down the slope leading to the river. The ground was littered with rocks and fallen leaves. He led me to a large limb which had broken off an old hickory tree, and motioned for me to sit down on it. Then he sat next to me, his hands on his knees.

"Now why don't you tell me what you mean," he said, looking intently into my face.

His hazel eyes blended with the yellow-green grass under our feet, the slant of the afternoon sun catching their flecks of brown and turning them to soft amber. I noticed, too, the play of light and shadow in his rich brown hair. The effect was spell-binding. I had to force my eyes away from his face in order to tell him anything.

"This is going to sound crazy, Cabe, but it's the truth."

"All right." He nodded soberly, keeping his eyes on me.

"My name isn't Katharine Walker. It's Katharine Garrett. This isn't my time or circumstance, Cabe. I won't even be born for more than ninety years from now. In some strange, unexplainable way, I have been transported back in time to this place. I have no idea how or why this has happened." I paused to catch my breath and measure the reaction on Caleb's face.

His eyes were wide, but there was no sign of skepticism in them. "Go on," he said in an even voice.

"It happened one particular afternoon while I was working for Professor Bowen. I'm Bowen's research assistant. He teaches at the college in Salt Lake and is writing a book about the Utah War. He asked me to take notes from some old pioneer diaries housed in the Church Historical Office. It had been a bad day. Professor Bowen misplaced some notes I'd taken earlier and things were generally in an uproar. I decided to get away from it all for a few minutes, so I took my lunch and went to the cemetery—Brigham Young's family cemetery—to eat while I enjoyed a little peace and quiet."

Caleb's eyes grew bigger, but he didn't comment.

I went on to tell him the whole story—about the old man with the pocketwatch and key, the abruptness with which I found myself at Brigham Young's graveside service, the astonishment I felt at being mistaken for one of the Walker children.

He listened to everything in silence, letting me tell my story without interruption. When I was through relating my experiences, he sat very still for some minutes, not saying anything.

"You don't believe me, do you?" I asked glumly.

He looked down into my face, his eyes narrow in concentrated thought. "I believe the fact that you believe it," he said after a moment.

162

I stood up impatiently. "I don't know if I even believe it anymore," I replied in desperation. "It's all so incredible. Like a dream. How could it have happened?"

Caleb shook his head. "I don't know. But that's not to say it couldn't have happened. Thomas is convinced that something happened to you."

"Thomas is?" I asked in surprise.

"Yes. While we were up at the pastures he told me a few of the things you'd said to him and how the two of you spent an afternoon searching for the old gentleman with the key."

"He did?" I echoed with excitement. I sat back down on the limb beside Caleb. "You never mentioned it to me, that you knew. Why didn't you?"

"I figured you'd tell me yourself if you wanted me to know." He gave me a sudden, warm smile.

"Weren't you the least bit curious?"

"Let's just say I was more interested in getting to know you here in the present."

I laughed. That simple action seemed to relieve the tension that had built inside me. Caleb laughed, too.

"You don't think I'm crazy, then?" I asked.

Caleb grinned. "I think . . ." he said mischievously, "that a little bit of craziness never hurt anyone."

I smiled in return. "I could tell you things about the 1990s that you'd never be able to even imagine," I said in a conspiratorial tone. "About computers and space shuttles, automobiles and television."

"Please," Caleb said, holding up his hand and chuckling. "I'd rather find out all in due time. Besides," he added, growing serious once more, "I'm primarily concerned with what's happening in the here and now. And here and now, Kate . . ." He took my hand in both of his, ". . . you're all I care about."

He leaned close to me, his eyes searching mine. I felt myself being drawn irresistibly to him. He let go of my hand and put his arm around me, drawing me near. His lips brushed my hair.

I felt a shiver of pleasure run down my spine. If this is all a dream, I thought desperately, I hope I never wake up.

The next moment he was kissing me. I lost all sense of time and place, wanting nothing more than to remain in his arms. But then he drew back, his eyes questioning.

"Does this mean your feelings match mine?" he asked.

I couldn't speak. I nodded, gazing into his face, trancelike.

A slow smile parted his lips. He passed a hand gently over my hair. "My lioness," he whispered. "How I love you."

I rested my head against his chest. I could feel the rapid beating of his heart. Slowly I let myself relax in his arms, reveling in the bliss I felt there. My anxieties and fears fell away like a snake shedding its skin. All of a sudden it didn't matter that I was not Katharine Walker. I was me—and Caleb loved me. Every other worry and concern vanished as I nestled in his arms.

Caleb stroked my hair as we sat together in silence. Finally, he spoke. "We have one problem, you know."

"Just one? I can think of at least half a dozen," I replied, partly in jest. Lacy's angry eyes flashed into my mind. I didn't relish the thought of explaining this to her.

He chuckled, a deep throaty sound that fell pleasantly on my ears. "I was referring to the fact that I don't think I can let you go out of my arms."

"That is a problem," I returned, leaning my head against his shoulder.

He lightly kissed the top of my head. "However, if we don't go soon, your father will be rounding up a search party for us."

I sighed and got to my feet. Caleb stood up, took my hand, and smiled at me. The fire smoldering inside me made my cheeks pink with heat. We started back toward the house, not saying much, just enjoying one another's companionship.

When we neared the house, reality and common sense descended on me like an unwelcome rain. "We really do have one immediate problem," I said, a frown creasing my brow. "Lacy is sure to stir up trouble for us."

"Lacy? Why is that?"

"We had an argument last night. Regrettably, part of it involved you."

Caleb's dark brows leaped in surprise.

"Lacy accused me of turning you against her. I don't know . . ." my hands came up in a gesture of helplessness. "Maybe she's jealous, or perhaps she's angry with me for teasing her about Silas, her beau in Salt Lake."

"I'll talk to her. Don't you worry about it."

"She won't be happy about this situation," I warned him.

"Let me take care of it. I want Lacy to understand how it is between us, you and me. And Thomas, and the rest of your family. I don't want to pretend about my feelings to anyone. Is that agreeable with you?"

I nodded, gripping his hand tighter.

We'd taken only a few steps more when he stopped in mid-stride. "Kate, about that experience of yours," he began in a firm tone of voice. "I don't know what to make of it, but I don't want you to hesitate talking about it to me if you feel you want to. I'll try to understand the best I can."

"Thank you, Cabe. That means a lot to me."

We walked the rest of the way in silence. When we reached the barn, Caleb kissed me then went inside to attend to his work. I floated the remainder of the distance to the house.

Thomas was seated at the kitchen table when I entered, eating a slice of bread smothered with gooseberry jam. I walked over to him and put my arms around his neck.

"Hey, what's this for?" he asked in surprise.

"I love you, Thomas. That's all." I kissed his cheek and flashed him a bright smile. I felt his startled gaze follow me out of the room. I hummed to myself as I mounted the stairs, barely feeling the wooden steps underneath my feet.

The rest of the day passed quickly. I wondered if Caleb had spoken with Lacy yet. She'd been in and out of sight most of the afternoon, her gaze always avoiding mine. After the evening meal, we retired to the parlor as usual. Mr. Walker seated himself in his favorite chair and took up his paper, while Aunt Lizzy set to work with a needle and thread. The rest of us occupied ourselves as we pleased.

We hadn't been seated more than twenty minutes when a knock sounded at the back door. Thomas went to answer it. I heard murmuring voices in the kitchen, and then Thomas returned to the parlor with Caleb at his heels.

"Father, Cabe wants to speak with you," Thomas said flatly.

I felt my skin grow hot and prickly. Caleb glanced at me as he walked over to Mr. Walker and sat down on the chair next to him. My heart started beating in double-time.

"Good evening, sir," Caleb began.

"Evening, Cabe. What can I do for you?"

"I want to speak with you, sir, about a subject which lies close to my heart."

Walker frowned slightly. "Do you wish to speak to me in private?"

"No, sir. I'd prefer the family to hear what I have to say."

I saw the ears on all three of Aunt Lizzy's boys perk up. Thomas, too, eyed Caleb with sudden interest. I was afraid to look at Lacy, to see her reaction.

"Go ahead then, Cabe. You may speak freely," Walker said, folding his paper and placing it on his knees.

"Well, sir, it seems that over the past few weeks as I have become acquainted with your daughter, Katharine . . ."

Every eye in the room shifted to me, riveting on my face.

". . . I have developed strong feelings for her. I told her of my affection only this afternoon." He paused, giving me a quick glance. "I've come to ask your permission to court Katharine."

The room was deadly still. No one even dared draw a breath.

Walker cleared his throat. "I see. Does Katharine share your feelings?"

Caleb's voice didn't waver. "I believe she does, sir."

Walker's gaze fastened on me. "Is this true, Katharine?"

I tried to speak, but the emotions raging inside me, compounded by Walker's unflinching stare, prevented me from uttering a word. I nodded my head.

"Well, then," Walker said in a booming voice, "you have my permission. And gladly given. You're a steady young man, Caleb. Honest. Smart. Katharine would do well with a young man such as yourself. I once heard Brother Brigham give a word of advice that bears repeating here. 'Young man,' he said, 'fit you up a little log cabin, if it is not more than ten feet square, and then get you a bird to put in your little cage.'" Walker nodded his head solemnly. "A sage piece of advice, is it not?"

"Yes, sir," Caleb answered. "I'll remember it."

My head was reeling from all that had transpired. Everyone in the room kept staring first at me, then at Caleb, and then back to me. I could feel the color rise in my cheeks.

"You're welcome to spend the remainder of the evening with us if you like, Caleb," said Walker.

"Thank you. I'd like that very much." Caleb got out of his chair and moved to one situated closer to me. He gave me a big, satisfied grin. I smiled shakily in return.

With Caleb by my side, I was able to summon up enough courage to glance in Lacy's direction. Her eyes rested on Caleb's face. She looked neither surprised nor angry; but like a little girl who has just lost her shiny new penny. Seeing that, my heart softened considerably toward her.

As if Caleb were reading my thoughts, he leaned over and whispered in my ear. "I told Lacy earlier this afternoon."

I raised my brows in silent question.

"She informed me that you planned to marry a fellow in Salt Lake named Horace Baumgarten."

My eyes rolled toward the ceiling.

"I hope Brother Baumgarten won't be too disappointed," Caleb added, a smile creeping to his mouth.

Caleb reached over and discreetly took my hand. From the

corner of my eye, I saw Reuben elbow his brother. All three of the younger boys watched Caleb and me in open fascination.

I spent a highly uncomfortable hour. In spite of Caleb's easy manner, I felt self-conscious and ill at ease under the family's scrutiny. I was glad when Mr. Walker finally folded his paper and set it aside. Caleb was quick to perceive the conclusion of this evening's visit. He hastily stood up, bid us goodnight and let himself out the back door.

The moment after evening prayer was pronounced, Lacy hurried up the stairs. I remained in the parlor for a few minutes longer and when I, too, climbed the stairs and entered the bedroom I shared with her, I found Lacy already in bed with the blankets pulled up to her chin. The lamp was out, but there was enough moonlight shining through the window for me to see that Lacy's eyes were tightly and irrevocably closed. I knew she wasn't asleep.

"Lacy?" I whispered.

She didn't move a muscle.

I walked over to the bed and bent down to her ear. "Lacy? I hope you're not upset with me. With Caleb and me."

She didn't respond except for a change in her breathing. It came faster and deeper than before.

I felt badly that she refused to speak to me; I hoped tomorrow she would view things differently and we could begin to establish a more amicable relationship. I sighed audibly. Ever since my arrival here, things had a way of getting more tangled in spite of my best efforts to sort them out. I quickly undressed in the faint circle of moonlight, said my personal prayers and climbed into bed. With all the emotional upheaval of the day, I thought I would have difficulty falling asleep. But before I could count even ten head of sheep, I felt the edges of consciousness growing fuzzy.

CHAPTER FOURTEEN

"HOW MANY OF THEM were there, do you think?" I asked Caleb.

"Four or five. Maybe more. When I got outside, I saw two of the coyotes skulking around the pens and heard the others a few yards off in the trees."

My skin prickled as I thought of the coyotes prowling around our sheep.

"You didn't hear them howling last night?" Caleb asked me.

Caleb and I were seated together on a large rock near the river, about a half mile from the ranch. It was mid-afternoon and we had stolen away to enjoy a few minutes to ourselves. It had been a week since Caleb had spoken with Mr. Walker about our feelings for one another, and since then we'd hardly had a minute to be alone. Although Caleb came "calling" at the house each evening, we had no privacy there. The entire family joined us in the parlor. And if we wished to take a walk, Mr. Walker insisted we be properly chaperoned—which meant Aunt Lizzy joined us. She discreetly lagged a few steps behind, but her presence disconcerted me, accustomed as I was to modern dating practices, although Caleb didn't seem to mind. So it was that we snatched a few moments together whenever we could.

"No, I didn't hear them," I answered in reply to Caleb's question. "And I'm glad I didn't, or I would never have been able to sleep afterwards."

Caleb smiled and drew my hand into his. "What's the matter, do you doubt my ability as a shepherd?"

"My confidence grows a little shaky when coyotes are involved," I replied, giving him a broad smile.

"You have a beautiful smile, do you know that? It lights up your whole face," he said, running his thumb slowly across my chin.

The feel of his hand sent shivers of pleasure shooting through me. I blushed under his gaze. "I know my hair pokes out in all the wrong places, my eyes are too small, and all my other features are quite ordinary," I returned lightly.

Caleb laughed. "But your smile is beautiful."

"I'll concede that one small point," I replied, looping my arm through his. "But if you want to see a really beautiful girl, you wouldn't have to look any further than my friend, Terri. She has long, wavy blonde hair. Gorgeous blue eyes. A darling figure. Terri looks like a model straight out of the pages of *Vogue*."

Caleb stood up, chuckling. "I won't even ask what *Vogue* is. I've never met anyone quite like you, Kate."

"That's probably truer than you imagine," I replied, thinking of my double life. "You know, I wish you could meet Terri. And my brothers and my parents, too."

Caleb pulled me up to my feet. "Why don't you tell me about them," he said as we started back toward the ranch at a leisurely pace.

"You mean it? You want to hear about them?"

"Of course," he replied, smiling down into my face. "Tell me about your parents."

I pictured Mom's smiling face in my mind. I saw her standing over the stove, her long-handled spoon in hand. "Oh, Mom's the greatest. She's a marvelous cook and takes enormous pride in keeping our home orderly. Both she and Dad are wonderful. Dad works for the Church. He travels a bit on his assignments, and he likes to take Mom and us kids along whenever possible. Although now, of course, there's only me left at home because my oldest brother, Mark, is away serving a mission on the island of Fiji, and my brother, Darrin, is at college." I paused, thinking longingly of my family. "But now I'm not even at home. I wonder what my parents think has happened to me," I said quietly.

Caleb put his arm around me, and pulled me close to his side. We walked in silence for a few moments. Then he asked, "And Terri? Tell me about your friend, Terri."

"You'd like Terri. Not only is she beautiful, she's vivacious, charming, and fun-loving." I frowned suddenly, thinking of some of the activities in which Terri and I had participated. Activities I knew Caleb would never have taken part in. I flushed with embarrassment. How could I have been so stupid as to disregard the teachings of my parents and the Church? I could see clearly now that I had been rushing headlong down a path which could only lead to disappointment and remorse.

"I don't know, Cabe. Maybe you wouldn't find Terri all that attractive. Maybe you wouldn't have found me attractive if you'd known me before."

Caleb hugged me against him. "I would have found you attractive in any time," he assured me.

I looked up solemnly into his face. "I've changed since coming here, Cabe. I'm not the same girl I was before. And I'm glad of it." I stood on tip-toe and kissed his cheek.

He stopped, took me in his arms and kissed me soundly. I felt my heart jumping like a jack rabbit underneath my prim brown muslin. When he let me go, I could hardly catch my breath.

"Who else?" Caleb asked as we began walking comfortably along again. "What about your Professor Bowen? Did you like working for him?"

"Oh, I could tell you a dozen things about Professor Bowen," I answered. "And Sally, too. Sally is the typist who works with us in the office. I wish you could meet them all." I squeezed his arm in excitement as another thought popped into my head. "I have a speedy little Mustang, too. How I'd love to take you for a ride!"

"You ride a mustang?" Caleb asked, wide-eyed. "If ladies ride wild mustang horses in the future, the world must surely be a different place than it is now."

I threw back my head and hooted with laughter. Caleb looked at me in bewilderment. When I was finally able to catch my breath, I said to him, "That statement is truer than you can imagine, Cabe."

Caleb flashed me a smile. I remembered when that grin seemed to me disagreeable and impertinent. I must have been blind—he had an absolutely charming smile. It was the feature which characterized Caleb's personality the most.

It wasn't long afterward that we reached the ranch. As we drew up alongside the barn, Caleb stopped, taking both my hands in his. "Listen, Kate. I won't be coming to the house tonight. I have an errand to run in town as soon as I'm through with my chores, and it may keep me past the time your father allows callers."

"All right. I don't suppose you're going to tell me what sort of errand you have in mind," I kidded him.

He bent down and kissed my mouth. "You'll have to wait and see, my lioness."

"Trying to conceal your real purpose, are you?" I said teasingly. "Now who's the lion in lamb's clothing?"

"You are, Kate," he replied in earnestness. "You're courageous, strong and proud. I love you for those very qualities." He kissed me again, long and tenderly.

I would have been content to stay in his arms forever. But like all enchanted spells, this one, too, inevitably was broken. Caleb gave me a parting kiss on the forehead, and sent me on my way.

As I neared the house Reuben came over to meet me, limping noticeably on his broken ankle. The collie, Buck, padded along at his side. Reuben seized my hand, wrapping it around his own smaller one.

"Hi, ya, Reuben," I said affectionately. I reached down and patted the collie trotting at Reuben's side.

"Hi, Katharine. Where you been? I've been looking for you."

"Out for a walk with Cabe," I answered in a conspiratorial whisper.

Reuben giggled. "I think you and Cabe make a nice pair. Are you going to marry him, Katharine?"

"I don't know, Reuben. That's a ways down the road yet."

"I think you should. I like Cabe."

"Me, too," I agreed.

We walked for a moment in silence.

"I've been taking real good care of Abby," he said earnestly.

"I know you have. I can see how fat and contented she looks. You're going to make a fine sheep rancher. Just like your father."

"I know a lot about sheep ranching already," Reuben boasted, puffing out his chest.

"I bet you do."

"I know about lambing, and shearing, and herding the sheep. Maybe next year Papa will let me go with the ranch hands up to the summer pastures."

"Would you like that?"

Reuben nodded enthusiastically.

We were almost to the house by this time. "You said you'd been looking for me. Did you want something in particular?" I asked.

"Lacy was asking for you, that's all."

"Oh?" I was surprised to hear Lacy had been inquiring after me. She hadn't spoken more than ten words to me all week. She was still angry over the situation with Caleb.

"Well, I'll go find Lacy and see what she wanted," I said. I bent down and kissed Reuben on the cheek. He bore the kiss patiently, then with a wave of his hand he hobbled off toward the sheep pens with Buck barking at his heels.

Lacy was seated at the kitchen table when I entered, bent over a magazine. As I neared her, I glanced at the drawings on the page. Evidently it was a ladies' magazine she was poring over, for the page was illustrated with the figures of half a dozen women dressed in stylish gowns. I paused to study the clothes shown on one of the models. She wore a fancy dress adorned with ribbons and bows. The neck was cut low off the shoulder, and edged with frilled lace. Attached to the bodice was an overskirt, short in front, caught up at the sides, and bunched out at the back. The underskirt was ruffled and heavily flounced. The sleeves were three-quarter-length, fitting tight to the elbows and ending with large frilled cuffs. Around the model's neck was a ribbon tied in a small bow with long ends dangling down the back. It was a very stylish outfit for the nineteenth-century woman.

The other ladies pictured on the page were equally well-dressed. Their hair was depicted in a variety of styles. One lady wore her hair piled on her head with a frizzy fringe of bangs across the front. A small ribboned bonnet sat atop her head. Another model's hair was shown waved and brushed back above the ears into a chignon. Loosely-curled ringlets hung down the back of her neck.

Lacy, knowing I was looking at the drawings over her shoulder, flipped to the next page. Here were pictured various examples of ladies' foundations to be worn under their skirts. Two or three different kinds of wire bustles were illustrated. I knew from my historical study that by 1877 the crinoline was out and the bustle had already gone through several adaptations. The skirts remained full at the back, with trailing trains. Ornamentation on ladies' dresses was very lavish with lace, braid, frogging, ribbon, and embroidery. Fabrics were dyed in purples, greens, reds, and royal blues. A mixture of fabrics and trimmings often went into one garment. Accessories included fans, gloves, and silk parasols. Bonnets had evolved into stylish hats, most of them with low crowns and narrow brims, embellished with feathers, ribbons, plumes, flowers, and tassels.

I knew clothing similar to that pictured on the pages of Lacy's magazine would never grace the Walker girls. Mr. Walker was very strict about the clothes his children wore. He did not allow frilly trimmings or loud colors. All the dresses kept in the trunk in Lacy's room were plain, modest, and of somber hue. I suspected that Lacy would have given almost anything for a gown like those printed on the pages in front of her.

I walked to the other side of the table and sat down across from Lacy. She didn't raise her eyes from the page or give any acknowledgement of my presence.

"Afternoon, Lacy," I said, after a few seconds of silence.

Lacy made no reply.

"Your magazine looks interesting. Did Aunt Lizzy lend it to you?"

"What business is it of yours if she did?"

"None. I was only trying to make conversation." Tired of her ill humor, I stood up ready to leave. I took a few steps and then as an afterthought commented coldly, "Reuben said you wanted to talk to me, but apparently he was wrong."

"Oh, that," she answered without raising her eyes from the magazine. "I only wanted to remind you that Father is planning to leave in the next couple of days."

"Leave?" I repeated blankly. "Leave where?"

"Here, of course. You know he never stays in Provo beyond the first week in November." She lifted her head and glared at me, sparks glinting from her eyes.

Lacy couldn't have knocked the wind out of me more effectively had she hit me in the stomach. I struggled to draw my next breath. My first hope was that she was lying in order to get back at me because of Caleb, but I realized that even though she enjoyed watching my distress, she was telling the truth. Certainly Mr. Walker would have to return to Salt Lake to care for his family and business there; and surely he would want to get started before the first snows fell. I should have been anticipating this, but I hadn't given it a thought. I was too wrapped up with Caleb and my experiences here on the ranch.

My breath came in a raspy wheeze. Lacy, staring hard at me, gave me a cruel smile. "I heard him tell Aunt Lizzy that he wanted to be back in Salt Lake by Saturday," she reported.

Four days. Saturday was four days from today. I had to tell Caleb. Make some sort of plans for us to see each other again. Tonight, when he came calling, I'd tell him about Walker's plans to leave and . . . I suddenly remembered that Caleb wouldn't be coming to the house tonight, that he was going into town instead. I turned away from Lacy's smug smile and stumbled up the stairs to my room. Shutting the door behind me, I flopped across the bed, hot tears stinging my eyes. For an instant I wished I had never met Caleb Hollister, then I wouldn't be feeling so miserable right now. I buried my head in my arms. From the hills, far in the distance, I heard the lone howl of a coyote.

At breakfast the next morning, Mr. Walker began talking about preparations for the return trip home. In spite of Lacy's malicious intent, I was glad she'd warned me that our departure was imminent; otherwise, I would have been unnerved by the talk at the breakfast table. If Aunt Lizzy was disappointed to see her husband leave, she didn't let on. She prattled in her usual cheerful manner, reminding us to pack various articles for the journey home. The boys, however, appeared downhearted. Walker was their father, and they hated to see him go. I wondered if Aunt Lizzy's boys ever visited the Walker household in Salt Lake. I concluded that they surely must, for it was only natural that they would do so; and Reuben seemed to be well acquainted with his half-brother, Jesse.

It was late in the afternoon before I had a chance to speak with Cabe. He hadn't breakfasted with the family, having taken some cold biscuits and cheese with him earlier to a spot out past the pens where he was doing some repairs. When I saw him stride into the yard from my vantage point at the kitchen window, I hastily threw a shawl around my shoulders and went outside to meet him. It was cold and windy. The gray sky threatened rain. I pulled my shawl tighter around me and hurried toward Caleb. His face broke into a smile when he caught sight of me.

"Kate, you're just the girl I was hoping to see," he said, grinning. He grasped my hands in his.

"Oh, Cabe, I've been wanting to talk with you," I blurted.

"And I've been wanting to talk with you," he replied, his eyes eager. "But it's too cold to stand out here. Let's go inside the barn to talk."

I glanced back toward the house just in time to see a corner of the kitchen curtain fall back into place. I suspected Lacy had been watching us. And probably still was. Caleb led me by the hand into the barn. It was warm inside and smelled comfortably of hay and animals.

Caleb sat down on a bale of hay and motioned for me to sit beside him. "I missed seeing you last night," he said, smiling at me.

"I missed you, too. In fact, I could hardly wait to see you so I could tell you . . ." I broke off, feeling suddenly foolish. Maybe Cabe wouldn't feel as forlorn as I did when he learned we were planning to leave Provo. Or perhaps he already knew. Working closely as he did with Thomas and Mr. Walker, they might have mentioned it to him.

"Yes, Kate?" He was looking intently at me.

"Well . . . I . . . Why don't you tell me first what you had to say," I answered falteringly.

"All right. I've been bursting all morning to tell you the news. Yesterday afternoon when I finished my chores I rode into town, as I told you I was planning to do." He paused, waiting for my word of encouragement.

"Yes?"

"I stopped at the Brigham Young Academy and spoke with the principal there, Mr. Maeser, about pursuing a possible career in law. He suggested I meet with Mr. Dusenberry."

"Who's Mr. Dusenberry?" I asked.

"Warren Dusenberry was the former principal of the Academy. He conducted the first term, then resigned to practice law. Mr. Maeser arranged a meeting later in the evening for me with Mr. Dusenberry, who was very helpful and obliging. Kate, Dusenberry invited me to study law under his direction."

Caleb's eyes sparkled and I could hear the excitement in his voice. "That's wonderful, Cabe. When do you start?"

"As soon as I can finish up here at the ranch. Another three or four weeks, perhaps, and then I can begin. I'm planning to speak to your father about finding a new hand to take my place."

Caleb took my hands in his and squeezed them. "Kate, do you know what this means to me? I've always dreamed of becoming a lawyer. Now I'm actually going to do it. Dusenberry is willing to defray my expenses until I'm able to pass the examinations and begin practicing, in exchange for assisting him in his law office while I'm pursuing my studies."

"It couldn't have worked out better for you, Cabe. I'm so happy for you." I tried to sound enthusiastic, but between his new plans to stay in Provo and my necessity of returning to Salt Lake, I could foresee our relationship disintegrating.

"I know I can be of assistance to the Saints, Kate. Our problems with the United States government didn't end with General Johnston's troops passing through the city. There are still issues to be resolved before the territory of Utah can hope to attain statehood. With some legal training, I can be a part of those solutions."

I forgot about my own disappointment in the face of his enthusiasm. I felt a growing sense of pride in Caleb and his ideals. I had no doubt he would be able to accomplish those things he so earnestly desired.

"Cabe, I'm so proud of you," I said with genuine feeling. "I know you'll be successful."

Caleb brought my hands to his lips and kissed them. "Thank you, Kate. I have you to thank for your encouragement and support."

"Me?" I said, laughing. "I didn't do anything. What you've accomplished has been brought about by your own gumption and perseverance."

He drew me to him and kissed me. "Wait a minute," he said, mid-way through the kiss. He pulled back and looked into my face. "I almost forgot that you had something you wanted to tell me. What is it, Kate?"

My first response was disappointment over the aborted kiss. Then I remembered what had seemed so important to me just a few minutes earlier. In light of Caleb's news, I felt silly bringing up the subject of my departure at all.

"What, Kate?" He pressed me for an answer.

I knew of no other way than to blurt the thing out. "We're planning to leave Provo at the end of this week to return to Salt Lake."

For an instant Caleb's eyes registered confusion; then came a stab of painful realization which he quickly masked. "I should have been expecting that, shouldn't I? I knew you were staying at the ranch only temporarily."

That had been my reaction, too, hearing the news from Lacy. But I didn't say that to Caleb.

"Well, then," he said, brightening. "I'll come to Salt Lake City to see you."

"How? You'll be busy with your studies and work."

Caleb grinned. "I'll come. You can count on it."

"Do you promise?"

"A tribe of wild Indians couldn't keep me from seeing you, Kate."

I felt better after that. "I'll let you come for a visit only if you promise to concentrate thoroughly on your studies. This training you're undertaking is no easy matter. If you're going to become an attorney, you might as well become one of the best."

"Yes, ma'am," Caleb said smartly.

"I'm not kidding, Caleb. It's rigorous work. You should see what efforts the law students go through in my day to success- fully pass their classes at the university, and then pass the bar exam, too."

"Well, Kate, luckily I won't have to compete against those law students. They're not even born yet." He flashed me a broad grin. My heart beat furiously at the sight of his smile.

He leaned over and kissed me long and hard. I felt the fire leap up inside me. It burned so hotly my eyes began to water with the heat of it. Or was it tears I felt, brimming in my eyes? All I was certain of was how much I was going to miss Caleb Hollister.

CHAPTER FIFTEEN

TUESDAY AND WEDNESDAY PASSED in a flurry of activity. Thomas and Mr. Walker were busy from morning until night taking care of last-minute chores around the ranch before we left. Caleb worked with them so much of the time that I barely got to see him—only the few minutes when he came calling at the house after supper. I missed the leisurely evenings spent with the family on the front porch or sitting in the parlor; but there was no time for that now. Lacy and I spent our hours helping Aunt Lizzy in the house and organizing our belongings for the return trip home.

On Thursday evening, however, the night before we were to leave, Mr. Walker didn't go back outside to his chores after dinner as he'd been doing. Instead, he called the family together in the parlor. Thomas came in from the yard, knocking dust off his pants with the brim of his felt hat. When he saw me seated in the parlor, he gave me a quick smile and I smiled back. I couldn't help remembering the first time I had met Thomas. Seated in the back of the Walkers' wagon as we drove away from Brigham Young's cemetery, he'd eyed me with a look of concern as I struggled to figure out what sort of strangeness had befallen me. His brown hair was longer now, his face leaner and harder from his work outdoors on the ranch. I had come to know him well, learned to read his moods, identified his likes and dislikes. And I had come to love him as a brother. I continued to smile at Thomas long after he'd taken a seat in the parlor and turned to his own interests.

Aunt Lizzy's three boys came tumbling into the room next. Emmett and Thorpe sprawled out on the floor, but Reuben came and sat beside me, putting an arm around my neck. I felt warm inside with Reuben's arm nestled about me.

Lacy was already seated. She slouched in her chair, a bored expression on her face. Next to her sat Aunt Lizzy, her hands folded in her lap, waiting expectantly for Mr. Walker to speak his mind.

Walker thoughtfully pulled at his graying chin whiskers some moments before saying anything. He was a tall, big man and his burly frame dwarfed the petite parlor chair he rested upon. He had combed his hair neatly into place and it glistened in the lamp light from the hair oil he had slicked on it. Walker cleared his throat, as he usually did when he had something important to say.

"I've been thinking recently about the bounties the good Lord has given us as a family," he began.

From the corner of my eye, I saw Lacy's shoulders heave with a sigh and her eyes roll toward the ceiling. She knew a sermon was forthcoming, and the prospect of it annoyed her. Thomas, too, shifted slightly in his chair. I seemed to be the only sibling eager to hear what Walker had to say.

"The farm and the ranch are doing well," Walker continued, nodding his head. "With a little sacrifice and hard work, we can expect to see a good profit this next year. The price of wool is up. If we can keep the flock healthy, we should see a handsome return on our labors. The Lord has, indeed, blessed our efforts." He paused, and then eyeing Thomas, called him by name.

Thomas's head jerked up. "Yes, sir?"

"I'll expect you to spend the greater part of your time next year here on the ranch. Lizzy needs your help, and it's time you started learning how to run the ranch yourself."

"But Father, you need my help on the farm," Thomas replied, a look of consternation springing to his eyes.

I knew Thomas's interests did not rest with sheep ranching. He enjoyed farming, and he was particularly interested in the new agricultural techniques which many of the younger progressive farmers were instituting. This revelation, that his father wanted him to run the sheep ranch, must have been distressing to him. I wondered if Thomas would speak his mind on the matter.

"Jesse is getting old enough to carry his weight on the farm. And I can hire hands at planting and harvest time. I want you to learn sheep ranching," Walker stated.

Thomas started to open his mouth, but then closed it again without saying anything. He slumped back in his chair, his eyes fixed on his hands. I knew it wasn't fear or timidity that kept Thomas from disagreeing with his father; he did so out of a deep sense of respect for his father's wishes.

"You're a steady young man, Thomas, and tenacious," Walker said after a moment's silence. "A credit to your namesake."

Thomas looked up at his father, his shoulders straightening slightly. "Yes, Father," he replied.

"The name you carry is one you can be proud of, son. Always remember that," Walker said in a quiet voice.

"I will, Father. I know Colonel Kane is a great friend to our people."

"Not only a friend, but a wise and just man. Brother Brigham once told Colonel Kane that the Lord had sent Kane to Utah with a work to do for the Saints. 'I want to have your name live with the Saints to all eternity,' Brother Brigham said to him. And that is the reason why you have been thusly christened," Walker said to his son.

I couldn't help myself after hearing that explanation. "Do you know Colonel Kane personally?" I asked Mr. Walker in awe.

"For heaven's sake, Katharine, you've heard Father's stories about Colonel Kane as often as I have," Lacy said irritably.

"But I'd like to hear them . . . again." I gulped, surprised by my own boldness.

Lacy heaved a great sigh and began drumming her fingers impatiently on the armrest of her chair.

"I agree with Katharine," said Thomas suddenly. "Tell us about the time you met Colonel Kane at Council Bluffs, Father."

I darted Thomas a grateful glance. "Yes, please do," I echoed.

"That's one of my favorite stories," Aunt Lizzy added.

Mr. Walker held up a hand to silence us. He didn't say anything for several seconds, then he slowly cleared his throat. I edged forward in my chair, holding my breath.

"You've heard me tell many times how Colonel Kane was instrumental in soliciting aid from the general government to assist the Saints. He labored diligently to gain permission for the Saints to occupy and safely cross Indian lands on their journey west."

Walker paused, and I was afraid he was going to say nothing more. But after a time he continued. "I was only a boy of thirteen or fourteen when I first met Colonel Kane. My family was camped at a place called Miller's Hollow with the other Saints during the summer of 1846. I remember it was hot—so hot that we had to stop frequently to water the oxen. I had been swimming in Indian Creek that morning with some of the other boys in camp, trying to keep cool. I had just gotten out of the water when I spied a tall, well-built man on horseback coming in my direction. I knew he was a stranger in camp by the way his eyes were taking in the surroundings.

"I quickly pulled on my trousers and shirt, never taking my eyes off him. When he drew near he greeted me and my friends, who by this time had gathered round, and asked us if this was the location of the Mormon camps. I told him it was. I remember how impressed I was by the stranger's military bearing, his cordiality and his striking appearance. He told us his name and his intention of spending a few days in our camp. I directed him to Brother Campbell's wagon, Brother Campbell being our captain of fifty. As Colonel Kane had to cross the creek to reach Brother Campbell's campsite, I offered to lead his horse to a shallow spot where he could cross safely. He said that he was much obliged for my help. I took hold of his horse's bridle—it was a handsome gray stallion, I remember, who held his head proudly—and led him around a marshy patch to a point thirty or forty yards downstream.

"Colonel Kane thanked me for my assistance and expressed the hope that one day he might return the kindness. Then he spurred his horse into the water. I watched horse and rider in fascination until they had crossed the creek and disappeared from view on the other side. Colonel Kane made a great impression on a young boy that day. He couldn't have been older than twenty-four or twenty-five himself at the time, but he had treated me as one gentlemen does another."

Walker smiled and stroked his beard thoughtfully. I was intrigued by his account. I wanted to ask a dozen questions about Colonel Kane, but I felt too bashful to do so.

Reuben, however, did not. "That was the time Colonel Kane got sick, wasn't it, Father?" he asked brightly.

"Yes, Reuben, it was. Colonel Kane fell desperately ill while in our camp. He spent the remaining part of the summer at Brother Brigham's headquarters. Brother Brigham's camp was some distance from our own, so I did not have the opportunity to see much of the Colonel while he was there. But I heard about him and was aware of his activities in readying volunteers for the Mormon Battalion and in striving to enlist assistance for our people to move west. It wasn't until I was much older that I learned how instrumental Colonel Kane was in securing permits of passage for us through Indian lands."

"Did you ever see Colonel Kane again?" Emmett inquired from his position on the floor near Walker's feet.

"Yes, Emmett," said Walker, bending down to rumple the boy's hair. "Twelve years later."

"Twelve years!" Reuben whispered in my ear. "That's older than I am."

"Yes, it is," I whispered back, giving him a hug.

"It was in the midst of one of our greatest struggles that Colonel Kane again came to our aid," Walker stated, looking down into Emmett's face.

"Your father has explained about the soldiers who were sent to Utah by President Buchanan," Aunt Lizzy reminded her son. "Colonel Kane was very courageous in coming all the way from Pennsylvania, where he lived, to try to settle the difficulties here with the soldiers."

Emmett nodded, remembering the story.

"It was a difficult trip for Colonel Kane," Walker said as he took up the narrative, "and he suffered greatly from the harsh winter cold and the hardship of the journey. He came not as an emissary from the federal government, but on his own responsibility and at his own expense, to do what he could to mediate the crisis between the Saints and the soldiers who were at our very doors."

"He came under an assumed name, didn't he, Father?" Thomas asked knowingly.

"Yes. Initially, he was introduced to the people as 'Dr. Osborne.'"

"Why didn't he use his real name?" asked Thorpe, putting his chin in his hands.

"I don't know the full reasons, son, but part of it was because Colonel Kane had heard some hard things about the Mormon people, and he wanted to find out for himself if they were true or not. He knew if he came to Utah under his true identity, the Saints would treat him cordially in return for his kindnesses to them in the past. But if the people did not know he was in their midst, then he could move among them as a stranger and ascertain the true nature of things."

"But, of course, Brigham Young and some of the other brethren knew who he really was right from the beginning. Colonel Kane never intended to disguise himself from his friends here in Utah," Thomas explained to Thorpe.

Thorpe nodded his understanding, then asked, "Did you

know it was the Colonel, Father?"

"Not right away," Walker replied. "Not until later when I had a chance to speak to him. Then I recognized him. But it wasn't until Colonel Kane arrived back in Salt Lake City from Camp Scott, with Governor Cumming, that I had that opportunity.

"You see, soldiers had been sent by President Buchanan to escort the new territorial governor into Salt Lake City and make certain there was no trouble about the people accepting him. At that time, Thorpe, the people didn't want Mr. Cumming to be their new governor, they wanted Brother Brigham to remain governing them. But even more important was the fact that President Buchanan had not informed Brother Brigham about the soldiers coming to Utah. Brother Brigham heard about the troops from reports given him by some Mormon men. He didn't know whether the army had come to drive us from our homes, as the militia mobs had done in Missouri and Illinois, or for some other reason.

"Brother Brigham decided if the army had come to drive us away, the Saints would not fight and cause blood to be spilled, but we would leave of our own accord. However, he was determined that nothing would be left for the soldiers. Brother Brigham gave instructions for every house, every barn, every field to be destroyed by our own hand if the soldiers entered Salt Lake City."

I watched Thorpe and Emmett as Walker related the story of the altercation between the Saints and the government. Their eyes grew big and round, and their mouths hung open in concentration. Of course, I knew well the facts of the Utah War, having researched it in detail for Professor Bowen. I had read about the non-Mormon federal appointees that President Millard Fillmore sent to Utah. In Mormon eyes these appointees were scoundrels, particularly the judges, so the Saints shunned the federal courts and settled their difficulties among themselves. The judges returned to Washington charging Mormons with disloyalty to the federal government, ignoring the laws of Congress, and showing disrespect for the presidency.

In 1857, the newly-elected president, James Buchanan, decided to replace Young as governor. Buchanan appointed Alfred Cumming, a former mayor of Augusta, Georgia, as the new governor. Anticipating the Mormon reaction, Buchanan sent a contingent of 2,500 soldiers under the command of Albert Sidney Johnston from Fort Leavenworth to Utah to ensure that the Mormons accepted their new governor. When Young heard about the army marching toward Utah, he mobilized the militia and laid plans for the evacuation and burning of the city.

It was during this tense period in the summer of 1857 that the tragic Mountain Meadows massacre occurred. One hundred and twenty emigrants from Arkansas and Missouri, bound for California, were ambushed and killed by Indians in concert with Mormons from Southern Utah. Brigham Young had learned that trouble was brewing between the Mormons and the emigrants. He'd sent a letter to the Saints in southern Utah discouraging any interference with the travelers, but it arrived too late—two days after the massacre. This incident was the worst single episode of violence in the Utah War.

As the United States troops neared the valley, the Mormons carried out guerrilla-like tactics against them. Operating from encampments in the canyons, they harassed the advancing soldiers by stampeding their livestock and setting fire to their supply trains. Preparations for the evacuation of the city began in the fall of 1857. Church records, livestock, farm implements, and 20,000 bushels of wheat were cached in Provo. The Mormon militia burned down Fort Bridger, which they had purchased from Jim Bridger, before the United States Army could get there. They also burned grazing sites where the army would camp.

Through the efforts of Colonel Kane a compromise was finally effected. Governor Cumming agreed to enter Salt Lake City without the army escort. Brigham Young would allow the U.S. troops to enter the valley provided the soldiers were not quartered in the city. To emphasize his stand, he ordered the city evacuated, leaving a few men behind to put a torch to the city if the troops stopped there.

Governor Cumming, in company with Colonel Kane, arrived in Salt Lake City on April 12, 1858. Nearing the city, the governor was dismayed to see the roads thronged with wagons and stock moving steadily southward. In ensuing days Governor Cumming made several trips along the moving line of wagons between Provo and Salt Lake City, urging the people to return to their homes.

Governor Cumming asked Brigham Young for help in persuading the Saints to cease their pilgrimage. Brigham's answer was clear and firm: when the troops were withdrawn from the territory, the people would stop moving. Governor Cumming and Colonel Kane left the city on the 13th of May, the governor to return to Camp Scott with promises to dissuade Johnston from taking up his march for the present, and Kane to return to Washington with dispatches for the President concerning the situation in Utah.

The crisis was settled with a "Proclamation of Pardon" for the Saints from President Buchanan. General Johnston's troops marched through a deserted Salt Lake City on the 26th of June and set up a post, Camp Floyd, thirty miles away in Cedar Valley. Four days later the people began returning to their homes. Johnston's army remained at Camp Floyd for three years, until the outbreak of the Civil War when it was recalled for service.

President Buchanan was criticized in many quarters for his mishandling of the whole affair. He had sent an army to Utah without first investigating charges made against the Saints, or informing the territorial governor, Brigham Young, of his intentions. The charges against the Saints proved false and the army, imprudently sent out too late in the season, suffered unnecessary cold and hardship. After Abraham Lincoln was elected President in 1860, T. B. H. Stenhouse, the Mormon representative in Washington, asked the President what his intentions would be towards the Saints in Utah. Lincoln answered in this way: "When I was a boy on the farm in Illinois there was a great deal of timber which we had to clear away. Occasionally we would come to a log which had fallen down. It was too hard to split, too wet to burn, and too heavy to move, so we plowed around it. That's what I intend to do with the Mormons. You go back and tell Brigham Young that if he will let me alone, I will let him alone."

"But Father," Thorpe persisted when Walker had finished his tale, "you said you spoke with Colonel Kane when he and the new governor got to Salt Lake City. Did he remember you from when you were a boy?"

"It wasn't in the city precisely where Colonel Kane and I exchanged a few words." Walker grinned and I thought I heard him chuckle softly. Then he leaned back in his chair and momentarily closed his eyes. "I was an eager young man of twenty-four the year Johnston's army came to the Utah territory. I was indignant that the United States government should send an army against its own people, a people who were patriotic and law-abiding. My young blood boiled when I thought of all the wrongs my fellow Saints had suffered under the hands of a government which claimed to protect all its citizens and guarantee them religious freedom. My own father and mother had perished because of religious persecution."

Walker paused, drawing a breath. "We didn't know the governor was coming until a few hours beforehand. I was a member of the militia at the time; our company was encamped at the head of Echo Canyon, guarding the passes. During the night we had great bonfires burning at different points in the canyon where our men were camped. I remember watching the long shadows cast by the militia men as they neared the fire to converse or warm themselves against the chill of the night.

"I was situated high up in the canyon walls where I could see the road going both directions for many miles. We had been alerted that another company of militia had met the governor's party at Quaking Asp Hill, and were conducting them to our encampment. The night was dark, but the light from the bonfires illuminated broad patches of ground and must have been an impressive sight from below.

"About ten o'clock in the evening, as near as I can recall, the cry went out that the governor's party had been spotted on the road. I scrambled down from my position on the mountain and stood at attention with the other men as the carriage carrying the governor and Colonel Kane came to a stop. As the governor alighted from his carriage, the men of the militia welcomed him and presented arms in honor of his coming. He looked a little discomfited, as if he weren't quite sure what to expect from us. To his credit, he gave a short extemporaneous speech, expressing his hope that the difficulties we had been encountering would soon be rectified."

"Was it then you spoke with Colonel Kane?" Emmett asked, picking up where Thorpe had left off.

"Not yet. Some of the boys in my company thought it would look impressive if a large group of militia men were gathered at each stop of the governor's carriage along his way through the canyon. This would make it look like our forces were greater than they actually were. As soon as the governor completed his speech, a group of us slipped away and dashed to the next encampment where the governor and Colonel Kane would be stopped by our militiamen."

Walker chuckled heartily this time. "We played that little joke two or three times, thinking ourselves very clever indeed. When the governor found it out later, he was not happy about being fooled."

Emmett started to interrupt again.

"Yes, Emmett, it was then I had the chance to speak with Colonel Kane. At the last encampment before the governor's carriage was to leave Echo Canyon, I approached Colonel Kane while he was visiting with some of the militia men. He looked older than the last time I had seen him. Lines rumpled his brow and his black wavy hair was beginning to gray at the temples. His bearing and manner were the same as I remembered, however—those of a proud, gentlemanly soldier. My respect for him was enormous.

"I introduced myself and we shook hands. After a few moments of small talk, I asked if he remembered the lad who had led his horse around the marshy bog to the river when he visited the Saints at Council Bluffs. He was quiet for a moment, his brow furrowed, then his face broke into a wide grin. 'Are you that lad?' he asked me. 'Indeed I am the same, sir,' I replied. 'And I want you to know that you have repaid me a hundredfold.' 'How have I done that?' Colonel Kane inquired, his dark eyes glittering in the dancing light of the fire. 'By accomplishing the impossible, sir. Bringing the governor to Utah without bringing the army.' Well, Colonel Kane threw back his head and laughed. Then he patted my shoulder, wished me well, and strode off into the darkness."

Walker stroked his heavy, gray-streaked beard wordlessly. None of the boys said anything, each of them lost in thought. As for myself, chills ran along my spine after hearing Walker's personal account of the war and his association with Colonel Kane. Before tonight, the Utah War had only been cold facts gleaned from a history book. Walker had made the war come alive for me. I would never again take an impersonal view of that struggle.

"And so you see, Thomas," said Walker abruptly, "Colonel Kane succeeded because he never gave up trying to accomplish that which he knew to be right and equitable. Be persistent in doing good, Thomas. A man of sound character and unflinching integrity will always be an asset to his country and to his God."

I saw a look of pride wash over Thomas's face.

"Yes, Father, I'll remember. And I'll try to do the very best job I can with the sheep ranch next year."

Walker nodded. "As for the rest of you," he said, eyeing each one of his children in turn, "I'll expect the best from you in all your endeavors. Look to your mothers as examples of charity, sacrifice, and hard work. Obey your parents. Heed strictly the tenets of the Church."

Walker's eye fell on Aunt Lizzy's three young boys. "Come here," Walker commanded, motioning to the three of them. Each one got up from his seat on the floor and went to his father. He embraced them as one, circling them in his arms.

"Now, my sons, tomorrow I will be leaving you for a little spell. While I am gone I want you to help your mother with every chore, willingly and happily. Will you do that?"

The boys' heads nodded in unison. I could see Reuben's eyes fill with tears. He clung to his father, struggling to keep the tears from flowing. Walker kissed each of them, holding their small faces in his hands. Although he kept his emotions concealed, I knew Walker's heart ached with the parting. My own eyes were wet, watching the scene before me.

Walker stood up, signaling the end of the evening's discussion. Aunt Lizzy rose to her feet beside him. She put her hand on his arm, and he covered it with his own work-hardened one. Thomas went to the fireplace and removed the Book of Mormon that rested there on the mantel, handing it to his father. Walker flipped through the pages, paused at a certain passage, then began to read aloud:

Behold, I can tell you—did not my father Alma believe in the words which were delivered by the mouth of Abinadi? And was he not a holy prophet? Did he not speak the words of God, and my father Alma believe them?

And according to his faith there was a mighty change wrought in his heart. Behold I say unto you that this is all true.

And behold, he preached the word unto your fathers, and a mighty change was also wrought in their hearts, and they humbled themselves and put their trust in the true and living God. And behold, they were faithful until the end; therefore they were saved.

And now behold, I ask of you, my brethren of the church, have ye spiritually been born of God? Have ye received his image in your countenances? Have ye experienced this mighty change in your hearts?

The tears rained down my face. This passage of scripture seemed meant especially for me. Had not I experienced a mighty change of heart? My heart was truly changed, my spirit lifted and strengthened. I had learned important lessons about repentance, humility, and obedience which would serve as a beacon for me through the remainder of my life. And I had come to love this remarkable family who lived life so simply and faithfully. I hated to leave Aunt Lizzy, Emmett, Thorpe, and dear, sweet Reuben. I wished we could take them all with us to the Walkers' home in Salt Lake.

When Walker finished reading, he closed the book and replaced it on the mantel. Without further comment the family knelt together in a circle, arms folded and eyes closed for prayer. Aunt Lizzy was voice, and she gave one of the most beautiful, heartfelt prayers I had ever heard.

I lay awake in bed for a long time that night thinking things over. When I fell asleep, it was with a grateful prayer on my lips.

CHAPTER SIXTEEN

WE WERE UP EARLY the next morning. Aunt Lizzy fixed a big, hot breakfast and packed a lunch basket for us to take on the road. Gus, Caleb, and the other hired men stood ready for last-minute instructions from Mr. Walker. The wagon, packed the night before, waited in the yard. The two collies raced about, yipping and frolicking in the early morning sunshine.

Although the sky was clear and the sun shone brightly, high above us in the east, it was a cold morning. I had put on my warmest shawl, but still the chill in the air seeped through. A thin layer of frost glazed the stalks of Aunt Lizzy's hollyhocks growing beside the door. I gazed at the solid little house, trying to memorize every detail of it. The house was still wrapped in morning shadows, looking snug and comfortable. I hated to leave it, for it represented security, solace, and spiritual reawakening to me.

As I stood looking at the house, Gus sauntered up to my side. I gave him a half-hearted smile.

"We're goin' to miss you folks around here," he said, squinting at a speck in the distance.

"Thank you, Gus. We'll miss you, too. Especially me. I've enjoyed my visit here at the ranch so much."

"I'm glad to hear that. Maybe you'll come back and visit us again one day."

I thought that was an unusual thing for Gus to say to me. Of course I'd be back to visit. Aunt Lizzy and her boys had come to mean a great deal to me.

"You have a nice trip, Miss Walker," Gus added, tipping his hat. Then he shuffled off toward the wagon where Thomas and Mr. Walker were working to secure the load.

"Thomas, tie down those boxes well," Walker was saying.

Mr. Walker and Thomas were on either side of the wagon, looping rope around a stack of boxes and tying it down. I watched as Caleb stepped forward to give Thomas a hand, holding the length of rope taut in his hands while Thomas knotted the end tightly to the rear of the wagon.

As he bent over the wagon, the morning sun captured the copper tones in Cabe's dark hair, turning it to burnished gold. I stared at him, mesmerized. Had he been wearing designer jeans and sunglasses, Cabe could easily have passed for a twentieth-century movie idol. I didn't know how I was going to manage until I saw him again.

Walker gave the loaded wagon a last quick appraisal with his eye, then he motioned to Lacy and me. "Into the wagon with you, daughters," he said brusquely.

Aunt Lizzy gave Lacy a big hug and kiss, and then the same to me. "Say hello to your mother for me, Katharine," she said. "And thank her for the gooseberry jam."

"I will, Aunt Lizzy." I hugged her again, squeezing my eyes shut against threatening tears.

Then Thorpe, Emmett and Reuben lined up for their hugs. "Be good boys, won't you?" I said in my best sisterly manner.

All three of the boys nodded their heads. Reuben threw his arms around my waist and clung to me. I bent down to kiss the top of his head. "I love you, Reuben," I whispered in his ear. When he looked up at me I could see tears glistening in his eyes.

"Say, Reuben, are you going to give anyone else a chance to say good-bye to Kate?" Caleb's voice came from behind me. When I turned, he was standing nearby grinning at the two of us.

"Aw, are you and Katharine gonna get all mushy?" Reuben asked him with a serious face.

"I don't know about Kate, but I'm certainly planning on it," Caleb replied, reaching out to rumple Reuben's hair.

Reuben pushed his hand away. "Well, I don't wanna watch this," he said emphatically, turning to walk away.

Caleb chuckled. I covered my mouth, trying not to laugh out loud. Reuben turned as he walked away, giving us both a disgusted look.

"I guess that pretty much discourages my plans for getting mushy," said Caleb, feigning a crestfallen countenance.

"You never had any such plans," I countered.

Cabe took my hand. "That's only because your father would pick me up by the scruff of my neck if I did," he answered, grinning.

"And you'd be well deserving of it," I quipped.

"You have a safe trip," Caleb said. The laughter disappeared from his eyes.

"I will. And you work hard on your studies."

"There'll be no doubt of that."

My confident demeanor faltered under Caleb's sober gaze. I dropped my eyes to the ground.

As if reading my thoughts, he clutched my hand tighter in his and said, "I'll come to see you, Kate, just as soon as I can."

I nodded, clinging to his promise.

He quickly kissed me, then helped me up into the wagon.

Lacy was already seated on the fresh straw and blanket that covered the floor of the wagon. Her face wore a sour expression as she moved aside to make room for me.

Caleb put a hand on the wagon and smiled up at me. "Just as soon as I can," he repeated quietly.

I wanted to jump down from the wagon and throw my arms around his neck, tell him how much he had come to mean to me and how much I was going to miss him. Instead, I just smiled back at him. The next moment Mr. Walker was swinging his tall frame up into the wagon. Thomas climbed up beside him, and before I could draw another breath the wagon lurched forward.

Aunt Lizzy and the boys waved until we rounded the bend and were out of sight. The dogs, barking furiously, raced after the wagon until Thorpe whistled for them to come back. I watched Buck bound out of sight, his tail wagging as he ran.

I settled down in my seat with a sigh. My eyes wandered to Lacy. She was leaning back against the side of the wagon, brushing bits of straw off the skirt of her dress. A slight frown wrinkled her brow. When she raised her head and saw me looking at her, her frown deepened and she deliberately turned away. Lacy had scarcely spoken to me since our disagreement over Caleb. In spite of my efforts, I had not been able to draw her out, to establish a rapport with her. I felt badly about that. I knew I should try to initiate some conversation with her, but I didn't feel like making the effort.

I closed my eyes and thought about Caleb. His tall, lean figure came easily to mind. My thoughts lingered over his dark hair, his wide hazel eyes, the curve of his nose and his impetuous grin. I smiled as I recalled the first time we'd met—and the arrogant impatience I had felt with him. Caleb had grown dear to me. He had taught me of the Good Shepherd in a way I had never contemplated before. He and the Walkers, by their example and their teaching, had turned my life around. I suddenly remembered the figurine of the shepherd with his lamb resting on Rachel Walker's mantelpiece in the parlor of her home. I realized then that it was no coincidence that she owned such a piece or that she chose to display it so prominently. The Good Shepherd played a pivotal role in the lives of all the Walkers.

The bed of straw where I rested was warm and cozy. I snuggled deeper into it, pulling my shawl around me. The sun was higher in the sky now, but the temperature was scarcely warmer. I found myself looking forward to reaching the Walkers' gracious home in Salt Lake City. In my mind's eye I built a picture of the house—the gabled roof, the tall rectangular windows, the inviting porch with its white wooden railing, and the handsome structure of ocher brick, yellow-pink in the afternoon shadows. I could see Rachel Walker bent over her herb garden, picking rosemary and thyme to season the family meals. Marinda and Jesse would be just rising, dressing in their work clothes for the day. Jesse would take his bucket to the barn where Elsie waited to be milked, while Marinda helped her mother with chores in the house. Suddenly, I could hardly wait to see Mrs. Walker, Marinda, and Jesse again. I wished Mr. Walker would hurry his horses along instead of allowing them to plod comfortably at their own pace.

I studied Mr. Walker's broad back. I had been wrong in my opinion of him. What I had first assumed to be harshness on his part was in reality an intense commitment to his family. I had thought Walker to be gruff and unapproachable, with his thunderous brows and his bushy beard, but I had mistaken his outward demeanor for his inner character. As I came to know him better, I recognized his deep concern for rearing his children properly. That same concern extended to neighbors and friends, evidenced to me by his ready willingness to help Mr. Gambit with his injured horse. The welfare of others always came first with Mr. Walker.

Mr. Walker and Thomas sat on the front seat of the wagon talking together. To help pass the time, I leaned forward to hear their conversation. They were discussing the sheep ranch, as I guessed they would be. I listened idly for a time, my ears on their words and my eyes taking in the scenery around me. I noticed a dusting of snow in the tops of the mountains that hadn't been there a few weeks ago when we arrived in Provo—like powdered sugar sprinkled on the peaks. Soon snow would cover the mountains completely, burying them in a coat of white.

"When we get home, Thomas, I want to see about selling our excess farm produce," Mr. Walker was saying. "We've hay and grain more than what we require for our own needs, and we should be able to turn a profit with the excess."

Thomas nodded his head thoughtfully.

"If we can clear a little extra ground this spring, we should be able to expand our opportunities further. 'Heaven never helps the man who will not act,'" said Walker resolutely.

I smiled at the quote Walker had just used. I was sure I knew who originated it. "Brother Brigham said that, didn't he?" I spoke up boldly from the bed of the wagon.

"No," Walker replied, turning to glance at me. "It was Sophocles who made that astute observation."

Sophocles? I shook my head in bemusement. I had never heard Mr. Walker quote anyone but Brother Brigham. I guessed living with the Walkers would continue to hold surprises for me.

"We could plow and plant the back quarter acre, Father. It should only take a couple of extra days," Thomas said, ignoring my interruption. "I've talked with some of the young farmers in town who are experimenting with a new and hardier strain of winter wheat. Perhaps we could plant a few acres in winter wheat, and then . . ."

Thomas went on to describe his ideas enthusiastically. My attention wandered away from the conversation, turning instead to the hunger pangs I was beginning to feel in my stomach. I eyed the covered basket of food Aunt Lizzy had packed for us, hoping lunchtime was not far away. I squinted up at the sun to determine its angle. It appeared to be almost directly overhead. Gray clouds were moving in, signaling a storm. A chilling wind had come up, carrying with it the breath of winter.

When I looked back to the road, my vision was blurred for a second or two from squinting into the sun. During those few seconds I thought I saw another wagon on the road ahead of us. I blinked and looked again. No, it wasn't a wagon, but a small buggy, coming toward us on the other side of the road. It was still some distance off, but close enough for me to see the buggy's shiny black color and the single horse pulling it along.

I thought it curious to see a lone horse and buggy on the road. We were miles from Provo by this time, with even further to go before reaching Salt Lake. The road between Salt Lake and Provo was long and usually traveled on horseback or by wagon. For some reason the sight of the buggy filled me with a strange foreboding. I shifted uneasily on my seat of straw.

"I'm hungry. Can we stop for supper now?" Lacy's whining voice startled me. For an instant I thought she was addressing me.

"In another half hour or so," Walker answered her. "We still have a fair piece to cover before we stop to rest the horses."

Lacy slouched down in the straw, a scowl on her face. She muttered something I could not hear.

"It won't be long," I said to her in a consoling voice. "Look. The sun's nearly overhead."

"Harump," is all she replied.

The sky was darkening rapidly now. Low black clouds covered the horizon. My eyes shifted from the sky to the buggy coming toward us. It was close enough now for me to see that it carried a single occupant. A man in a dark suit, his head bare, was handling the reins.

Mr. Walker noticed it too and said, "I wonder who that is. Do you recognize him, Thomas?"

"No," Thomas replied, shaking his head. "I don't think I've ever seen that horse and rig before."

"We'll stop to say hello, then," Walker said.

A trail of goosebumps went down my arms. For some reason which I didn't understand, I hoped Walker would not stop and talk to the stranger in the buggy. The feeling of foreboding I had experienced earlier pressed upon me.

Thomas and Mr. Walker continued to converse, but not a word registered with me. My attention was riveted on the advancing buggy and the man driving it. I heard Lacy make some comment at my side, but I paid no attention to it.

The buggy was nearly abreast of us when Walker called out a greeting. The driver's face was hidden in shadow so that I could not at first see his features. But I knew he was looking intently at me. I could feel his gaze. He reined his horse to a stop just a few feet from us. It was then that I saw his face clearly. I froze, my fingers gripping the side of the wagon. Saying nothing, the old man reached into his vest and pulled out a pocket watch attached to a chain. A large black iron key hung from the chain.

The man snapped open his pocket watch to glance at it. Then his eyes captured and bore into mine. Deep, dark, bottomless eyes that held my gaze locked in his. In that instant I knew exactly what was going to happen.

"Wait!" I cried out. "Not now. Not yet!"

I felt myself falling forward, as if his eyes were pulling me into their very depths. A tumbling sensation seized hold of me, and I closed my eyes tightly against it, resisting its pull with all my will. Still the sensation persisted. Tumbling. Turning. Falling through space and time.

"Caleb!" I shrieked. The word was muffled in my ears. It echoed farther and farther away until I could not hear the sound of it at all.

The hum of a small plane's engine overhead brought me abruptly to my feet. I shaded my eyes with my hand and looked up into the flawlessly blue sky. The plane skimmed past unobstructed to my view. With a start, I realized that there was not a trace of a cloud where only seconds before the sky had been lowering with an approaching storm. I looked around me, jerking my head this way and that. Where was I? Where was the dusty, rutted road we'd just been traveling?

A plump young woman dressed in rust-colored slacks and an orange blouse was sitting nearby on the grass. She looked up briefly from the paperback book in her hands. If she noticed the frantic darting of my eyes, she didn't indicate it. She went back to her reading, oblivious to my distress.

Slowly the thoughts spinning in my head took shape. Piece by piece I remembered coming to the cemetery, strolling about, then sitting down to rest under the ivy-cloaked tree. The memories came into my mind fragmented, like looking into a cracked mirror. With jarring abruptness, I suddenly remembered the old man with the key. I whirled around to look at Brigham Young's grave. No one was about. No old man. No gate set in the spiked iron fence. No jingle of a key in the lock.

I frowned and rubbed my eyes hard with the palm of my hand. Had I dreamed everything? Had I fallen asleep under the old gnarled tree and dreamed all of it? That was impossible! Impossible! I could not have dreamed up the old man. I could not have imagined Mr. Walker, Thomas, Reuben, and the others. They were as real to me as my own family. As real and as dear. A wave of despair washed over me as Caleb's face pushed to the forefront of my mind. Caleb with his steady manner, his quick sense of humor, his compassion, his spiritual strength. Surely Caleb was not a dream! Suddenly I felt forsaken and alone. I clung to Caleb's memory, unwilling to surrender it to the present which pressed unmercifully upon me.

A breeze came up, rustling the leaves of the trees in the cemetery. Though it was only a light April breeze, it chilled me through and unconsciously I pulled my navy blue suit jacket tighter around me. My blue jacket. My plaid skirt. I brushed my hand over the smooth fabric. What had happened to the ankle-length homespun calico I didn't even dare to contemplate.

Drawing a deep trembling breath, I started toward the street which lay outside the cemetery. The closer I got to the gate, the faster became my pace. I was anxious now to be gone from this place. To leave it behind me. To leave the memories behind me. I could not deal with the memories just now. They were too vivid. Too tied to my emotions. I slipped through the black wrought-iron gate, carefully averting my eyes from the initials of President Young woven into the ornamental ironwork. I hastily walked down First Avenue, not allowing myself to think about the ground beneath my feet—the ground that should have been a dusty dirt road, packed and hardened by countless carriage wheels, instead of concrete and asphalt.

I hurried faster, nearly running, until I reached my car parked at the curb. I fumbled in my pocket for the keys, jammed them into the ignition, and heard the engine leap to life. The tires screamed as I jerked the wheel around.

My mind was reeling as I drove the short distance to the college. I hurried into the building, raced up the short flight of stairs and into my office.

Sally was sitting at her desk, her fingers marching over the keyboard. She paused when she saw me enter the room.

"Where have you been?" she asked in her clipped military manner. "Bowen's been asking for you all afternoon. He's hopping mad."

"What time is it, Sally?" I asked breathlessly.

Sally consulted her wristwatch. "It's after four. I tried to call you at the Historical Office, but they told me you hadn't been there."

I put my fist to my head. "Oh, my gosh. The diaries. I completely forgot about them."

A frown appeared on Sally's brow. "How could you forget about the diaries? I thought that was the reason you left the office. Are you feeling all right, Kallie? You look a bit pale."

"Yes, I'm fine. That is, not really. I guess I'm not really feeling very well."

Sally gave me a perplexed look.

"I just need to catch my breath," I told her. I walked over to my desk and sat down. My eye fell on the stack of papers piled on the desk. The bold writing across the top sheet set my hands trembling: THE UTAH WAR.

Mr. Walker's face leaped into my mind. I heard his strong voice recounting an incident from the war. I shut my eyes tight against the image.

"Kallie?" Sally's voice came to my ears as if from a great distance. "Kallie, do you want me to get you a glass of water or something?"

"No, I . . . perhaps I ought to go home," I replied in a raspy voice. "I feel a little faint. Would you tell Bowen that I'll be here early in the morning? Tell him I wasn't feeling well. Tell him I'll have those diary entries on his desk first thing tomorrow morning."

Sally stared at me as I stumbled out of my chair, collected my purse, and headed for the door. I prayed that I wouldn't run into Professor Bowen. I didn't think I could face a confrontation with him.

The drive home seemed to take an unusually long time. I squirmed in the seat of my car, deliberately holding back on the gas pedal. I was anxious to arrive home, but at the same time I was almost afraid to get there. What if my parents' house was not there, not where it should be? What if I was suspended somewhere between the past and the present? I willed my foot not to bear down on the accelerator. It was a huge effort. Patience, I counseled myself. Just be patient . . .

A few moments later the house came into sight—the familiar red brick rambler nearly hidden by the tall spruces in the yard. From the road I could see Mom's brightly-colored tulips growing from the rock planter box alongside the porch. I heaved an audible sigh of relief. I parked my Mustang in the driveway, hurried to the back door, and let myself inside.

"Mom? Mom, where are you?" I shouted.

"Here, Kallie," came Mom's voice from the hallway. An instant later she appeared, carrying a dust cloth in her hand.

"Oh, Mom!" I cried as I hugged her. "I've missed you so much. I can't tell you how good it is to see you," I said in a rush of words.

Mom patted my shoulder. "It's good to see you too, Kallie." She pulled away from me and looked intently into my face. "Is something wrong?"

Her expression showed mild concern, but nothing more to suggest that she had been unduly alarmed about me. I realized with a start that she must be thinking I was behaving quite strangely.

"Uh, it's just that I've had a difficult day," I replied, dropping my gaze. "A little hectic at work, that's all."

When I looked up into her face again, I saw her concern fade. "Well, a good hot meal will do you a world of good," she said briskly.

I kissed her cheek. "That's exactly what I need, Mom."

"Dinner will be ready soon, dear." She bustled back down the hall, leaving me to myself.

I sighed contentedly. It was good to be home. My eyes took in the familiar surroundings, bringing me a measure of peace. I walked into the living room and sank down into Mom's brand new Queen Anne chair. Its fabric was silky smooth, not like the coarse horsehair chairs in Mrs. Walker's parlor. Mrs. Walker's kindly face formed in my mind. I pictured her black hair drawn up into a neat bun, her smiling eyes, her humble demeanor. I felt her warm embrace as she hugged me good-night.

A sudden sense of loss enveloped me. Mrs. Walker had disappeared from my life, along with all the others I had grown to love. Tears welled up in my eyes. No, the intense emotions I was feeling were not imaginary. Surely the Walker family had not been a figment of my imagination. Their every word, their every action burned in my mind with brilliant clarity. I didn't know how it had all happened, but I knew my experience with the Walkers did happen. The memories were too overpowering to be less than real.

I moved through the remainder of the day in something of a daze. I was as thrilled to see Dad when he arrived home from work as I had been to see Mom. The talk at the dinner table was reassuringly ordinary. I didn't say much. I mostly listened to Mom and Dad discuss the events of their day and their comments concerning my brothers who were away.

I retired to my room early. The familiarity of my own things was comforting. My eyes followed the trail of ruffles along the bottom of the mauve curtains covering my bedroom window. I passed a hand over the rough bindings of my books, set in their customary place on the shelf above my bed. My fingers brushed the polished cherrywood headboard as I eased down onto my bed. How soft and comfortable the mattress was—no straw tick here, I thought, feeling a trace of disappointment. I lay down, still dressed in my street clothing, and closed my eyes. In my mind's eye, I reassembled every detail of the bedroom I had shared with Lacy and Marinda—the colorful rag rug covering the wood floor, the bedside table on which rested the blue-flowered bowl and pitcher, and the big trunk squatting at the foot of the bed, filled with homespun dresses. Although I was glad to be home in my own bed, still I felt a longing for that other time and place I had known.

That night I dreamed about Caleb Hollister. I dreamed we were walking hand in hand through Aunt Lizzy's fields. Caleb was talking to me about the Good Shepherd, and I was entranced by his every word. His eyes captured the green of the fields, and his hair gleamed in the sun like polished chestnuts. When I awoke at dawn, tears were wet upon my cheeks.

CHAPTER SEVENTEEN

I SEARCHED EVERY CORNER of my office for the notes on Colonel Thomas L. Kane, but they were nowhere to be found. Curiously, I was not upset by it. I knew more about Thomas Kane and his part in the Utah War than any history book could ever teach me because I'd heard a first-hand account of it. Of course it would be quite impossible to put down on paper my thoughts and feelings concerning the war. I couldn't write objectively about it now; I was too intimately acquainted with the people and circumstances involved.

"Do you plan to do the research over again?" Sally asked me from behind her computer.

"No. I don't," I replied.

Sally looked puzzled. "What are you going to do, then?"

"I'm not sure yet."

Sally had been giving me suspicious glances ever since I'd come in to work that morning. I didn't think I'd done anything to warrant her curiosity, but apparently something about me aroused her interest. She said nothing more, but continued to watch me as I shuffled papers from one end of my desk to the other, looking for the notes.

"Did you know that Colonel Kane and Brigham Young formed a fast friendship?" I mumbled as I checked the crack between my desk and the wall.

"No," Sally answered slowly.

"Yes, they did. And Brother Brigham told him that the Lord had sent Kane to Utah with a work to do for the Saints."

"Really?" Sally's eyebrows arched.

I nodded vigorously, my eyes still sweeping the room for the lost notes.

"Kallie?"

I looked up. Sally was eyeing me with a grave look.

"What's going on with you, Kallie?"

"What do you mean?"

"I mean, why are you behaving so strangely?"

I was genuinely taken aback by her question. "I didn't know I was."

"Come on, Kallie. You're not in the habit of discussing your research with me. Especially in such mystical tones."

"Mystical? I don't know what you're talking about, Sally."

"It's your whole attitude. You just seem—different."

"I guess I'm a little preoccupied." I sat back in my seat behind the desk. Mr. Walker's face appeared in my mind, his eyes sharp and solemn. "I'll be glad when this project is finished," I said to Sally.

"It'll have to be soon. I know Professor Bowen isn't planning to stay the summer."

"I suppose he's nearly finished with the research he came out here for," I replied, frowning. I thought about his file of anti-Mormon literature. Bowen was anxious for me to add to it by providing him with "appropriate" excerpts from pioneer diaries. That thought weighed like a heavy stone in my stomach.

Sally straightened a page from the manuscript which rested on her desk.

"You're not a Mormon, are you, Sally?" I asked on impulse.

She looked startled by my question. "No. I don't practice any religion."

"What do you think of Professor Bowen's proposed book?" I asked, leaning forward on my elbows.

Sally shrugged her shoulders. "I don't know. I don't have any feelings about it one way or the other."

"Do you think he's presented his information in an impartial manner?"

Sally gave me a perplexed look.

"Let me put it another way." I rubbed my forehead, trying to couch my thoughts into words. "If you knew that someone was deliberately trying to persuade others to his point of view by presenting half-truths and slanted arguments, what would you do about it?"

"Nothing, I suppose," she answered after a long pause. "People are free to believe what they want to believe."

"Even if the information given to them is false?"

Sally stared at me, her eyes as dark and hard as dried raisins. "Are you accusing Bowen of giving false information?"

"I'm not accusing anyone. The question is a moral one. It has to do with personal integrity." I could feel the color rise in my face as my agitation mounted.

"I think," Sally answered slowly, "that one should mind his own business and attend to his own work."

"Yes," I replied, nodding my head. "That is what I thought, too. Yesterday."

Sally shook her head at me. No more was said between us, and a moment later I heard the martial step of her fingers on the keyboard.

Neither of us spoke again the rest of the morning. I took a short lunch, then worked steadily through the afternoon. I had difficulty staying with my task, for my thoughts were far removed from it. I kept wishing I could talk with Caleb; the answers were always so clear-cut for him. He never seemed to be hampered by gradations of shade. The answer was either black or white, wrong or right, and he acted accordingly. I wished he could advise me now.

I remembered his explanation of the parable of the Good Shepherd, and the light in his eyes as he recounted it for me. I recalled the intense suffering I'd felt, wondering if I was numbered among Christ's sheep. The night Caleb and I found Reuben injured in the cave, I had promised the Lord that I would obey his every commandment. I realized now that my feelings in that regard had not changed, and my commitment had not lessened. This came as a surprise to me. I had not expected to find within myself a changed heart.

If my experience with the Walkers had not really happened, then why this change in me? It did happen. It *must* have happened. What else could account for the spiritual stirrings I felt? While I sat pondering these things, the time slipped by. It was only when Sally turned off her computer and began to gather up her belongings that I noticed the afternoon shadows stealing across our office walls.

"I'll see you tomorrow, Sally," I said absently.

Sally nodded and walked out of the office, closing the door behind her.

I left shortly afterward. I was grateful that I hadn't seen Professor Bowen all day. I'd heard him come into his office between classes, but he'd stayed there working and hadn't disturbed Sally or me. Traffic was heavy as I made my way home on the freeway.

Mom, Dad and I ate a leisurely meal together, then I went to my room to relax. I hadn't been there long when the telephone rang. Mom answered it.

"It's for you, Kallie," she called from the kitchen.

"Thanks, Mom. I'll get it in here."

Terri Gilbert was on the line. "How's it going, Kallie?" she greeted me.

"Good. Hey, it's great to talk to you!" I said enthusiastically. I hadn't realized how much I had missed visiting with Terri while I'd been away at the Walkers'.

Terri chuckled at my ebullience. "I thought I'd go out for a coke. Do you want to come along?"

I wanted to go, but I was exhausted from my day at work. "I don't think so, Terri. I'm dead tired."

"Okay. Have you managed to get out of that trip to California yet?"

I knew her question was asked innocently enough, but for some reason it rankled me. "Well, actually, I've decided to go. My parents are counting on it."

"You're kidding," Terri exclaimed. "You *hate* going on those trips with your parents."

I hardly knew how to respond. "I think I ought to go this time."

"That's a new one," Terri replied. I could hear the sarcasm in her voice.

"Yeah, well, it might be kind of fun," I stammered.

"All right. You're sure you don't want to come with me, just for the ride?"

"No, I'd better not."

"Well, let's take in a show tomorrow night, or something. Do you want to?" she asked brightly.

"Sure. That'll be fine."

"Okay. I'll talk to you tomorrow."

"Yeah. See you."

I hung up the phone, feeling oddly out of sorts with Terri. I pictured her sitting in her lavishly furnished house, with her long, wavy blonde hair combed perfectly into place. The image disturbed me, though I didn't know why it should. I sat on the edge of my bed, thinking back on some of the activities Terri and I had participated in. I felt uncomfortable even recalling many of them, and I was glad Caleb didn't know about some of the things we'd done. I doubted that he would have looked on me with much favor if he had, and I knew he wouldn't have approved of Terri's actions. That was it—that was what was nagging me about Terri. I would have been embarrassed to have Caleb meet my best friend.

My face flushed thinking about it. I focused my thoughts on Caleb. How I missed him! How I wished I could see him again, talk with him, feel his arms around me. My mind went over every detail of his strong face. I yearned to be with him, to be near him as he tended the sheep or went about his work on the ranch. I knew he would be preparing for his studies in law under Dusenberry's tutelage, and I wanted to be there to share in his excitement.

I lay down on the bed and flung my arm across my eyes. Tears threatened; I willed them back only with great effort. As much as I wanted to believe that my experiences with the Walkers were real, that Caleb was real, there was no way of being certain. Was I longing for someone who did not exist except in my imagination? I flopped over onto my stomach, picking absently at a speck of lint trapped in a crease of my lavender quilted bedspread. If my experience with the Walkers really took place, how did it come about? And why? But if I had only imagined the whole episode, or dreamed it, why was the memory of it seared into my mind?

I couldn't make any sense out of either argument, so I gave up trying. Rising from the bed, I quickly changed into my nightclothes. Pulling the curtain aside, I glanced out into the night. The moon was full and a few stars twinkled through a thick cloud cover. I could smell rain in the air; a spring shower was brewing. It was hard for me to remember that it was early May, not mid-November when Mr. Walker was anxious to return from Provo to Salt Lake. I thrust the image of Walker out of my mind. I wouldn't allow myself to think about it any more tonight. It was all too confusing for me to sort out.

I rummaged in the bottom drawer of my bureau, looking for the Bible I had carelessly put there many months ago. Retrieving it, I sat down and turned to the book of John in the New Testament. I read again the passage about the Good Shepherd. Then I knelt down and offered a prayer. When I was finished, I put out the light and drifted into a fitful sleep.

The next morning I overslept and was late for work. To my dismay, Professor Bowen was standing beside my desk when I arrived.

"Good morning, sir," I said hastily, hoping he wouldn't notice my tardiness.

"Ms. Garrett," he growled, "you're late. You were also late in returning from your lunch break the other day. Are you planning to make this a habit?"

"No, Professor Bowen, I'm not. It's just that I . . ."

He put up a hand to cut me off. "Please, spare me your excuses. I'm interested only in knowing if you've finished your work in the diaries."

I gulped, and the sound of it was distinct. Sally sat at her desk, watching our exchange with interest. I swallowed again nervously. "No, I'm not through," I replied in a surprisingly calm voice.

"And why not?" he demanded, glaring at me. I noticed the color begin to rise in his face. "I've warned you before, Ms. Garrett. My time here is limited, and we still have much to do."

"I understand that, but . . ."

"I'll expect your notes from the diaries on my desk before you leave this evening."

I nodded slowly.

He cast Sally a gruff glance and disappeared into his office.

I slumped in my chair. The kinds of details he wanted from me were going to be difficult to dredge up. And truthfully, I no longer was interested in pursuing the project. If Professor Bowen wished to write a derogatory book about the early Mormons in Utah, it was his prerogative to do so. But I didn't wish to be a party to it. My experiences with the Walkers had convinced me of the genuine commitment and faith most Latter-day Saints possessed.

Suddenly, the thought struck me that today was no different than it had been in times past. My own parents had always been examples of Christlike living. But I had not been paying attention. I had not given heed to their teachings, even though they had lovingly and tenderly tried to encourage me. I saw my sins in all their scarlet apparel—but I knew that through Christ's atoning sacrifice, I could be forgiven and my sins washed away.

The struggling of soul I had experienced gave way to a sweet peace and a desire to do what I knew was right.

Righteous living begins with righteous choices, that much I knew. And here, placed before me, was an opportunity to make a righteous choice, to exercise some degree of personal integrity. It had been a long time since I'd taken a stand for truth or righteousness.

Abruptly, I got up from my chair. I knew my face expressed the determination I felt. I gathered up Professor Bowen's file of anti-Mormon literature and started toward the door with it.

"What are you going to do, Kallie?" Sally's voice was unusually animated.

I turned around to face her. "What I should have done from the start."

Sally's eyes grew big. "You're going to speak your mind to Professor Bowen, aren't you?"

"That's right," I said.

"You'll be sorry, Kallie. You'll lose your job."

"Maybe. But I'll gain my self-respect."

I left the room while Sally sat shaking her head. In spite of my determination, my hands trembled as I crossed the hall to Professor Bowen's office. He answered my timid knock with a curt command to enter.

I found him leaning back in his chair, reading from a handful of my notes. His brows came together when he saw me standing inside the doorway.

"Yes?" he said impatiently.

"Could I speak with you for a moment?" My heart fluttered like a bird cornered in the bush.

He indicated with a wave of his hand for me to take a chair.

I sat on the edge of the leather-bound chair, my knees knocking. "I've come to tell you that I'd prefer not to continue our research in the direction we've been taking."

He looked genuinely startled. "You'd prefer not to . . ." he repeated, scratching his balding head.

"Yes." I held his files up so he could see them. "The kinds of things you're writing about the Latter-day Saints are not entirely accurate, sir. You're not giving a true picture."

Bowen's face flooded with red. He stood up and took a step toward me. "You insolent pup. What gives you the right to dictate what I will or will not write?"

"I'm not dictating to you, Professor Bowen. I'm telling you how I feel about it. I can't be part of a project which compromises my values and beliefs."

"Then, by heaven, you shall not be a part of it!" he thundered. The veins in his bulbous nose swelled, and his lips quivered with rage. Even the sparse hair on his head bristled. "You're fired, Ms. Garrett! Fired!"

His words stung me even though I was expecting them. I struggled to compose my voice. "I'm sorry to cause you this inconvenience." I handed him the file of literature. He snatched it from my hand.

"Get out of here, Ms. Garrett. I've heard enough of your whining."

I stood up and walked stiffly out of the room.

When I returned to my corner of the office, I found Sally sitting motionless at her desk. Her expression told me that she'd heard the whole conversation. I silently started to collect my personal belongings from the desk.

"Now what?" Sally asked in a flat tone of voice.

"I guess I'll be looking for another job," I replied, giving her a half-hearted smile.

She stared at me for a moment, then asked, "Do you think what you just did is going to change anything?"

I paused, thinking about her question. "No," I finally answered. "I'm sure Professor Bowen will still write his book. I'm sure people will continue to believe what they want about the Latter-day Saints. But I feel good about the choice I've made. In fact, it's the best I've felt in a long while."

I straightened the notes I had made on the Utah War into a

tidy pile. Then I stacked the books I'd been using for research next to them on the corner of the desk.

"If the notes on Colonel Kane show up, give them to Professor Bowen for me, will you?"

"Bowen didn't tell you?" Sally asked. "He found the notes in the bottom drawer of his desk, underneath a pile of papers."

I smiled, shaking my head. "I'm not surprised. I figured Bowen had them all along and had just misplaced them." I gathered the rest of my things, cast a final glance around the tiny office, and started for the door.

"Kallie?"

I turned around.

"It was nice working with you," Sally said quietly.

"You, too, Sally."

I took a firm hold of the knob and let myself out.

CHAPTER EIGHTEEN

I FELT LIGHT-HEARTED as I drove home from the office. Even though I had no idea where to start looking for a new job, I wasn't too concerned about finding one. I pulled into the driveway and parked the car. The mid-morning sun seemed to heighten the color of Mom's spring flowers growing beside the porch. Red tulips alternated with yellow daffodils to create a brilliant visual pattern. I paused to enjoy the blaze of color. The fresh smell of a neighbor's newly-cut grass lingered in the air. The scent and sight of spring lifted my spirits even more.

"Mom?" I called, as I came through the back door.

"Kallie, is that you?" I heard her reply from somewhere in the depths of the house.

"It's me."

Mom came scurrying into the kitchen. "For heaven's sake, what are you doing home this time of day?"

"Don't look so worried, Mom. Everything's fine. I quit my job."

"You *what?*" she replied, her eyes wide.

"Well, technically I got fired."

"Fired!" Mom shouted.

"It's okay, Mom. I feel good about it."

I set my purse on a kitchen chair and walked into the living room. Mom trailed behind me, open-mouthed.

"What do you mean, you got fired?" she asked. "What happened?"

I dropped into our comfortable wing-backed chair. The TV was on, and I caught a glimpse of a talk show host questioning a gorgeously-gowned Hollywood starlet. "There arose a little difference of opinion between Professor Bowen and myself," I explained. "You would have been proud of the way I handled it, Mom."

She sat down in the chair next to mine. "Tell me what happened, Kallie."

"It's a long story, and the reasons behind it are kind of confusing. The important part is that I know I did the right thing." I patted Mom's hand in the same reassuring way she often patted mine.

Mom looked a bit bewildered.

"Now that I have some extra time, let's spend it together, Mom. You want to go shopping this afternoon? We can have lunch out and do some shopping."

"All right," Mom answered slowly.

"And you know what?" I continued enthusiastically. "I can give you a hand around the house while I'm not working. I bet there's a million jobs I can help you with. Why, I can clean the ashes out of the fireplace, and turn the mattresses, and churn the butter."

"Churn the butter?" Mom repeated, laughing.

"Oh, Mom, you can't imagine all the chores I know how to do. I can be a big help to you."

She just smiled at me.

It was a wonderful afternoon. We talked and laughed as we hadn't done in years, and we even bought silly matching T-shirts with big yellow ducks appliquéd on the fronts. I told Mom how much I loved her and appreciated all she'd done for me. She hugged me and said she loved me, too.

After dinner, Terri Gilbert picked me up for the movie we'd decided to see. When I got into her car, the smell of cigarette smoke assaulted me. The odor clung to my clothing and hair. I knew Terri smoked occasionally, but I disliked the malodorous habit.

"Hey, that's some snazzy T-shirt," Terri said as she slid into the driver's seat.

I knew from her tone of voice that she intended the comment to be sarcastic. "You want one for yourself? I'll pick one up for you," I retorted.

"I was kidding, Kallie. What's with the shirt, anyway?"

"I like it. That's all."

Terri reached over to my shirt and stretched the shoulders up for a better look at the picture and the slogan printed across the front. "'Going Quackers.' What does that mean?"

"It doesn't mean anything," I replied, pulling away from her grasp. "It's just a big yellow duck with an exasperated look on its face. Going quackers, you know. A play on words."

One of Terri's blonde brows hooked up sardonically. She pulled out of our driveway and into the flow of traffic. "You a little edgy tonight?" she asked, glancing at me.

"Maybe. I lost my job," I replied simply.

"You're kidding, aren't you?"

I shook my head. "Nope. I got fired this morning."

"What for?" Terri asked. Her eyes darted to my face, then back to the road.

"It has to do with the book Bowen is writing. He was putting things in his book which are not altogether true."

Terri glanced at me again. "So?"

"So I told him I didn't want to be a party to his dishonesty." I watched Terri's face, waiting to see her reaction.

Her expression remained the same, except for a slight lift of her brow. "He fired you for that?"

"Yep. I guess he didn't appreciate my criticism of his work."

"Why did you say it?" She increased her speed now that we were on the open highway.

"Because it was true. Because I couldn't let it go unsaid."

"That doesn't make sense, Kallie. Why do you care what Bowen writes?"

I paused before answering, considering whether or not I should tell her about my experience with the Walkers. "Haven't you ever felt something so strongly that you had to act on it, no matter what the consequences?" I asked slowly.

"Yeah, sure. I felt that way last Friday night with Brandon Davis." Terri laughed harshly.

Her comment settled any question in my mind about discussing the Walkers with her.

"Hey, I'm sorry," Terri said, touching my arm. "Seriously, what are you going to do about a job?"

"I don't know yet. I'll look around," I said stiffly.

We had nearly reached the movie theater by now. Terri slowed to make the turn into the theater parking lot.

"I know just the thing to cheer you up," she said brightly. "We'll throw a big party next Sunday night. Invite everyone we know. You haven't forgotten, have you, that Kevin is bringing his roommate home with him for the weekend? We'll invite him to the party."

"Sure, Terri," I replied sarcastically. "Your brother's friend is really going to love your kind of party."

"He might—if he's not an old stuffed shirt like Kevin."

"No thanks. I'm not interested in partying or in meeting Kevin's roommate."

"What are you talking about, Kallie?" Terri replied, nudging my arm. "Kevin says his roommate is a cool guy. How many cool guys have you met in the last little while? None, right?"

Caleb's face sprang to mind. It brought an excruciating wave of loneliness. I turned my face to the window so Terri couldn't see the pain in my eyes.

"A party is just what you need, Kallie. It will take your mind off your troubles," Terri insisted as she wheeled the car into an empty parking space.

We climbed out of the car and started toward the theater.

The night air was chilly, raising goosebumps along my arms. I wished I'd brought my sweater with me. Or a shawl. I could almost feel the fuzzy softness of Katharine Walker's wool shawl around me. It was a curious thing how Katharine's clothing had fit me so well. I hoped she didn't mind that I had worn her dresses. I wondered what the real Katharine Walker would have thought of Caleb. If she had known him, would she be missing him like I was? Or did her heart belong solely to lean, lanky Horace Baumgarten, her beau in Salt Lake?

I was glad when we entered the cool darkness of the theater and took our seats. It felt good to have my mind occupied with nothing more weighty than the capriciousness I saw on the screen. I settled deeper into my seat, determined to let the movie chase away my blues.

I spent the next day helping Mom clean house. As I worked, I thought about the evening Terri and I had shared together. I had come home feeling disappointed because I had not been able to tell her about my experiences with Caleb and the Walkers. I had wanted to tell her everything—to get the whole story off my chest. But I sensed that she would not be receptive to it or able to appreciate the changes in me. Nevertheless, it was clear to me that I had changed. I noticed that my relationship with my parents was not the same as before. I recognized a difference in my feelings for the gospel. And, sadly, I felt a change in my attitude toward Terri. She and I were no longer alike; a fundamental difference existed between us that hadn't been apparent before. I realized that Terri's friendship was no longer attractive to me.

That realization was unsettling. Terri and I had been best friends for several years. But at the same time, I felt an odd sense of pride. I was moving away from the person I used to be, becoming more the person I wanted to be. Without a doubt, the Walker family had contributed to that evolution. They were people of simple, childlike faith. Their example of obedience and sacrifice was an inspiration to me. I admired their self-reliance and their ability to work together to make the family unit successful.

By now, Mr. Walker would have arrived back home from Provo. In my mind's eye I could see him hitching the big strawberry roan draft horses to the hay wagon. He and Thomas would be busy laboring on the farm, clearing the fields and storing the last of the crops.

I wondered how Thomas was getting along. I smiled to myself as I recalled his somewhat stubborn and skeptical nature. Soon he would be returning to Provo to run Aunt Lizzy's sheep ranch. I knew his heart was with farming, and I admired his integrity in respecting his father's wishes.

Lacy, too, would be home by now. I felt a pang of guilt as I pictured her cold, angry countenance. I had earned her displeasure and I should have made more of an effort at reconciliation. I wondered what kind of relationship Katharine and Lacy had had before I intruded. Had they been close, and had I provoked an estrangement between them? I silently apologized to Katharine Walker if I had.

I paused in the midst of scrubbing the kitchen floor, letting the memories flood through my mind. I pictured the younger Walker children, Jesse and Marinda, who held a special place in my heart, as well as Aunt Lizzy's boys. I chuckled aloud remembering Emmett, Thorpe, and Reuben racing outside to greet their father on his arrival at Aunt Lizzy's.

Reuben's memory evoked my tenderest feelings; I missed him perhaps more than any of the other children. At this moment I could almost feel his soft hair against my cheek, his little arms around my neck. Reuben had been the means of teaching me a great lesson. His devotion to the one sick sheep had taught me about the Savior's unconditional love. As in the story of the shepherd who left the ninety and nine to seek after the one sheep which was lost, I had been the sheep in need of rescue.

"My, but you're helpful today," Mom smiled, coming into the kitchen where I was bent over my task.

Her intrusion scattered my chain of memories. "You haven't seen anything yet, Mom," I replied, giving her a smile.

"I don't believe I've ever seen this floor so sparkling clean," she observed.

"Do you realize how easy we have things, Mom? When you think back to a hundred years ago or so, the women then had to work in their homes all day long. They worked hard, too, cooking over a coal stove, raising their own food, making their own candles and soap. Imagine trying to run a household without electricity or indoor plumbing. Those women were pretty remarkable. They possessed stamina and great strength of character."

"I hadn't thought of it in exactly that way," Mom replied.

"Have you ever thought what kind of woman you'd be if you lived back then, Mom?"

Mom considered the question for a moment. "Well, I guess I'd be pretty much the same person I am now. Wouldn't you?"

My thoughts went back to Lacy Walker. I recalled an incident which had occurred during one of the Walkers' family prayers. I remembered Lacy kneeling with the rest of her family in prayer, only Lacy's eyes were wide open and her expression clearly showed that her heart was far from the humble sentiments being offered. Eventually I came to understand that Lacy was unmoved by things of a spiritual nature. She had grown rebellious, proud, and resistant to her parents' teachings—much as I had been, I realized with a stab of guilt.

"I don't know, Mom," I answered quietly.

She leaned down to kiss my cheek. "I'm sure you would have been a fine young woman."

She left to return to her own chores after that. We worked in the house until dinnertime. Afterward, I read for an hour or so, straightened up my room, and went to bed.

The next morning I awoke early. The sky outside my window

was gray and a drizzling rain fell. I had planned to spend the morning working outside in Mom's flower bed, but it looked like the damp weather would mean a change of plans. I considered getting the newspaper to study the employment section for some leads on a job, but I was too comfortable lounging in my bed to stir just yet.

I closed my eyes to think about Caleb. A fuzzy, muddled image came to mind. I sat up abruptly, painstakingly framing his face in my thoughts. I could see his tall, sturdy build and dark brown hair, but his features refused to come into focus. I desperately worked to recreate his likeness, but his face lingered just beyond the edge of my consciousness where I couldn't reach it, like the dim memory of a dream.

I tried to picture Mr. Walker. To my consternation, it was the same situation. And the same with Thomas, Lacy, and the others. I leaped out of bed, alarmed over the sudden dimming of their memory. The experiences I'd shared with the Walkers were still vivid and clear, but all of the players' faces were hazy.

I threw on my bathrobe and went out to the kitchen. I could hear the murmur of Mom and Dad talking together in their bedroom. I poured myself a cold glass of milk and sat down at the table. What had happened? Why couldn't I remember the Walkers' faces? Why couldn't I remember Caleb's? I put my chin in my hands, staring glumly out the window. The rain pattered against the kitchen windowpane. I felt as bleak and gray as the weather outside.

"You're up early," Mom said from the kitchen doorway.

I was so wrapped in my thoughts that I hadn't heard her come in. "Morning, Mom."

She cast a sidelong glance at me as she crossed the floor to the refrigerator. I watched dully as she took out a carton of eggs and the partially empty bottle of milk.

"Feel like some scrambled eggs this morning?" she asked me.

"Sure. That's fine," I mumbled.

The clicking of the metal spoon against the bowl as she beat the eggs matched the rhythm of the falling rain. I turned again to stare out the window.

"Why so gloomy this morning, Kallie?" Mom asked. She gave me another quick look from the corner of her eye.

"I guess it's the weather," I answered, avoiding her glance.

"Good morning." Dad's booming voice announced his presence in the kitchen. He was dressed for work in his suit and tie. He gave Mom a kiss and a pat on her waist, then he bent to kiss me. I could smell the freshness of his scrupulously clean white shirt.

"Kallie's feeling a little down this morning," Mom informed him.

"Oh?" Dad replied as he took a seat at the table across from me.

Mom dropped two pieces of bread into the toaster and served the eggs. After Dad said a blessing on the food, he started heartily on his eggs and toast. I picked at the food on my plate. I wasn't feeling very hungry.

"Do you have a busy day planned?" Mom asked Dad as she sat down next to him with her breakfast plate.

"Yes. I have a meeting this morning and another this afternoon."

I listened half-heartedly to their conversation.

"We should be getting a letter from Mark today or tomorrow," Mom commented, a hopeful note in her voice. "It's been more than a week since we've heard from him."

"I hope the missionary work is going well in Fiji," Dad said.

I tried again to bring Caleb's face to mind. It evaporated before the picture was complete.

"You know, Kallie," Dad said, turning to me, "I think your spirits would pick up if you were to find a job. You're probably feeling a little nervous and depressed over what to do."

"Yes, I guess so, Dad."

"Why don't you spend the day looking around a bit? You can check the newspaper and make a few calls."

"All right," I replied.

"I'll make some inquiries, too. Maybe we can find you a job before the week is out." Dad smiled broadly and patted my shoulder.

"That would be great, Dad," I said without much enthusiasm.

"Good. Now I'd better run." He kissed Mom and me again, and shortly afterward I heard his car pull out of the garage.

I puttered around the house most of the morning. I did take time to make a cursory check of the want ads, but found nothing there of much interest. In the afternoon I ran a few errands for Mom. When I returned home, she told me that Terri had called. I didn't return her call, and she didn't telephone again that evening.

The next couple of days slipped by quietly. I knew I should get serious about finding a job, but my heart wasn't in it. With each day, the memories associated with Caleb and the Walkers became more obscure. I was beginning to believe that the whole experience with them had been nothing more than a dream. In thinking back on that afternoon when I visited Brigham Young's family cemetery, I decided that I must have fallen asleep under the old gnarled tree and dreamed the entire episode. But that conclusion saddened me, because my experiences with the Walkers had seemed so real. I felt as if I had suddenly lost my best friends, and I was depressed and apathetic. I knew Mom and Dad were concerned about me. That must have been part of the reason Dad was so enthused to tell me, a few nights later, about a possible job opening.

"Apparently, Kallie, this man has an extensive rock collection and needs someone to catalogue it for him."

"But Dad, I don't know anything about rocks."

"You can learn. You're an historian, aren't you?"

"Where is this job opportunity?" I asked, shaking my head.

Dad gave me a downtown address and suggested that I go see the fellow first thing in the morning—"before someone else snaps up the job," he said.

I tried to summon a degree of enthusiasm as I drove downtown the next morning. I found the address easily enough, located in the heart of the business district, and boldly presented myself to the gentleman in question. He was a small, wiry man with a short haircut and ears that seemed too large for his thin face. We discussed the position; he said he would let me know his decision, but I figured he had already made up his mind. I actually felt relieved knowing that he probably would not hire me, for I did not share his interest in the beauty and mystery of minerals.

Since I was in the downtown area with nothing pressing to occupy my time, I decided to walk around a bit. I wanted to compare the memories I still had of my extraordinary dream with the actual setting. I walked slowly along Main Street, mentally clicking off the names displayed on the modern glass and steel buildings. I saw no saddle and harness shops, no millinery or tailoring establishments, and no stout adobe homes sandwiched between commercial buildings. There was no Wells Fargo and Company situated on Main Street, no Deseret National Bank. I felt a vague despair settle over me. I would have given almost anything to see a familiar 1877-period building.

Suddenly I brightened as I remembered that there was such a building still standing—the oldest commercial building, in fact, in downtown Salt Lake City. I quickened my pace along Main Street until I came to First South. There, on the corner, stood the Eagle Emporium. I clapped my hands together and laughed aloud. The building, of course, didn't house William Jennings's old mercantile, but the white stone structure appeared nearly exactly as I remembered it. I delighted in seeing the stately columns set on either side of the door, and the carved eagle with spread wings perched atop a handsomely crafted beehive. Even though the sign on the building read "Zion's First National Bank," to me it was still the Emporium.

Looking up and down the street, I visualized the old buildings which used to stand there. The old sandstone Council House had been replaced by the Deseret News building. Godbe's drugstore and the original Walker brothers' bank had grown into tall bank buildings. Through the block, I glimpsed a corner of Dinwoodey's furniture store. The three-story brick building which housed Dinwoodey's had been constructed in 1873. How did I know that? I thought with a start. How did I know anything at all about the early buildings along Main Street? I squeezed my eyes shut, concentrating on exactly how I had learned these facts. As hard as I tried, I couldn't be sure whether I had picked them up from doing research for Professor Bowen, or whether I had actually seen the buildings as they stood in the late 1870s.

This sequence of thoughts was very unnerving. I retraced my steps back to my car, my eyes on the sidewalk, as I tried to sort out the images and memories crowding my mind. I had parked on State Street, near the Mountain States Telephone building. As I walked past it, my eyes chanced to fall upon a metal plaque set into the side of the building. The plaque commemorated a structure which had once stood on this spot. Pictured on the plaque was a handsome building with broad steps leading to an entrance flanked by Grecian columns. The roof was hipped with a promenade on top. People dressed in nineteenth-century clothing were arriving by buggy or walking, ready to make their way into the building. I recognized the building depicted on the plaque without having to read the inscription. It was the Playhouse, the old Salt Lake Theater. Tears gathered in my eyes as I leaned close to read the poem printed on the commemorative plaque:

> *Long, long be my heart*
> *with such memories filled,*
> *Like the vase in which roses*
> *have once been distill'd.*
> *You may break, you may shatter*
> *the vase if you will,*
> *But the scent of the roses will*
> *hang round it still.*

That verse said it all for me. I still didn't know if my nineteenth-century experience had been a dream or had truly happened, but suddenly it didn't seem to matter quite so much. I would cherish its memories, and I would never forget or ignore its lessons. Caleb, the Walkers, and all the others had affected me in a most profound way. Whether imagined or real, they had taught me lessons that I could have learned in perhaps no other manner.

I caught a flashing image of Gus, the grizzled old foreman of Mr. Walker's sheep ranch, weaving willows into a chair for Aunt Lizzy. What was it Gus had said to me that day, when Walker and the other men were away gathering the sheep from the high summer pastures? I couldn't remember his exact words, but he had spoken of a change of heart, and now I understood what he'd meant. Gus knew I needed the old man's help to return home. Not only could that old man unlock the passageway to the past and back to the present, but the key he carried represented that mighty change of heart called repentance.

Dad had once said it would take a miracle to turn me around, and he was right about that. But the miracle I experienced had little to do with my journeying into the past. That journey was only symbolic of the real miracle in my life brought about by the power of repentance. I had traveled the difficult road one step at a time until I had felt the peace, joy, and redemption which come with forgiveness of sins.

I wiped the tears from my eyes and smiled to myself. With the most tender feelings, I ran my hand over the raised surface of the commemorative plaque. Two people walking by gave me suspicious glances, but I didn't care. I must have stood there beside the plaque for several minutes. When at last I climbed back into my silver Mustang, my heart was calm.

CHAPTER NINETEEN

"KALLIE, CAN YOU COME OVER?" Terri's voice was charged with excitement.

I hadn't talked to Terri for over a week. Truthfully, I'd been trying to avoid her. Hearing her voice now over the telephone annoyed me. I swallowed my irritation. "No, I really can't, Terri. I'm in the middle of filling out this job application. I have to get it in first thing tomorrow morning."

"Oh, is it something that might work out for you?" Terri asked. I could tell that her question was asked out of duty, not interest.

"I think so. It's a position that's opened up at one of the county-operated historic sites."

"Sounds great. Listen, Kallie, Kevin is here from BYU with his roommate. The roommate is a hunk; you've *got* to come over and meet him."

I frowned. I didn't care a whit about meeting Kevin's roommate, particularly if it meant spending the afternoon with Terri. "I'm sorry, Terri. I'm afraid I can't make it. I'm sure you've already captivated him with your charms, anyway."

Terri laughed. "I won't deny that I've been trying. Come on, your application can wait an hour or two. They're only going to be here through the weekend, and Kevin would like to see you, too."

I pictured Kevin's face in my mind. He was light-haired, like Terri, but he had soft brown eyes and a ready smile. I liked him for his grace and openness.

"You'll be sorry if you don't come," Terri purred. "This guy is *hot*. Besides, I've already told him all about you. He wants to meet you."

I cringed inwardly. There was no telling what Terri might have said about me. "I'll call you tomorrow afternoon if I get some time, all right?" I said in a half-hearted effort to appease her.

I hung up the phone and turned my attention back to the application in front of me. I felt fairly excited about this job. The work sounded interesting and would challenge my skills. I carefully filled out all the information requested, then tucked the application form in my bureau drawer to wait until morning.

By that time it was getting late. I undressed, put on my pajamas, said my prayers, and slipped into bed. I lay there for some time, letting my mind wander. My thoughts did not dwell on Caleb Hollister or the Walkers. By now I had reconciled myself to the fact that they did not exist—that they had never existed, except in my imagination. I dallied with the idea of purchasing some new clothes for my trip to California with my parents. I needed a new pair of shorts and a T-shirt. I fell asleep making a mental list of things I wanted to pack for the trip.

Traffic was heavy the next morning as I drove to the county offices. I turned in my job application and was given an appointment for an interview the following week. After I left the office building, I did a few errands and returned home around noon. Changing into my grubbiest pair of levis and a baggy blue and white checkered blouse, I went outside to weed Mom's flower garden. Although the weather had been cool and rainy the last several days, this afternoon the sun was shining brightly through clear skies.

Using a hand tool, I began to dig up the stubborn weeds infesting Mom's tulips. I should have worn garden gloves for the work, but I liked the comforting feel of the soft, moist earth between my fingers. The smell of spring was strong in my nostrils as I spaded up the soil. A bird's song, floating in the air, filled me with simple delight. The sun warmed my back as I bent over the garden, and I hummed a tune while turning the soil with my spade.

I hadn't worked for more than half an hour when I heard the sound of wheels grinding to a stop in front of the house. When I saw that it was Terri's car, I felt a flicker of impatience. I stood up from the flower bed, brushing the dirt from my hands onto my jeans. Terri jumped out of the car and waved to me. The door to the passenger side opened and Kevin climbed out. Behind him, from the rear seat, another fellow of about Kevin's age emerged.

"Hi, Kallie. We were hoping you'd be home," Terri said as she walked toward me.

I shaded my eyes with my hand. Kevin was following behind her with the other fellow at his side. I noticed that the young man was slightly shorter than Kevin, but broader in the shoulders. He had light hair and wore round, wire-rimmed glasses.

I nodded at Terri, and then to Kevin I said, "It's good to see you. How's school going?"

"All right," he replied. "How's everything with you?"

"Good." My eyes slipped past Kevin's slender face to the fellow standing beside him. Terri had paused to wait for him, and now she linked her arm through his. I saw a fleeting look of dissatisfaction cross his face.

"Kallie, this is Jeff Colton. He's Kevin's roommate. Jeff, meet my friend, Kallie Garrett," Terri said ceremoniously.

Jeff Colton put out his hand. "Nice to meet you," he said in a resonant voice.

"You, too," I replied, offering my hand. He had a strong, confident grip. When I looked up into his face I saw that his expression, too, was firm and self-assured. Dark blue eyes peered at me from behind his stylish wire-rimmed glasses. His nose was well-proportioned and his mouth attractive. He gave me a brief, controlled smile.

"Jeff is a senior at the BYU. He's majoring in business. Is that right, Jeff?" Terri squeezed his arm and flashed him a dazzling smile.

"That's right," Jeff answered. I watched him discreetly disengage his arm from Terri's.

"He plans to be a big business tycoon," Kevin said, giving me a wink.

I nodded.

Kevin's light hair was cut shorter than the last time I saw him, and he was wearing a pair of dress slacks and a blue pin-striped shirt. I'd never seen Kevin dressed in anything slouchy. He always looked as if he'd stepped out of a men's clothing advertisement.

Suddenly, I realized how awful I must look in my dilapidated jeans and shapeless blouse, with dirt from the garden smudged all over my clothes and hands. I winced with embarrassment.

"How's the research going?" Kevin asked.

"It's not," I replied, knocking the loose dirt off my jeans. From the corner of my eye I saw Jeff looking at me. His stare made me feel even more self-conscious about my appearance.

"What do you mean?"

"Well, Professor Bowen fired me."

Kevin's expression registered concern.

"Actually, I don't mind. I have my eye on another job."

"What kind of job is it?" It was Jeff who asked the question. He'd taken a step away from Terri, which put him closer to me. I could easily see the deep, vivid blue of his eyes.

"It's a position with the county." I stumbled on my words. What an impression I must be making on Kevin's friend, I thought miserably, with my dirt-stained clothes and the ignominy of losing my job.

"Doing what?" Jeff persisted.

"The county has restored an original pioneer log cabin and opened it to the public. The position I've applied for is Director of Exhibits at the site."

"That sounds interesting," Jeff commented.

"I think so. The Director of Exhibits makes sure all exhibits are handled and displayed appropriately, catalogues existing

234

exhibits, is responsible for acquiring new exhibits, and things like that."

I knew I was rambling, but Jeff's gaze unnerved me. Something about him was familiar to me. I couldn't quite put my finger on what it was. I wondered if perhaps we'd attended the same school. I thought about asking him where he'd gone to high school, but decided the question would sound stupid.

"When will you find out about the job?" Kevin asked me. His intense brown eyes indicated his interest.

"I have an interview set up for next week," I answered. "What about you guys? Are you working while you go to school?" My gaze took in both Kevin and his friend.

Kevin chuckled. "I'm serving up sandwiches in the Wilkinson Center cafeteria when I'm not in class. It helps fill the belly, but it doesn't put a lot in the pocketbook. You know how it is, Kallie. You need every spare minute to study."

Jeff nodded in agreement.

"Do you work at the cafeteria, too?" I asked Jeff.

"No. I have a scholarship I'm trying to hang on to."

He smiled briefly, and again I got the feeling that I knew him from somewhere. It bothered me that I couldn't remember where.

"Are you from Utah?" I asked Jeff, no longer able to contain my curiosity.

He shook his head. "No. I grew up in Arizona."

"Phoenix?" I inquired.

"A small town near Phoenix."

I had never spent any time in Arizona, so it was not possible for our paths to have crossed there. I shrugged, and gave up trying to place him.

Terri had been standing quietly while I talked with Kevin and Jeff. Now she moved to Kevin's side and carelessly rested an arm on his shoulder. "There must be a million girls who go through that cafeteria line," she said to her brother. "What an opportunity for you, Kevin."

"I don't have much time for girls," Kevin replied, giving Terri's cheek a playful pinch. "It's all work, work, work."

"Yeah, I'll bet," Terri snorted.

"We keep our hands to the plow, don't we, Jeff?"

"Every minute," Jeff answered soberly.

I smiled at the boys' banter. While they kidded with Terri, my eyes kept wandering back to Jeff Colton. I couldn't help noticing the snug fit of his levis and the way his beige pullover molded to his shoulders and chest. The sleeves were pushed up to his elbows, revealing muscular arms. His hair was parted and combed into a casual style. The round, wire-rimmed glasses gave him an intellectual air.

"Since you boys are so deprived of female company, I'll make you an offer," Terri said coyly. "Kallie and I are throwing a party Sunday night, and you're welcome to come. I guarantee there will be plenty of girls in need of companionship."

Before Kevin or Jeff could answer, I blurted out in consternation, "Terri, I told you I'm not coming to any more parties. Especially one held on Sunday."

For a second Terri looked at me with bewilderment, then a frown flickered across her face. "Whether you come or not is up to you, Kallie. But I don't get it."

I knew what she meant. Terri couldn't understand the change in me, and she didn't like it. I lowered my eyes, not knowing what to say next.

"Thanks for the invitation, but I'm afraid I can't make it either," Jeff told her. His voice was unfaltering.

I looked up at him. He stood tall and straight, his arms folded across his chest. I had a difficult time pulling my eyes away from him.

"Don't look at me," Kevin added, holding up his hands in mock horror. "I've been to one of your parties before."

"No you haven't. You wouldn't be caught dead there, Kevin." Terri stiffened her arms and strained her neck up tight—the perfect imitation of a person stuffed into a shirt.

I giggled, even though I probably shouldn't have. I saw Jeff smother a chuckle, too. As I glanced at him, our eyes met. He gave me a big, open grin.

At that moment, my heart surged in my breast as I recognized with vivid clarity what was familiar about him. Jeff was wearing Caleb Hollister's smile! I stared at him in astonishment. My eyes traveled over every feature of his face, searching for some resemblance between him and Caleb. They shared nothing in common except that extraordinary smile.

"Guess you'd better forget about a party," I heard Kevin say. "It sounds like nobody's coming."

Terri sniffed. "You just keep your nose in your books, Kevin. That's what you're good at."

Kevin put an arm around Terri's neck and playfully pulled her to him. "Come on, Terri. Show some respect for your big brother."

"Knock it off," Terri retorted as she wriggled out of his grasp.

I listened in a daze to their exchange. I kept wondering if my mind was playing tricks on me. Had I just imagined seeing Caleb's smile on Jeff's face?

"I guess it's back to the books for us," Kevin was saying. He shot Jeff a woeful look.

"All kidding aside, I really do have to get back to Provo soon. I have an exam on Monday I need to study for," Jeff replied. He looked at me as he spoke, and I detected a note of disappointment in his voice. I felt immensely disappointed myself.

All of us started walking back to Terri's car. "Is it a business class you're having an exam in?" I asked Jeff. I wanted to delay his departure as long as possible. I found myself enormously attracted to him, which was unusual for me. It generally took some time for me to decide if I liked a new fellow or not.

"Yeah," Jeff replied. "Business law."

"Sounds like a hard class," I remarked. I noticed how blue his eyes looked in the glare of the afternoon sun.

"It is, but it's an interesting one. Actually, I'm kicking around the idea of applying for law school. I've kind of developed an interest in the area of constitutional law."

"Oh?"

"Yeah, well, I haven't decided for sure. I'll see how this business law class goes."

We had nearly reached the car by now. Jeff was walking close to my side, and with him so near I was finding it difficult to keep my breathing even. I tried to think of something intelligent to say. "Do you like the professor?" I asked. It was the best I could come up with.

Jeff glanced over at me. "Of the business law class? Yeah, I do. The professor is a woman, and she's tough. I've never had to work harder in any class than I do in this one. The prof is a small, delicate-looking woman, but she's ferocious. A real lioness in lamb's clothing."

My mouth dropped open. I stood rooted to the spot, gaping at Jeff.

I felt Terri nudge my shoulder. "You're staring, Kallie," she said, laughing harshly.

My eyes stayed riveted on Jeff's face. Terri nudged me again; I pushed her away. "Excuse me, but what did you say?" I asked Jeff in a hoarse voice.

Jeff's look was a question.

"Just a second ago. What did you say to me?"

Jeff glanced at Kevin with a puzzled expression, and then back at me. "About the business law professor?"

"Yes!" I fairly shouted.

"That she's tough. A lioness in lamb's clothing." Jeff shrugged, not understanding my urgency. "It's just an expression."

I stared at him, my eyes nearly popping out of my head and my heart racing.

"Come on, Kallie," Terri murmured. I heard her titter nervously at my side.

"I'm sorry," I whispered, trying to pull myself together. The phrase Jeff had used was Caleb's pet phrase. And it was Caleb's smile on Jeff's face. But this was not Caleb standing next to me, looking at me with a perplexed expression.

"Is there a problem?" Kevin asked innocently.

"No. No problem," I replied. A warmth began to spread through me, filling the void, the sense of loss I'd experienced over the last couple of weeks. I felt at peace, and indescribably happy.

"Good," Kevin declared. "Then we'll be on our way. Kallie, it was nice seeing you again."

"You, too, Kevin." It took enormous effort to take my eyes from Jeff's face long enough to bid Kevin good-bye.

Kevin and Terri climbed into the car. Jeff paused a moment before joining them. "Are you going to be around next weekend?" he asked me.

"Yes," I answered eagerly. "Oh, wait a minute. I almost forgot. I'm going on a trip with my parents next weekend."

He nodded. "Well, it was nice to meet you."

I hoped he would pursue the matter, but he didn't. He just got into the car with no further comment.

Kevin shut the car door. "See ya," he called as Terri stepped on the accelerator.

The car roared away, leaving me standing alone beside the road.

The next few days passed quickly. My interview with the county personnel went well, and I hoped I would get the job at the historic site. I helped Mom get things ready for our trip to California. Although I still wasn't terribly excited about going, I knew it was the right thing to do. Mom and Dad were looking forward to our spending the time together.

As it turned out, the trip was enjoyable. Mom and I laid out beside the motel pool during the day while Dad attended his meetings, and in the evenings we all went out to dinner and afterwards took in a concert, museum, or show. I was sorry to see the trip come to an end.

We arrived home on Tuesday night of the following week, and I spent the next day giving my room a good cleaning. I washed and ironed the mauve curtains which hung at my bedroom window, and straightened my clothes closet. On Thursday evening I received a telephone call.

"Hello. This is Jeff Colton," came the voice over the phone.

My heart leaped uncontrollably. I tried to keep my voice calm. "Hey, Jeff," I answered. "How are you?"

"Good. How was your trip?"

"Really nice. We had a great time. I hated to come home." I held my breath, afraid of rambling on in my excitement.

"I'm glad you had a good time. How did your job interview go?" he asked.

"Great. I got the job! They called me about it today."

"That's terrific," Jeff said. I could hear the pleasure in his voice.

"Yes, I'm excited about it. I start work on Monday morning."

"The new Director of Exhibits, huh?"

"That's right." I chuckled in delight over the sound of my new title.

"Way to go, Kallie."

"Thanks. What about you? How did your exam go?"

"Well, my scholarship is still intact for the moment."

I laughed. "Good for you."

I heard Jeff draw a breath. "Hey, there's going to be a concert down here on Saturday night. I wondered if you might like to go with me."

I danced a little jig, phone in hand. "Yes, I'd like that very much."

"You would?" He sounded surprised.

"Of course. Did you think I wouldn't?"

"I don't know. I wasn't sure I made the right kind of impression on you when we met."

I rolled my eyes. "I didn't think I'd made a very good

impression on you. Dressed in my grubbiest clothes, telling you about losing my job—that can't be very impressive."

He laughed. I could visualize the smile on his face, and it sent a wave of warmth flowing over me. "I was impressed," he said, still chuckling.

"Well, honestly, I didn't think you'd call," I told him in a more serious tone than I'd intended.

"I almost didn't."

His reply brought me up short. "You—you didn't?" I managed to stammer.

"You want to hear the truth?"

"Sure."

"After meeting your friend, Terri, I was prepared not to like you."

I swallowed. "Oh? What changed your mind?" I asked in a squeaky voice.

There was no hesitation in his answering. "You stood firm for the principles you believe in. That's what impressed me."

"When did I do that?" I asked, genuinely puzzled.

"'I'm not coming to any more parties. Especially one held on Sunday.'"

My own words echoed over the phone.

"You see, Kevin had already told me about his sister. I wasn't interested in meeting her. Or her friends. This may sound corny, but when I got home from my mission I decided that I wouldn't date girls who didn't have the same standards and goals as I did."

I listened to his explanation, my breath nearly stopping in my throat.

"I've been accused of being narrow-minded, but I think it's important to have friends who can help lift you up, not drag you down."

I didn't know what to say in reply. I was totally caught off guard by his candor.

There was a long pause and then Jeff said, "So, do you still want to go with me Saturday night, or have I turned you off with my ranting?" His voice carried a trace of self-deprecating humor.

This time I knew exactly what to say. "You haven't turned me off, Jeff. In fact, I want to thank you for being frank with me. What you've just said convinces me that I've made the right decision in dealing with some important changes in my life."

Jeff didn't say anything for some seconds. I heard him clear his throat. Finally he said, "You know, this sounds crazy, but I feel like we've already known each other a long time."

I smiled to myself. I felt warm and tingly inside, as if I were sitting by an open fire with Caleb's kiss fresh on my lips. In my conscious mind I knew that Jeff was not Caleb Hollister, though their personal and spiritual qualities were similar. Yet deep in a corner of my heart, I believed that Cabe had kept his promise to me. I still had no idea how this whole circumstance had happened—but I was quite sure how it was going to turn out. And my heart soared.

"I suppose it's possible," I replied. I allowed a hint of mystery to creep into my voice. "Perhaps we've met somewhere in the past."

The Passageway

Laurel Mouritsen

About the Author

Laurel Mouritsen grew up with a passion for history and literature. She holds a degree in history with a minor in English literature, and teaches creative writing for adult and community education programs. She also teaches classes in genealogy and enjoys speaking on the topic of family history.

In addition to reading and writing, Laurel enjoys skiing, golfing, horseback riding, and traveling with her family. She and her husband Robert have four children. They live in Sandy, Utah.